ONLY ONE WAY HOME

THE REWINDING TIME SERIES
Inspirational Novels of History, Mystery & Romance

book 2

DEBORAH HEAL

ISBN: 1507578652
ISBN-13: 978-1507578650

This is historical fiction. While every effort was made to be historically accurate about the real people and events of the past, they were fictionalized to one degree or another. As for the contemporary characters, any resemblance to actual living persons is purely coincidental.

Other Novels by Deborah Heal

Available in e-book and paperback, The Rewinding Time Series:
   Once Again (book 1)
   How Sweet the Sound (book 3)

Available in audiobook, e-book, and paperback, The History Mystery Trilogy:
   Time and Again (book 1)
   Unclaimed Legacy (book 2)
   Every Hill and Mountain (book 3)

"I am the way, the truth, and the life."

John 14:6

For my Great, Great Grandmother Mary Ann Jones Bohannon,
the "Indian Woman," and for my brother Kenny Woods
who inherited his good looks from her.

CHAPTER 1

Merrideth Randall ran a strand of blond hair through her flatiron. She took the time to do it every morning, because she figured if she had to have flat hair it might as well be shiny flat hair. But it was a tiresome process, made worse by her inadequate bathroom. For one thing, the mirrored medicine cabinet had been installed at a height suitable for her apartment's ten-foot ceilings—if the person trying to use it was also of gigantic proportions—but since she was only five foot two inches, she had to stand on tippy-toes if she wanted to see what she was doing. She reminded herself that at least her calves got a good workout.

Besides, it was impossible to be annoyed on such a glorious day. The window behind her claw-foot tub was filled with golden sunlight, and if the weatherman hadn't lied, temperatures would be more typical of April than January. More importantly, it was the Friday morning of a four-day weekend, her grading was caught up, and she would not have to be back at McKendree College until her Tuesday afternoon freshman history class. Furthermore, she would be spending the day antique-hunting, one of her favorite pastimes, with her best friends Abby and John Roberts.

Rising on tiptoes once again, she examined her hair. It actually looked pretty good, and so she added "good hair day" to the weatherman's propitious forecast. Setting the flatiron on the ledge of the pedestal sink, she bent to get her little zippered cosmetic case from the cardboard box on the floor. She took out her bottle of honey-beige foundation and wedged the case behind the faucet. Although she'd lived there for over five months, her grooming paraphernalia and towels were still in boxes. Although the bathroom was large, it had little actual storage space. But today, if all went well, she would bring home a small antique dresser in which to put all her stuff.

Since her apartment was part of a historic old house—one of the many that graced Lebanon, Illinois—something antique was the only rational choice. She figured the price for a solid wood dresser would probably be only a little more than the plastic (horrors!) shelving units at Walmart. Something in cherry or mahogany would be nice, although pine would be acceptable—and probably less expensive. She felt confident she would find something that would work. Antique dealers from several states would be at the Marion Cultural Center for the annual two-day event called the Egyptian Caravan of Antiques.

She smoothed on a bit more foundation and then put the bottle back in the case and took out her mascara. In the process, her elbow bumped the flatiron. It skittered over the porcelain surface, but she caught it right before it would have landed in the basin under the dripping faucet. She was grateful to have good reflexes, because getting electrocuted would have really put a damper on the nice day. Grinning at her thought, she unplugged the flatiron and set it back down. The cord snagged on the cosmetic case, sending it to the floor. The bottle of foundation shattered on the black and white checkerboard tile, splattering honey-beige makeup to the four corners of the room.

Drat! It was almost seven o'clock, and like her, John was habitually prompt. She would have to hurry in order to get downstairs before he and Abby arrived. She got paper towels from the kitchen and wiped up the broken glass and the worst of the gloppy mess. The doorbell rang. The floor was still smeary, but there was no time to mop it. John hated to be late. The doorbell rang again.

"All right. All right. Hang on, would you?" She washed the makeup from her hands and hurried to the living room where she got her keys from the faux mantel of her faux fireplace and her coat and oversized leather shoulder bag from her lumpy couch.

She opened the door, expecting to see John. Instead, Brett Garrison stood there, hand raised in mid-air. Grinning, he pretended to knock on her forehead. As usual, his smile made her stomach do flips. As usual, she forced it to stop its gymnastics.

2

Today, instead of his usual suit and tie, he was decked out in jeans, blue chambray shirt, and work boots. And instead of a briefcase, he carried a shiny red tool box. He looked like Hollywood's version of A Working Man when he was, in fact, McKendree's youngest physics professor and thus a man who used his brain rather than his hands to make a living.

Brett's get-up should have made her laugh. Instead, it made her cranky. He looked just as attractive in it as he did in his elegant professional attire, and like everything else he wore, it seemed to accentuate his good looks. It was annoying, given her determination to keep the man at arm's length and firmly in the *friend* category. No way was she going to sabotage her position at McKendree by getting involved with a colleague. It was a small college in a small town, and rumors flew like carrier pigeons.

She made a show of looking at her watch. "Kind of early for a visit, don't you think?"

"I figured since you're an early bird you wouldn't mind. I did try to call, but your phone isn't working."

"Oh! I forgot to charge it." She dug in her shoulder bag for it. "Speaking of phones, I don't seem to remember calling a repairman...er...carpenter or whatever you're supposed to be."

"Sure you did," he said, edging his way past her into the apartment. "You've been complaining for weeks about your sticky doors." He strode across her living room like he owned it when, in fact, he'd only been there a couple of times.

She laid her bag down and followed him, nearly running to keep up with his long stride. "Well, then where's the Acme Construction label on your shirt, Mister? I insist on Acme for all my construction needs."

"The only one I know who uses Acme is Bugs Bunny."

"It's really nice of you to take an interest in my doors, Professor Garrison. But they're happy as they are, in spite of all my griping. And I'll be moving anyway...as soon as I find a place to buy."

"Well, you might as well have decent doors while you wait. Is that the one?"

"That's one of two."

The bathroom floor looked even worse now that the smears of makeup had dried in a honey-beige glaze on the black and white tile. Brett shook his head and clucked in mock dismay. "You really should think about switching to Mr. Clean, Merri."

3

"My cleaning products are perfectly fine, thank you very much. I just didn't have time to mop."

He set his tool box down in the hall and pulled her bathroom door toward him until it stuck with a creak on the tile floor a full three inches from closing. She knew because she had once measured it.

"If I want to shut it completely, I have to win at a very spirited game of tug-of-war, which I don't like to do because the door knob is loose." Like the rest of the house, the door had its original china knobs, just one of the quaint features that made it worth living in what Abby called "chic squalor."

Brett swung the door back and forth a few more times. "Pretty typical with old houses. Everything settles over time."

"My landlord Mr. O'Connor keeps promising to do something about the doors. But he's so decrepit that I don't think he can actually make it up the stairs to my apartment any more, much less do any repairs once he got here."

"That's where I come in."

"You can fix it?"

"Sure. It's a simple matter of planing a little off the bottom of the door."

"It would be great if you could fix them, Brett, but today's not good. We'll be gone all day."

"We? Where are *we* going?"

Oh great. Now she had roused his raging curiosity. It was one of his most annoying traits. When she didn't volunteer her itinerary for the day, he put on a bland expression as if he had lost interest. But she wasn't fooled by it for one minute. From experience, she knew that he would continue to try to weasel information out of her. He seemed to have an insatiable need to know every detail of her life. Too bad, because she didn't care to tell all her business to everybody who asked. The blasted man should be grateful. She had already shared more with him than she did anyone else except Abby and John.

"So you should go on home now," she said.

"Always the polite hostess, aren't you?" Completely ignoring her request, he bent and got a hammer and chisel out of his tool box. Then he went into the bathroom, pulling her after him, and shut the door as far as it would go.

"What on earth—" she squeaked. With him in it, her bathroom

no longer seemed so large after all. And the air was noticeably deficient in oxygen. He was frowning, so maybe he noticed it, too. "I need you to help me get the doors off before you leave. So where did you say you're going?"

"Aren't you full of nosy questions?"

"It only seems like a nosy question to someone who guards her secrets like the gold at Fort Knox. As for me, I'm an open book."

"Okay, then I've got a question for you." She had her own share of curiosity, truth be told. For weeks she had been dying to ask him about something he had said.

"Ask away."

"A while back you told me that everyone has family secrets."

"And you're asking what mine is?"

"I guess I am. Let me remind you that you know mine."

"But you didn't tell me. I discovered it on my own."

"Which you did by snooping!"

"I did not. Your father's letter from Joliet Prison was right there for anyone to see on your couch." He put the chisel to the upper brass hinge and tapped it with his hammer. The pin popped up like a turkey thermometer, and he pulled it out and set it on the floor. "My secret is that I'm not a real Garrison. Thus, I am not related to those heroic ancestors you found for Aunt Nelda's family tree." He didn't wait for her to respond to that bit of news, just started in hammering on the middle hinge.

When the racket stopped and the second pin was out, she said, "Of course you're a Garrison, Brett. You look—" Merrideth shut her mouth and turned away so he wouldn't read her face. She had been about to remind him that he looked just like his ancestor James Garretson—the same glossy black hair and emerald eyes, even the same jaw line.

She knew because she had gotten a first-hand look at James Garretson back in November, courtesy of her *Beautiful Houses* software. The thought still made her shiver with excitement and wonder. True, she had taken only virtual trips back to Garretson's time in the 1780s, but it was amazing all the same. Undoubtedly, Brett would be fascinated by a computer program that allowed users to circumvent a few of the supposedly immutable laws of physics in order to virtually rewind time. But if she told anyone it was working again after all these years, it should be Abby and John, and she didn't have the guts to do so in case they insisted she stop using it. They had always thought it was too dangerous to let word of *Beautiful Houses* get out, fearing someone would adapt it to use for spying on everyone's thoughts. But the technology was just too precious to give up—for her historical research and for her sideline genealogy consulting business.

Behind her, Brett grunted. "I never would have taken you for a snob, Merri."

She whirled to face him, saw that he was frowning, and mentally kicked herself for taking so long to respond. "I do not care one iota what your last name is or whether your parents were blue-blooded aristocrats or…or… orangutans."

His frown was replaced with an amused smile. "Oh. Sorry. Here, take these," he said, handing her his hammer and chisel.

"What am I supposed to do with them?"

"Now you do the bottom hinge while I hold the door."

"Are you getting tired?" she said sweetly. "Maybe you should go home and take a nap."

"I'd do it myself, but these old doors weigh a ton, and if I don't hold it level it will torque and get jammed, making it more difficult, if not impossible to—"

"Okay, okay. I got it." She knelt and positioned the chisel as she had seen him do and then hit it with the hammer. It wasn't as easy as he had made it look. The pin only moved up a quarter of an inch. She looked up at him. "So what makes you think you're not a Garrison?"

"You hammer. I'll talk."

"Just don't let the door fall on me."

"I won't," he said, rolling his eyes.

She went back to hammering, or rather lightly tapping. She didn't want to get the pin out too quickly or she might lose the opportunity to pump him for information.

"Mom died when I was eight."

She looked back up at him. "I'm sorry, Brett."

"Don't look so tragic, Merri. I was used to her letting me down."

"It hardly seems fair to blame her for dying."

"It is, if the cause of death was booze."

"But alcoholism is—"

"A disease. I know it now. But try telling that to an eight-year-old. Fortunately, Aunt Nelda scooped me up and took me to her farm, so I didn't have to watch Mom drink herself to death."

"It must have been horrible." It was obvious from his expression that he didn't want her pity, so Merrideth went back to tapping on the hinge. "What about your father? Where was he during all this?"

"My alleged father died before I was born. He got food poisoning in Athens."

"I presume you have a reason to believe he wasn't your real father."

Before he could answer, the pin finally came out and clattered to the floor. Brett lifted the door off the hinges, lugged it into the hall, and leaned it against the wall. "Is that the other one?" Without waiting for an answer he started down the hall toward her bedroom.

"Wait!" She slid past him and stuck her head in the door. Seeing him approaching her room had given her the sudden fear that she had left bras hanging from the bedpost or forgotten to pick up her underwear and dirty socks from the floor. But everything was as neat as always. "All right, the coast is clear."

He smirked as if he knew very well what she had imagined. After a ridiculously short time, he had the first and second hinge pins out and handed the tools to her again. "Okay. You know the drill."

She saw right away that she wouldn't have to fake it this time. The blasted pin only budged a couple of millimeters with each swing of the hammer. "You were explaining why your father was of the *alleged* variety."

"To be my real father, he would have had to be present for my conception. But he was gone on a three-month business trip to Rome during the pertinent time period. He was gone a lot during my childhood. I guess Mom got bored and had a little fling. Or a dozen, for all I know."

"Maybe you were born prematurely."

"Not at eight pounds, fourteen ounces, I wasn't. No, dear old "Dad" was gone the spring I was conceived, on loan to the European branch of SysCom in Rome."

"He worked for SysCom?"

"He was the chief financial advisor of SysCom."

"Even more impressive. But you said he died in Athens?"

"He was attending a technology conference there, one of

SysCom's charitable deals for developing nations. Unfortunately, the conference was cut short, because a lot of people got sick with food poisoning, and a few, including my dad, died. My alleged dad, that is."

"I'm sorry, Brett." Once again his face turned wooden, so she looked away and went back to tapping half-heartedly with the hammer.

After a moment, he said, "Aunt Nelda doesn't know that I know, so I'd appreciate it if you didn't mention it to her. And I'd appreciate it even more if you'd get that pin out of the hinge this century."

"I'm trying. How did you find out?"

"Aunt Nelda told me, although she doesn't realize it. She made me a little scrapbook when I first came to live with her. She put things about the family in it so I'd be proud of my Garrison roots. Ironic really, because it was the scrapbook that revealed to me that I wasn't a Garrison at all. One of the things in it was a newspaper clipping about Dad's work in Rome. I saw the significance of the dates right off. It's that number and pattern recognition thing I have."

"At age eight?"

He laughed. "I was an old hand at it by then. In kindergarten I used to amuse my teacher Miss Nelson by reciting the multiplication and division tables I'd seen on the big kids' notebooks. And the license plates of all the cars in the school parking lot. And how many smiley face stickers Miss Nelson had awarded over the course of the year and to whom. When I pointed out that Jimmy Owens had only gotten three all month, she started giving him more. It was a relief, because I had determined that I should probably give him some of mine."

She laughed because she knew he was trying to turn the conversation away from painful memories. "That was nice of you."

"We'll never know if I would have done the noble deed or not."

"Merri?" It was John's muffled voice coming from somewhere in her apartment. "Sorry I'm late. Aren't you ready to go?"

"I'm nearly ready," Merrideth called through the door. "Just hang on a second."

"Who's he?" Brett said.

"Who's *he*?" John said from the other side of the door.

"Oh, great, Brett," Merrideth whispered. "Now you've done it."

She put the chisel back to the hinge and banged on it with the hammer. The pin rose enough for her to get a grip on it, but she lacked the strength to pull it out.

The door handle rattled. "Are you all right, Merri?" John sounded intense.

"Turn loose of the door, John," Merrideth said. "You're going to make things worse."

"Stand back, Merri, I'm coming in."

"Don't be a moron," Brett called through the door.

"The moron is going to rip this door off if you don't tell him what's going on."

"I'm going to take it off myself if you give me a minute," Brett said.

"And why exactly would you want to do that?"

"He's going to fix it, John."

"Why didn't he say so?" he said huffily.

Merrideth banged on the chisel again, and at last the pin came out. Brett lifted the door and carried it into the hall.

Then John was there, scowling first at Brett's retreating back and then at her. "Don't you know to have someone with you when you have repairmen here?" he growled softly. "Especially in your bedroom?"

"For crying out loud, John, he's not a repairman."

Brett set the door down next to the other one, then came back toward them wearing a matching scowl.

"John, this is Brett. He's a colleague of mine at McKendree."

"The physics guy?" John said, extending his hand.

"And yet so many people call me Dr. Garrison."

Their handshake might have been the quickest one on record.

"Dr. Garrison," Merrideth said with a heavy coat of sarcasm, "may I present John Roberts, Attorney at Law."

"We should go, Merri," John said.

"And where are you two going, Merri?" Brett said. "I think you owe me that much."

"Do you really think so?" John said. It was one of his favorite Atticus Finch lines from *To Kill a Mockingbird*, and he often trotted it out for legal opponents in the courtroom and anyone else he considered a fool.

Merrideth rolled her eyes. "We're going to an—"

"I'm growing old waiting for you two, and something's wrong

with your phone, Merri." Abby appeared in the hall, studying her cell phone.

"I forgot to charge it," Merrideth said. "I'll do it on the way."

Abby stopped and looked up from her phone.

Merrideth expected her to scowl, too. With the two men standing one on either side of her, hackles raised like angry dogs, they must have made an interesting tableau. But instead, Abby smiled widely and came forward with her hand out. "Hi, I'm Abby."

Brett politely lowered his hackles, put away his frown, and shook her hand. "Brett Garrison. Pleased to meet you."

"He's going to fix my doors."

"Is that what they're calling it these days?" John muttered testily.

Merrideth glared at him.

Abby ignored her husband's stupid comment and continued smiling like she had the winning lottery ticket in her pocket. "You're the professor at Merri's college. Well, not *her* college, but you know what I mean. I'm Merri's… *friend* hardly covers it. More like—"

"She's the sister I never had," Merrideth said. She pointed a thumb at John. "And that… that is my over-protective idiot big brother. Pretend big brother, mind you."

"Oh. So he's not your…" Brett smiled. "You're Merri's family. She went to your house for Thanksgiving and Christmas. You have two girls, Lauren and Natalie, right?"

"Yes," Abby said. "We just dropped them off at my folks' house for the day."

"The day that is quickly passing," John said.

"I've been hoping to meet you," Brett said.

"Well, now you have," John said.

"And I've been dying to meet you," Abby said.

The gleam in her eyes indicated that she had gone into matchmaking mode again. It didn't matter how many times Merrideth explained that she didn't have time for dating while she was getting her career securely launched. Abby was dedicated to finding a man for her—any man, it sometimes seemed.

"You look nice, Merri. Doesn't she look great, John?" Abby said it with a sidelong glance at Brett that made Merrideth want to wring her neck.

"Of course she does. Same as always," John said, looking at his watch.

"Love your outfit. And great earrings, kiddo," Abby said, tapping one with a nail. "What a clever design. They look like little silver rivers."

"Brett's Aunt Nelda made them for me."

"Really? Brett, when Merri told me N/A Garrison actually lived in the next county I was astonished. I have two of her poetry books on my bookshelf."

"I could take you to meet her sometime. She would be happy to autograph them for you and show you her latest jewelry designs. She's been after me to bring Merrideth out again soon."

"How sweet of her," Abby said.

And devious. Nelda's tactics to get Merrideth and Brett together were as creative as everything else she did. She had tried to manipulate the situation so that Merrideth would have to accompany Brett to her house in order to get the earrings. But Merrideth had no intention of being managed, no matter how nicely, and had circumvented her ploy. Now every time she wore the earrings she felt a pleasant sense of triumph.

"Okay, then," John said. "We'd better go. My trailer is jutting out into the street more than I like."

"Are you going camping?" Brett said.

"Not likely. It is January, you know," John said.

Brett continued to ignore John's bad humor. It spoke well of his forbearance, but curiosity fairly radiated off him. Merrideth decided to put him out of his misery. It seemed only fair, since he had told her her huge family secret.

"We're going antique-hunting," she said. "Although I don't know why we need the trailer. These two couldn't possibly cram another antique into their house."

Abby laughed. "Which is why we're going to be mostly looking for things you need to put in your apartment."

"Really? I think it looks great as it is," Brett said. "My condo, on the other hand, looks like a dentist's waiting room."

"You should come antique-hunting with us, Brett," Abby said brightly. "Merri can help you find things to liven up your place. It will be fun."

"I'm sure it would be fun," Brett said, "but I don't like to leave a job once I've started it."

"Well, you can't hang around in Merri's apartment while she's gone." John said. After a pause, he added, "On second thought, maybe you *should* fix the doors while she's gone."

"He's right, Merri." Brett smiled when he said it, apparently unfazed by John's verbal jabs at him. "This way, you won't have to have me and my mess in your way, and you'll come home to doors that actually shut when you want them to."

"That sounds wonderful. But are you sure?"

"I'm sure."

CHAPTER 2

Merrideth threw herself into the car, slammed the door, and put on her seatbelt. "You were completely out of line, John."

"Much worse than usual," Abby said. "I theorize that it was because of seeing Brett come out of your bedroom, Merri."

John put the car in gear and pulled away from the curb. "How was I supposed to know the guy was fixing her doors? Besides, he's not her type."

"That's no excuse for being such a jerk," Merrideth said.

John huffed, but after a moment he said, "I'm sorry, Merri. You're right. It's just that—"

"Do not qualify that, John Roberts," Abby said. "You *were* being a jerk, and *I* was being a meddlesome busybody. I apologize, Merri."

Merrideth sniffed. It was impossible to stay mad at them. "That's all right. Just try not to do it again."

The car fell silent, and after a moment Merrideth's thoughts returned to Brett's unexpected visit. It was a wonder she'd been dressed, much less had her hair and makeup done when the annoying man dropped in unannounced.

The flatiron! Had she unplugged it or not? Yes, of course she had unplugged it. So she wouldn't get electrocuted. That's when the cord caught on her makeup case. That thought led to a worse one—her mascara! In all the confusion she had forgotten to put it on. It was bad enough that the public would see her with invisible lashes. But so had Brett! He had probably been wondering what was wrong with her eyes, not admiring her hair.

Merrideth grabbed Abby's shoulder. "Why didn't you tell me? What kind of a person lets a friend leave her house without mascara?"

"Oh, no. I'm sorry, Merri. That's one of the cardinal sister-friend rules."

"It is?" John said.

"Mercy yes! Right up there with being on the lookout for chin hairs. Do you have any in that suitcase you call a purse?"

"I don't think so," Merrideth said, reaching for her shoulder bag on the floor. But maybe an extra mascara would miraculously turn up among the million and one things she kept there. Drat! In the confusion, she had forgotten to take her laptop out. Now she'd have to lug around the extra weight all day. Worse, it was a risk to the security of *Beautiful Houses*—one-of-a-kind *Beautiful Houses*. The fact that Abby and John were within a few feet of the software made her nervous and caused a surge of guilt that she masked with annoyance. "You would have noticed I wasn't wearing mascara the minute you walked in my door, if you hadn't been ogling Brett."

Abby turned to look at her and snorted a laugh. "Hah! Why should you care, since you say you're not interested in him? And for your information, I was not ogling Brett. I was scoping him out for *you*, which as you well know is sister-friend Rule Number One."

"You'd better not be ogling," John muttered grumpily.

"There's a Gas 'N Grab just up ahead," Abby said brightly. "Don't you need to fill up, honey."

"Oh, right. Do either of you need anything?"

"Mascara," Merrideth said. "If there's any in my bag, I can't find it."

※※※

They arrived at the Egyptian Caravan of Antiques before ten o'clock. In spite of the name, there was nothing the least bit exotic about the event, just row after row of vendors hawking their wares—everything from huge pieces of antique furniture to little knick-knacks and historical oddities. They paid the entry fee and were each given a canvas tote bag imprinted with the name of the event beneath a row of blue camels. Merrideth was glad they had decided to come on Early-Bird-Friday instead of the weekend. The convention center wasn't at all crowded, and her slight—but frustrating—agoraphobia wasn't showing any signs of kicking in.

As they started down the first aisle, she reminded herself sternly to stick to her goal of finding a suitable dresser and not get sidetracked by all the intriguing pieces just begging for her to take them home. But right off, her eyes were drawn to a beautiful little wooden bell. It was darkened with age but had only a few small dents and imperfections. She succumbed to her need to pick it up and then realized that it was not a bell at all, but a butter mold engraved with tiny flowers and leaves. The tag said *circa 1880*. It also said the price was thirty dollars. Merrideth put it back on the shelf with a sigh.

Abby reached in to pick it up. "That would look so sweet on your kitchen window sill, Merri. You should get it."

Merrideth ignored her comment. If she showed the least bit of interest in the butter mold, Abby would insist on buying it for her.

Merrideth heard a faint jingling coming from her shoulder bag and pulled out her phone. "It's Brett." She turned away and said, "Hi, how are the doors coming?"

"Maybe you should have insisted on Acme after all."

"Why, what's wrong?"

"I broke one of the china door knobs. It fell off and hit the tile floor."

"Too bad. I love those knobs."

"I figured. That's why I'm calling. I thought you could keep an eye out for something similar while you're there."

"Good idea."

"Sorry. I should have been more careful."

"Don't be silly. I'm quite certain you didn't do it on purpose."

"Okay, I've got to go. Have fun."

"I'd say the same, but it's hardly fun spending your day off repairing my doors."

"I don't mind in the least, Merri. I forgot to ask when you're coming home."

"I'm not sure. I only want one thing, but you know how that goes."

They said their goodbyes and she turned to see that Abby was trying unsuccessfully to look bored. "He was calling about the doors."

"Right."

"He was. One of the knobs broke. I'm supposed to look for a

replacement."

"I still think you should have invited Brett to come along with us—as a friend, if you're determined not to date."

"He would have attached way more importance to an invitation to spend the day together than I'd like."

"If you say so. We'd better catch up with John. He is not to be trusted in places like this. Last time I had to beg him not to buy a ginormous wagon wheel that he wanted to put on our front porch."

They found John admiring a display of antique hand tools hanging from a battered peg board. He was deep in conversation with the vendor but looked up and smiled at Abby before she was even within ten feet of him. Merrideth sighed. She often teased them about their gooey sweet relationship, all the while secretly hoping she'd find the same for herself one day.

"I was thinking some of these would look good mounted on the wall over the sofa in my man cave," John said, studying Abby's face for her reaction. "It's like art, really. What do you think?"

"They certainly look manly enough for the job, more like weapons than farm tools. That one in the middle looks like the Grim Reaper's whatchamacallit."

"It would be a great conversation starter," John said.

"Practical, too. It could double as a Halloween decoration." Abby put her arm around his waist and studied the tool thoughtfully. "I think you should buy it, sweetie. Just think how handy it would be for keeping overzealous shoppers from snapping up the antiques I want to buy."

John laughed a little sheepishly. "I guess I'd better think about it a little more."

The vendor tried to nail down the sale, but when he saw he wasn't making any headway, he thrust business cards at them and turned to look for paying customers. Abby turned and winked at Merrideth as if to say, "That, my friend, is how to prevent monstrosities from accumulating in your house."

Merrideth smothered a laugh.

"You should open an antique store, Merri," John said, oblivious to the interplay. "Customers would love all the historical background you could give."

John and Abby continued down the packed aisle, stopping to study whatever caught their attention along the way. Merrideth trailed along, still thinking about what John had said. There was a magnificent old home across town that she had been lusting after ever since she'd seen it was for sale. She had dismissed the idea of buying it because it was huge, ridiculously large for one person. But if she lived on the top floor and filled the bottom with antiques.

"Oh, look! See, Merri? By that pregnant lady."

"I don't see any dressers," John said.

"Not dressers, door knobs," Abby said.

"Where was I when you segued into door knobs?"

"Oh, good," Merrideth said, hurrying across the aisle. A conglomeration of door knobs, hinges, and other salvaged findings filled several wooden bins. After only a short time of rummaging through it, Abby found a set of china knobs still on their brass face plates, and they were dead ringers for the ones in Merrideth's apartment. And the price was not bad at all. The vendor was talking to the pregnant woman, but, sensing a sale, he abandoned her and came over.

"I'll take this," Merrideth told him. "It's perfect."

While she was paying for it, the pregnant woman next to her turned toward them. "Abby? John? What are you doing here?"

A smile lit up Abby's face. "Patty Ann Frailey!" Abby took her hands into her own. "Just look at you. You're all grown up."

"And out," she said, patting her belly. "The baby's due to arrive in two weeks."

"Congratulations," John said.

Patty tapped the wedding ring on Abby's left hand. "And congratulations to you two. I thought then you made a perfect couple."

"How long has it been?" John said.

"Fifteen years," Abby said. "Since the summer I tutored Merri. Speaking of whom, here she is."

"Hi, Patty Ann. Merrideth Randall."

"You're *Merrideth* now and I'm just plain *Patty*. I thought Patty Ann sounded a bit much with Anderson." She gestured to the woman beside her. "This is my mother-in-law Louise Anderson. Louise, this is John and Abby...."

"Roberts," John added helpfully.

Louise Anderson awarded them a cool smile. She didn't offer to shake hands. "How do you do?" Her tone as cool as the smile had been.

"They stayed at my parents' house while they were doing genealogy research in the Equality area. John and Abby, that is. Not my parents."

"I did not suppose you meant Benjamin and Darlene." Louise seemed to lose interest in the conversation, and Merrideth had the sense that she would have liked to turn back to the antiques but was too well-bred to be so impolite.

"How are your parents?" John said. "I still remember your dad sitting on the front porch playing his guitar while you and your mom sang old bluegrass tunes."

"Mom and Dad both still play and sing, only now it's for their fellow residents at the assisted living home. The farm is gone now, everything strip-mined away."

"Just as you feared," Abby said sadly.

"But now we have the water park the coal company built," Louise said. "You have to admit Sherman Coal has brought a lot of tourist dollars into the local economy, Patty. Besides, now you're an Anderson, you can roam the vineyards to your heart's content."

Patty grimaced, turning away so her mother-in-law wouldn't see.

Abby and John had gone to Equality on the prowl for information about her roommate Kate's ancestors. Merrideth hadn't been with them, but they had told her all about the bright teenage girl who had served as an unofficial guide and co-conspirator. She seemed like a nice woman—too nice to have an ice queen for a mother-in-law.

"You've heard of Anderson Vineyard and Winery, of course?" Louise said.

"No, sorry," Abby said.

"Really?" Louise said, looking insulted.

"But I noticed your signs this morning as we came into town," John said.

She looked somewhat mollified by his comment.

"So, tell us about your husband, Patty," Abby said. "Do you have a picture?"

"No, not with me. I wish you could meet Alex. He's wonderful." She put just a smidgeon of emphasis on the pronoun *he*. "Unfortunately, he's in Texas on business."

Louise pulled a designer wallet from her designer handbag and opened it to show them several photos of her son Alex. If he had any siblings, she didn't carry their pictures. They all complimented Alex's photo. Indeed, he was a handsome man with the same striking silvery blond hair and blue eyes as his mother. Merrideth hoped he hadn't inherited her personality and that he made up for Patty having to have Louise for a mother-in-law.

Louise's phone rang. Excusing herself, she turned away and spoke into it. She sounded agitated. When she turned back, her cheeks were splotched with red.

"I need to go to the winery, Patty. The fool distributor sent the wrong wineglasses again."

"Just a second, Louise. I want to get this toad for Alex's birthday."

The amphibian in question was from a display of various fanciful animals artfully crafted from scrap metal. They reminded Merrideth of the tin chickens Nelda made.

"I'm sorry, Patty," Louise said. "We have to go. Don't you think Alex would prefer something from the mall anyway?"

"We can take you home, Patty," John said.

"Perfect," Louise said before Patty could answer. She gathered her shoulder bag close. "I'll leave you all to get caught up on old times."

Patty showed no sign of being angry at her mother-in-law's unwillingness to wait the sixty seconds it would take for her to make the purchase. Actually, she seemed positively happy to be rid of her. Merrideth couldn't blame her.

"Sorry about that," Patty said. "I'll just get my toad, and we can move on."

"You should get one for Brett's apartment, Merri," Abby said. "It would be cute."

"No, I have an idea," John said. "Let's get him that grim reaper scythe. He can hang it over his bed as a reminder of what to expect if he ever—"

"Oh, that's really funny, John," Merrideth said.

Abby gave her husband a look and then adroitly turned the conversation back to the summer they'd met Patty. After several minutes of reminiscing, it became obvious that Patty was tiring and needed to sit. Abby offered to take her home so that John and Merrideth could continue browsing. But John wouldn't hear of it, so they got their hands stamped by the attendant at the door and left.

On the way to Patty's house, she gave a summary of her life since John and Abby had last seen her. Stated baldly, it was a dismal history, but Patty told it without the least bit of self-pity. She had earned a state scholarship and gone to Southern Illinois University for three semesters. But then she'd had to drop out to care for her parents, both of whom had developed health problems after the stressful years of fighting with the coal company to save their farm. With the farm gone, they had moved to Marion, where Patty got a job working at Anderson's Vineyard, met Alex, and fell in love. She assured them Alex wasn't anything like his mother. Eventually, Patty had been promoted to office manager, in name if not actuality. Louise butted her nose into every aspect of the winery's business.

"I want to go back to college after the baby's in school," Patty said. "Turn right at the light, John. The house is in the next block."

Merrideth was surprised by the opulence of Patty's house. Judging from Abby and John's description of Patty's humble farm house in the hills, it must have been a huge step up for her. She led them into a formal living room nicely decorated in muted shades of sage green. The furniture was sleek and modern, but Patty had interspersed touches of country-inspired art—paintings of farm scenes and clever pieces of Americana made of pine. The combination of styles shouldn't have worked, but somehow did. Patty set the scrap-metal toad she had bought on the coffee table, and it looked right at home.

Merrideth joined John to study a large painting over the sofa. The artist's perspective was from high on a hill overlooking a green valley. A silvery stream seemed to be actually flowing through the painting.

"I know this spot," John said. "Abby, come look at this."

"It's Eagle Creek," Abby said. "Below your farm."

"Yes," Patty said. "I like to remember the way it was."

John stooped and looked closer, then let out a small grunt. "You painted this, Patty?"

"Yes. All of them. It's a hobby."

"Holy cow, girl!" Abby said. "This is no hobby. Please tell me you're going to major in art."

"I hope to," Patty said, smiling shyly.

She went to get iced tea, and they wandered into the adjoining dining room to look at the art there. On the table was a file folder overflowing with papers. Next to it, a large scrapbook with a pink padded cover lay open to a family tree. Alex Anderson's ancestors were listed on every branch of the left side. Patty's Frailey's were only sparsely represented on the right.

"It's Toad's baby book," Patty said, setting a tray of glasses on the table. "Please, have a seat."

Chuckling at everyone's confusion, Patty put a hand to her belly. "We haven't decided on a name yet, so Alex calls her our little toad."

"Hence the toad you bought today," Abby said, smiling. "Your Alex will love it."

"It will be nice for Toad to know her family history," John said.

"If I don't get going, she's only going to know about her Anderson roots." She rubbed her belly fondly. "But I want Toad to know her heritage—from both sides of the family."

Abby smiled at John and then Merri. "I just had a déjà vu."

"The Old Dears," John said, smiling nostalgically.

Merrideth smiled, too, thinking of Eulah and Beulah's lopsided family tree. The three of them had helped the twin sisters fill in the blanks on their father's Buchanan branch.

"Toad's tree doesn't look as lopsided as some I've seen," John said.

"Turn the page," Patty said.

When he complied, they saw that Patty had attached a fold-out addendum to the genealogy chart. On the left side more Anderson names abounded. The right side was blank.

"I see what you mean," John said.

Patty passed around the glasses of iced tea. "I was able to get a few things from Grandma Ethel's Bible," she said. "I wish I had asked her more about the family while we still had her with us. It was only after I started working on the family tree a few months ago that I realized how little I really knew about the Fraileys. Dad never did talk much about the family. Now with his dementia, he can't. I may never know."

John grimaced. "My dad has Alzheimer's. It's stealing him away before our very eyes."

"I know just what you mean." Patty closed the baby book and busied herself tucking the papers on the table into a folder. "I don't suppose you guys still do genealogy work? I'd pay for your services, of course." She said it reluctantly, as if unwilling to presume on old ties.

"Sorry," Abby said with a nervous laugh. "We don't. Not since that one summer."

"I've often wondered about your computer program. It was amazing what you were able to do with it. Or did I just dream that?"

Merrideth felt her eyes go wide. Somehow Abby and John hadn't gotten around to mentioning to her that they had revealed *Beautiful Houses* to Patty. From the looks on her cohorts' faces, they were wishing Patty didn't know about it. John cleared his throat and exchanged a look with Abby.

"Yes, it was real. Emphasis on *was*," Abby said. "It stopped working right after I found my roommate's family."

"What a shame. I guess it wouldn't work in my situation anyway."

Patty was right. The software only went into what Merrideth called "miracle mode" when it was run in an old building. Without a house connected to the Frailey family, it would be useless as a genealogy tool. If Patty only knew that the software *was* working again—well, it would be just one more reason to mourn her family's strip-mined farm. If any of the buildings had remained, Merrideth would have been able to easily track her family.

Abby looked at Merrideth, the obvious question in her eyes.

"But I happen to do genealogy consulting," Merrideth said. "As a sideline to my teaching. I'd be glad to help with your Fraileys."

"That would be wonderful," Patty said.

Without the program, finding Patty's family would have to be done the old-fashioned labor-intensive way. But even so, Merrideth felt a strong desire to take on the project. Patty Frailey Anderson was obviously important to Abby and John. And even if she weren't, if Merrideth could be instrumental in putting Patty on equal footing within the Anderson family she'd feel like it was a job well done. And if she could find a hero or two like she had for Brett and Nelda Garrison, maybe the Ice Queen would thaw toward her daughter-in-law a little.

Merrideth took one of her business cards out of her bag and handed it to Patty. "I'll give you my friend discount."

Patty smiled. "That's nice of you, Merrideth, but really not necessary. Alex will be happy to pay your normal fee. As a matter of fact, he'll probably insist on it. He's generous to a fault."

Merrideth took her laptop from her shoulder bag and set it on the table. "Then let's get started."

"You really do have everything but the kitchen sink in that thing, don't you?" Abby said.

"Yeah, well, I didn't mean to bring it, but since I did—"

"You should get back to the Egyptian Caravan before all the good things are gone," Patty said.

"Merri's awesome," Abby said, ignoring Patty's comment. "It won't take her long at all to find some juicy facts."

"I can't guarantee that I'll find much, but I'll try. Do you have any documentation for what you have listed in the baby book?"

"A few things. It's all in here," Patty said, handing the file folder to Merrideth.

Inside was her grandparents' marriage license and several other mostly unhelpful documents. The rest were sheets of handwritten names and other notes, which Patty explained were what she remembered from her dad and grandma. Altogether, it wasn't much to go on, but it was a starting place.

Merrideth shooed the others away so she could concentrate. "You might as well spend your time visiting with Abby and John," she said when Patty offered to help. "This part is going to be tedious. I'll call you if I have questions." They obediently went into the living room.

Armed with the information from Patty's file folder, Merrideth logged onto her Ancestry.com account and began the hunt. She quickly got several hits, but they turned out to be New England Fraileys and completely unrelated. When she discovered that *Frailey* was sometimes the Americanized spelling of the German name *Froehlich*, she followed a promising lead to a man named Gerhardt Froehlich who appeared on a list of Illinois prisoners convicted of theft. She wasted several minutes on him until she realized the dates were all wrong. She didn't mind. Red herrings only made the hunt more fun. From time to time laughter came to her from the living room, and then later the sound of Patty singing and playing her guitar. It was a pleasant accompaniment to Merrideth's work.

Eventually she sniffed out the right Fraileys and soon found several online family trees posted by other genealogically-minded Fraileys around the country. Most listings lacked any authoritative, verifiable documentation and contained maddening contradictions and discrepancies. But a handful of them had census reports, marriage and death registries, cemetery lists and other helpful documents attached to their trees. Following each of those trails yielded tons of new data for Patty's tree.

After two hours of work, Merrideth leaned back in her chair and stretched. She had mined all she could via Ancestry.com. If the others were willing to wait while she worked, she would check her other resources.

"Did you find anything?"

Merrideth turned from staring at her monitor and saw Patty standing shyly in the doorway. She smiled. "I did. You can come in, you know. It *is* your dining room."

Patty waved at Abby and John, and they all came in and took seats at the table.

"Okay, Merri, quit looking mysterious and give," Abby said.

"I'm stymied," Merrideth said with an apologetic look at Patty. "I can't find Matthias Frailey's father for anything. I thought for a while that your family must be German. But you're not, which is good because then you would have a convicted thief on your tree. I think you're actually Scottish because—"

"Back to this Matthias you found," John said.

"Oh. Sorry. I guess I was rambling. Matthias Frailey was your great, great, great, great grandfather, Patty."

"Did you say four greats?"

"I did. There are no Fraileys listed in the 1840 census for Gallatin County, but in 1850, Matthias appears there as the head of a household. His age is listed as thirty-two, so he was born about 1818. His son Luke had a son named...well, it got real biblical. Matthias begat Luke. Luke begat Mark. Mark begat Matthew. And Matthew begat John, your grandpa."

"Wow! I had no idea you'd find so much so quickly." Patty put a hand to her belly. "Toad says thank you."

"I told you Merrideth's good," Abby said, smiling smugly.

"A lot of it is pure, blind luck."

"Don't listen to her, Patty. She's being modest," John said. "It takes a lot more than luck and genealogy software to do what she does."

"Oh, stop. You're making me blush," Merrideth said. "I'm sure I can find more Fraileys, Patty. There are a bunch of them in Pope County that I want to check out."

"Why Pope County?" Patty said. "My family has owned our

farm in Gallatin County for generations."

"According to the Illinois registry, Matthias Frailey was married in Pope County to a woman named Emmaline Jones. By the way, I think Emmaline was married previously, because the 1850 census lists a Tobias Jones, age eleven, residing in Matthias' household. The boy could be from her first marriage. But you never know. He might be a nephew or cousin they're raising along with their own children."

"Or maybe Emmaline's brother," John said.

"Right," Merrideth said. "Which is why we don't know whether *Jones* is her maiden name or her first husband's name. But there are a slew of Joneses in Pope County, so if you want me to, I can look into that branch. Fortunately, there aren't as many Fraileys to wade through. I found a Lachlan, age seventy in the 1850 census, and Duncan, Angus, and Simon, all in their thirties, presumably his sons. I'm thinking Matthias is another, but so far I haven't proved it. I had hoped to find him in the 1840 census, but unfortunately, he's not there. At least not as a head of household."

"Maybe he was young enough that he was still living with his parents in 1840," Abby said. "That would tell you their names."

"Don't I wish. But the thing about census records before 1850—here, let me show you."

Merrideth navigated her way back to the 1840 Pope County census and then to the photographic image of the actual ledger page where the Fraileys were listed. She explained that because of the way households were numbered, she had deduced that the census taker had visited each one consecutively. In other words, their properties abutted each other. Together with the Scottish origin of their given names, it was clear that the four Frailey men were related. She pointed out that in 1840, only the names of the men were recorded. Under each one, the other un-named members of his household were enumerated, indicated as ticks on the page, sorted by categories of age, race, and status as slave or free.

"So one of those ticks in Lachlan's household might very well be Matthias," Merrideth said.

"I don't understand the system," John said. "There are ticks all over the place."

"That's because some are bleeding through from the other side of the page."

"Which is why you're stymied," Abby said.

"Which is why I need to make a trip to the courthouse," Merrideth said. "The only way to tell what's what is by visually inspecting the original physical ledger."

"You mean now, Merri?" John said. "Today?"

"Why not? It's only about an hour away, so I might as well go take a look at it while I'm down here. And they may have other records that aren't available online yet."

"But you'll miss your antique show," Patty said, looking distressed.

Merrideth smiled. "Don't worry about it. I'd rather hunt for ancestors than antiques any day." She looked at the time on her computer. It was nearly noon. "I should be back by three o'clock, easy."

Abby turned to John and they did their silent communication thing. Without a word between them they reached a consensus and turned together to face Merrideth.

"We'll come with you, Merri," John said. "I wouldn't feel right about you going alone."

Abby slung an arm around Merrideth's shoulder. "As for the antiques—we can always come back down tomorrow."

"Don't be silly," Patty said. "You can spend the night here. I'll have dinner ready for you when you get back."

"And hopefully, I'll have more ancestors ready for Toad," Merrideth said.

CHAPTER 3

Golconda, the governmental seat of Pope County, was a river town on the Ohio, making its population of 861 some of Illinois' southernmost citizens. In a town that size, the brick courthouse was easy to spot. John parked and they walked up the front sidewalk.

To the right of the double doors, a stone monument with a brass plaque caught their attention. According to it, the founder of the town was a woman named Sarah Lusk. In 1796 her husband Major James Lusk had led a party of thirty-five hearty pioneers from South Carolina and settled on the Illinois side of the Ohio River in what would eventually become Golconda. It was the first permanent white settlement between Kentucky and Kaskaskia. While James turned his attention to setting up a ferry service between Illinois and Kentucky, Sarah hired a surveyor and laid out the new town, which they named Sarahville in her honor. Years later, when the Lusks were only a faint memory, the town fathers changed the name to Golconda.

"She must have been quite a woman," Merrideth said.

"Doesn't seem fair to change the town's name," John said.

Abby ran her hand over the plaque. "At least someone remembered her."

They went inside, and a pleasant secretary in the county clerk's office cheerfully directed them to the records room on the second floor of the courthouse.

A waist-high slanted counter ran down the center of the room.

A man stood at it with piles of books and papers spread out before him. He looked up briefly and smiled distractedly. He reminded Merrideth of some actor she had recently seen on TV, although she couldn't pull the name from her mental file cabinet. He had the looks for Hollywood. His mouth quirked in an attractive manner, and his eyes were a swoon-worthy shade of blue. But no tinsel town actor would be caught dead wearing outdated glasses, a button-down plaid shirt in hideous shades of green, and shabby cargo pants.

Abby nudged Merri's side and whispered, "Cute, huh? Ryan Gosling playing the role of small town nerd. And I don't see a ring either."

Wow. Two attempted matches in one day. It was a new record for Abby. Shaking her head, Merrideth strode into the room, her friends trailing after her. The guy *was* kind of cute. Her eyes were drawn against her will to his left hand, and she saw that Abby was correct. She mentally shook herself and turned to the business at hand.

She found the census ledgers on the far wall. The earliest one was for 1820, the latest for 1940. But the one that she had specifically come to see was not there.

"I'm, sorry," Merrideth whispered. "I guess this was a wasted trip." Then she had a thought. She went around the counter and stood beside the man until he looked up at her. "Excuse me. Do you have the 1840 census ledger by any chance?"

He blinked owlishly at her. "What? Oh. Sorry." He shuffled the papers in front of him.

One of them ripped and Merrideth gasped. "Shouldn't you be more careful with those documents?"

He looked up at her in surprise. "Oh. Don't worry. These aren't official. I'd never— They're just my notes. For a book I'm writing." He extracted a ledger from the pile and handed it to her. "Here you go."

"Thanks." She turned and found Abby looking like a hawk ready to pounce on a mouse. So much for her promise to mend her ways. John put a restraining hand on his wife's arm and sent her a nonverbal warning to settle down, already. The unsuspecting man beside her hadn't yet realized he was in Abby's sights. Unfortunately, the reason he hadn't noticed was because he was staring at Merrideth as if he had never seen a woman before.

He shoved more papers aside to make room at the counter for her. "Sorry for hogging the whole room. I get a little carried away when I'm on the hunt."

"I have a friend like that," Merrideth said, sending Abby a warning glare. She set the ledger down on the counter next to him.

"I'm Nick Landis," he said, extending a hand.

"Hi. Merrideth Randall."

"And we're Abby and John Roberts," Abby said at his other side. "What's your book about?"

Nick Landis seemed a little taken aback, as if he hadn't noticed them there. "I'm writing about the Kaskaskia-Cahokia Trail." He drew their attention to the map in front of him on the counter. "It was one of the earliest roads in Illinois, here more than a century before the Americans came on the scene."

"I know. It's fascinating, isn't it?" Merrideth said. "First the buffalo, then the French trappers, and finally the Americans."

He looked surprised, but then most people didn't go around spouting obscure historical facts off the cuff. Merrideth chuckled. "I'm a history professor at McKendree College. I did some research recently on the trail as it passes through Monroe County."

"Merrideth was instrumental in finding Fort Piggot," Abby said.

"Lots of people helped."

"I read about that," Nick said. "It was an amazing discovery. Why are you here?" His face grew pink. "Sorry. That was rather abrupt."

"Nothing as dramatic as Fort Piggot. I'm doing genealogy research for a friend. I traced her ancestor Matthias Frailey to Pope County."

Merrideth opened the ledger and carefully thumbed through the fragile pages until she reached the Frailey entries. And there they were: Lachlan, Duncan, and Angus—the Fraileys of Pope County. Seeing their names in faded brown ink made her stomach flutter, as it did every time she handled old documents.

"But no Matthias Frailey," Nick said. "Too bad."

Merrideth looked up and was startled to find that he was close enough to read the ledger.

"Oh, sorry for butting in," he said, stepping back. "I get excited." He took another step back. "I mean, with historical things. Not women I just met."

Merrideth smiled. "I knew what you meant."

She turned back to study the page. Even though the ink was faded, it was clear enough to plainly see that the census taker had made only three ticks in Lachlan's household, one in the 60's age bracket and two in the 20's. "They are just the right ages," Merrideth said. "One of the twenty-somethings is undoubtedly Simon, still living with his parents before he married, and the other one just may be our missing Matthias."

"Not unless Matthias is a girl," Nick said. "The tick is in the female column."

"What?" Merrideth squinted at the page again. "Drat! You're right."

"You don't suppose the census taker made a mistake," Abby said.

Sighing, Merrideth closed the ledger. "I suppose it's possible, but I doubt it."

"Then what do we do next, Merri?" John said.

"We can check the probate records, deed books, stuff like that, unless you're in a hurry to get back to Marion, in which case I could do that online when I get home."

"I'm not sure all of that has been digitized yet," Nick said.

"We've still got time," Abby said. "You should take a look at what they have while we're here."

"They're over here," Nick said, pointing to the shelves behind them.

They found the Fraileys listed in several indices. And, dividing the books between the four of them—Nick insisted on helping— they began the tedious business of hunting down every last reference to *Frailey*. Most of them concerned Lachlan Frailey who made multiple land purchases and had a thriving lumber business at Frailey Landing on Lusk Creek.

"They were smart to locate there," Nick said. "Lusk Creek empties into the Ohio. From there, Lachlan Frailey could get his lumber to the Mississippi and then on to New Orleans with its shipping connections to ports around the world. As for ground transport, there was Lusk Road, our present-day Highway 146, which went to Kaskaskia, the seat of government for Illinois at the time. This means the Fraileys' operation was smack dab where all the early immigrants were flooding into Illinois needing lumber to build their cabins and commercial buildings. Whole towns were springing up."

"Shrewd businessmen, the Fraileys," John said.

"And prosperous," Abby said.

Nick smiled. "Indeed. And another major benefit for the Fraileys' lumber business would have been the Golconda Ferry. Major James Lusk built it and an inn called the Ferry House in 1797."

"He was an enterprising man," John said.

"Very," Nick said. "Lusk also constructed another corduroy road from Golconda to a point on the Mississippi River across from Cape Girardeau, Missouri, where there was another early ferry. This virtually guaranteed that the flow of pioneer immigrants heading west used Lusk Ferry. And then during the Removal—"

"Oh, that's right," Merrideth said. "They came through Golconda."

"Who?" Abby said.

"The Cherokee on the Trail of Tears," Merrideth explained. "They came across the Ohio on the ferry at Golconda, traveled across the state, and then entered Missouri at Cape Girardeau."

"A lot of people don't realize they came through southern Illinois," Nick said. "They camped west of town."

"It must have been quite a sight," Merrideth said.

"I could show you the trail they took," Nick said. "There are clues if you know where to look for them."

"Maybe some other time," Merrideth said. "We need to focus on our task and not go off on tangents, no matter how interesting."

"Sure. I understand."

They got back to the hunt. Most of the Frailey references were mundane and useless for their purpose, but still each one had to be checked. Merrideth was just closing the last ledger in her stack when Nick grunted with excitement and said, "I found something."

Merrideth looked over his shoulder. "It's Lachlan Frailey's will."

They crowded around him to read it. Legal jargon was difficult enough to read from a modern typed page, and this was handwritten in faded brown ink on a mottled page decorated with fly specks. But the gist of the will was crystal clear: When Lachlan Frailey died in 1868 at 91 years of age, he bequeathed 1000 acres of prime land to his "beloved sons Duncan, Angus, and Simon." There was no mention of a son named Matthias.

Merrideth sighed in disappointment. "Well, that stinks."

"Maybe he predeceased his father," John said.

"I don't know Matthias Frailey's death date, but he was still in Gallatin County for the 1870 census."

"Don't worry, Merri," Abby said. "Patty is thrilled with what you already found." She smiled at Nick. "Thanks for helping."

"Not a problem. It was fun." Although responding to Abby's thanks, he kept his eyes on Merrideth.

"Good luck with your book," Merrideth said, picking up her shoulder bag from the floor.

"Thanks." Nick was still watching her when they left the room.

"Don't look back, Merri," John said with a smirk. "Or he'll get up the nerve to follow you. He's dying to ask for your phone number."

"John and I can make ourselves scarce if you want to let Nick show you around town."

"No,

we cannot," John said. "I'm not about to let her go off with a strange man and—"

"Oh, you're not, are you? Merrideth said.

"What I meant to say was—"

"Save it, John, I have absolutely no interest in Nick Landis."

"Are you sure?" Abby said.

"I'm sure. And even if I did, I wouldn't dare show it with the dragon here." Merrideth stabbed a finger into John's chest. "Nick Landis is a nice man doing historical research just like we are, which I suggest we get back to doing, okay?"

"I thought we were done here," John said.

"I was thinking we should try to find the Fraileys' property."

"Why?" Abby said.

"Would you think I'd gone all woo-woo if I told you that despite the lack of evidence, my intuition is still screaming that Matthias was related to the Golconda Fraileys?"

John grinned. "Maybe you are woo-woo, but I think it makes sense to go take a look at the property. For all we know, there could still be Frailey descendants living there. Maybe even evidence of the old sawmill, which would be totally cool to see."

It *would* be cool, but not for the reason John thought. If she could find any buildings from Lachlan's time still standing on the Frailey property, she could set up *Beautiful Houses* and time-surf back to find out whether or not he and Matthias were related.

"Then let's go. Only can we hurry?" Abby said, looking at her watch. "I want to get back to antique hunting."

By the time they reached the car, Merrideth had the navigational app up on her phone.

"Do we know specifically where the Frailey land was?" Abby said.

"Nope," Merrideth said. "Those court records aren't much help unless you have the corresponding plat map. And even if we had one, there's little to go on while driving along down the road. But if you follow Lusk Creek we'll have to come to it eventually. Turn left onto Decatur Street at the stop sign, John. According to my map, it parallels the creek."

There were too many houses to see anything until they reached the edge of town, and then Abby spotted Lusk Creek flowing by on their right. It was a surprisingly small and unremarkable stream.

"That's Lusk Creek?" John said. "It could barely float a rubber ducky to the Ohio, much less a load of lumber."

"Streams change sometimes," Merrideth said. "I saw the same thing when I was looking for Fort Piggot."

When they reached the city limits, the street downgraded into a country road. Five miles later it curved to the west to circumnavigate a small lake. When they got past it, the creek was somewhat larger. They drove for another five miles but there were no clues to indicate where Frailey Landing once was. There were certainly no old buildings beckoning her to come time-surf.

"You might as well turn around," Merrideth said.

"Well, it was a nice drive," Abby said.

John pulled the car into a driveway and then turned back toward Golconda. "I just thought of something. You know that lake we passed?"

"My map calls it Lack Land Pond," Merrideth said.

"The Frailey property had to be near there, because wouldn't they need a mill pond to run their sawmill?"

"Lachlan Pond!" Merrideth said. "Not *Lack Land*. I'll bet you five dollars."

John slowed down as they came to the pond again. "I'm going to keep my eyes on the road. You two look and tell me what you see."

Merrideth trained her eyes over the landscape. "I don't see anything man-made."

"Unless you count that rickety picnic table," Abby said.

"If the Frailey's lumber business was ever there, everything is gone now," Merrideth said. "Sorry for the wild goose chase. We can leave now."

"It was worth a look," John said.

Merrideth's phone rang. It was Brett again. The last thing she wanted to do was have a conversation with him while Abby and John were listening in. But what if he had run into some other problem with the doors and needed something to finish them? She angled herself toward the window and spoke just above a whisper into the phone. "Hi. We found a door knob."

"I can't hear you," Brett said.

She gave up on the notion of privacy. "I said, we found a door knob."

"Is he stalking you?" John said.

"Hold on, Brett. I've got interference." She muffled the phone with her coat sleeve and glared at the back of John's head. "Do you mind?"

"Oh, sorry."

She put the phone back to her ear. "Now, what were you saying?"

"I said that it's good that you got the knobs. I finished your doors. Now I'm thinking maybe I should paint my condo."

"Wow, you are in a home-improvement mood, aren't you?"

"Yes, well I had planned on something else entirely for the weekend, but then that fell through at the last minute."

Had that something else involved her? She wouldn't have agreed anyway, so it was just as well he was getting useful work done.

"I'd be glad to help you paint." It was something friends did, didn't they?

"I wasn't asking for that. But I am hoping you could help me pick the color. I've been told I'm a complete dunce in that department."

She laughed. "I really doubt that. But I'll see if I can help. What did you have in mind?"

"Well, I like the colors in your apartment. They're so...colorful."

"My walls are a neutral tan. Do you mean my throw pillows and curtains—things like that?"

"Right. Those."

"Well, you can't paint your walls red, blue, and green, Brett."

"Why not?"

"I don't know. You just can't."

Abby turned in her seat. "You should make some for him, Merri."

Merrideth muffled her phone. "Make what?"

"Curtains and throw pillows."

Helping Brett paint was one thing. Delving into the domestic arts for him was quite another. "I don't know how to sew."

"Don't be silly." Abby turned further in her seat and called out, "You should have seen the great Halloween zombie costume she made, Brett."

He laughed. "I wish I could have."

"Well, it didn't require sewing skills," Merrideth said.

"I could teach you," Abby said.

"I think I'm going to like your friend Abby." Brett's voice was filled with laughter. He knew very well what Abby was up to, and what Merrideth thought of it. "That's all right, Merri. I'll think of something to liven up my dentist's waiting room."

"Abby made mine, but there are plenty of colorful curtains, pillows and throws and such at the mall."

"Thanks for the tip."

"Glad to help."

"One more question. What's a throw?"

"A blanket to snuggle up with on your couch. Not *your* couch necessarily. I should have said *one's* couch."

"Then I'm definitely getting one of those."

"Goodbye, Brett."

He was laughing again when she hung up.

They were just entering Golconda. Merrideth tried to imagine what it had looked like back in its early days as Sarahville. A few of the commercial buildings looked old—or at least old-ish. But certainly none dated back to the 1790s.

John started rubber-necking, and Abby said, "What are you looking for?"

"Some place to eat. I don't think I can wait until dinner."

"I'll see if I can find something," Merrideth said, studying her phone app. "There's Cousin Eddy's, but that sounds like a bar." Then she let out a squawk. "Or how about the Ferry House! It's on Water Street. Turn right at the intersection."

"Why the excitement?" John gave her an amused look in the rearview mirror. "I thought I was the one who squealed like a baby at the thought of food."

"Because I'm hoping it's the original inn," Merrideth said. "You know, the one Nick told us about."

"Oh, I hope so," Abby said. "I love old buildings."

"Really?" John said ironically. "I had no idea."

When they came to the intersection, they saw the Ohio straight ahead. John turned onto Water Street and they drove alongside the river.

"There it is," Merrideth said, pointing out her window.

The Ferry House sat overlooking the river at the intersection of Water and Main Streets.

John parked in a lot across the street from the restaurant, and Merrideth got out and studied the building. "It's old," she said with satisfaction. "Very old."

A porch spanned the whole front, which was covered in wide wooden planks totally unlike siding used in modern homes. Dormer windows on the upper floor were covered with homey curtains, indicating someone lived there. Residing above a restaurant surely wasn't ideal, but whoever lived up there had to have a good view of the river.

The riverbank below the Ferry House was paved with irregular, moss-covered stones, indicating where the landing had once been. Weary travelers would have stepped off onto a dock then walked up the landing and into the inn for a meal or lodging. Locals would have gathered there, too, for mugs of beer or just to hang out and shoot the breeze.

What better place to time-surf than the local watering hole? Probably everyone in the whole area—the men at least—came to the Ferry House at one time or another. If she couldn't go to the Fraileys' home, she'd wait and let them come to her. Merrideth retrieved her bag from the car and slid it onto her shoulder.

"I could lock that in back for you," John said.

She instinctively hugged it to herself. "No, that's all right."

"Suit yourself," he said, pocketing his keys.

Abby smiled at her and took her arm. "Merri, you look as excited as a kid going to the fair."

Merrideth snapped out of it and plastered on what she hoped was a semi-bored look. "I'm just looking forward to lunch."

And a chance to time-surf back to Matthias Frailey's time. That is, if she could think of a way to slip away from them to set up *Beautiful Houses*.

Although it was nearly two-thirty, the restaurant was still crowded and noisy. Merrideth studied the layout as the hostess led them to their table. The building was not as large as she had thought it would be. Certainly there were no quiet alcoves where she could set up without being noticed. Even if there were, Abby would come looking for her if she were gone more than a few minutes. And it would take a good bit of time, even if she were lucky enough to find the Fraileys right away.

Someone grabbed her arm, and Merrideth turned in alarm.

"Merrideth, you're still here." A smile lit Nick Landis' face as if he'd just won a prize.

"And us," John muttered.

"My booth is right over here."

The hostess realized they were no longer following her. "I can seat you with him," she said. "I'm running out of tables anyway."

"That's great," Merrideth said, because what else could she say?

When they were seated, Abby said, "This is a cool building, Nick. Do you know how old it is?"

"It's not the original Ferry House, I'm sorry to say. But it *is* old. It was rebuilt on the same site back in the 1870s. There are two apartments upstairs. I'm going to rent one of them as soon as Mr. Starnes—he's the owner of this place—gets the lock changed. The previous tenant absconded with the only two keys."

"But the Buel House is the one that is really old," Nick said. "Its claim to fame is that during the Trail of Tears, the Buel family gave pumpkins from their garden to the hungry Cherokee. You should take the tour."

"Are you from around here, Nick?" Abby said.

"Born and bred. As a matter of fact, the Landis family was one of the first to settle here."

While the others made small talk, Merrideth tried to contain her frustration. The current Ferry House was not old enough. Matthias Frailey would have been long gone by the time it was built. She studied the quaint antique signs covering the restaurant's rough-cut cedar walls. Like the building itself, the signs were only reproductions. Then something Nick had said bubbled to the top of her brain.

"But they built it on the original foundation, right?" Merrideth said. She could tell from everyone's expressions that she had blurted that out apropos of nothing they had been discussing. She felt her cheeks grow warm.

But Nick smiled as if she'd said something brilliant. "Yes."

Merrideth smiled. "That's a relief...I mean, isn't it fascinating?" It was difficult to contain her excitement. Her software might still work even if the current building wasn't old enough! After all, she'd picked up enough vibes from the foundation of the Garretson's blockhouse fort to make it work there. Merrideth made an effort to tune in to the others' chit-chat.

They talked about their respective jobs, about local history, and about Nick's book. Merrideth found it difficult to concentrate when all she could think of was her laptop—more specifically, the software on it. She managed to hold up her end of the conversation. Mostly. But toward the end of lunch she realized she must not be doing so well, because Abby and John did that wordless telegraph thing they were so good at and then they raised their eyebrows in identical expressions of confusion.

"Are you all right, Merri?" Abby said.

"Sure. Why wouldn't I be? I was just thinking. That's all."

"Then let's get going back to Marion." John laid money on the table and rose. "If we hurry we can still get in a little antique hunting."

Nick stood to let Abby out. She started to scoot out of the booth, but Merrideth put a hand on her arm. "Wait! We can't leave yet."

Abby's eyes went wide, and Merrideth realized that her tone had set off her friend's uncanny radar.

"I mean I have to use the restroom."

"Oh. Me, too." Abby shot John a look, and his eyebrows rose in curiosity.

Nick seemed oblivious to the interplay. He sat back down and picked up the dessert menu, obviously not intending to leave any time soon. Sighing, John sat down across from him.

The moment Merrideth stepped inside the restroom, Abby turned piercing eyes her way. "Okay. What gives?"

"What do you mean?"

She snorted. "I mean you freaked out when John suggested we leave. Furthermore, you hardly said a word all through lunch. You just sat there stroking your backpack like Gollum did the ring. What's in there anyway? Do you call it 'My Precious'?"

Telling Abby and John about *Beautiful Houses* had always been a foregone conclusion. But she had hoped to have a little more time to use the program—and more time to think of a good way to let them know she'd been keeping it a secret from them. But if she didn't tell them now, they'd leave the Ferry House, and her opportunity to find Matthias Frailey would be lost.

She expelled a deep breath. "You know that time the girls and I camped out in your attic."

"Last Halloween."

"Right. Well, in the middle of the night, I got the blue-light special."

"You went to K-Mart?"

"Don't be silly. You remember the way the light would come on in the night, don't you?"

Abby gasped. "Oh, *that* blue light special. How?"

"John's old laptop. It was in a box on your storage shelf."

"I forgot all about it being up there."

"Anyway, when I went to investigate the light, there it was on the screen—*Beautiful Houses: Take a Virtual Tour.* And it works, Abby! Just like before."

"And so you've been using it ever since."

"Yes."

"Whatever happened to our Three Musketeers pact? One for all and all for one—and all that?"

"I'm sorry, Abby. I know we agreed to only time-surf together, but you and John weren't there, and well, it seemed as if I were being given permission to use it again."

"And you have it there in your backpack?"

"I do. On a new computer, that is."

"Then what are you waiting for? Go find Matthias Frailey."

"Here?"

"Lock yourself in one of the stalls. I'll go try to shake your boyfriend." She smiled mischievously. "I should tell him you've contracted a stomach virus and are in here puking up your socks."

Merrideth let out a relieved breath. "Thanks, Abby."

"You're not off the hook yet, girlfriend. John's going to be mad. At both of us."

"I figured.".

CHAPTER 4

Someone knocked on the stall door, and Merrideth jerked in alarm. She blinked several times to clear away the confusion. "What?"

"Merri? You didn't fall in, did you?"

Abby was back. Merrideth took out her earbuds and opened the door. "I need more time. I just heard someone mention the Fraileys."

"Sorry, kiddo. You're fresh out of time. You've been in there for twenty minutes and the natives are getting restless."

"I have? It seemed like only couple of minutes. I saw Sarah Lusk. She was a strong-minded woman. Beautiful, too. Oh, and William Henry Harrison was here in 1804 when he was the Territorial governor. He came to help sort out some legal problems Sarah was having after her husband died. A bully was trying to take the ferry away from her. When Harrison reached the ferry on the Kentucky side, the bully refused to let him board. Sarah and her little maid took their guns and went storming over to Kentucky to get the governor. Harrison got the problem all straightened out for Sarah, and she managed the ferry for years. He was a good man. I met him when I did that work for Brett's Aunt Nelda."

"You can tell us all about it later. Right now it's time to make an appearance before Nick decides we should call an ambulance for you. He is so crushing on you. The guys should be back any minute."

"Where did they go?"

"John convinced Nick that he wanted to see his apartment upstairs. He told him some Banbury tale about wanting to look out

40

over the river."

When they got back to the dining room, Nick and John were just entering it from the opposite doorway. Nick gave Merrideth a concerned look. John smiled toothily at her. It was more like the kind of smile displayed by psychotic killers in horror movies, than what friends and acquaintances typically sent her way. So Abby had already told him, then.

Merrideth put a smile on her own face and spoke out of the side of her mouth to Abby. "What are we going to do?"

"I have no idea. Maybe John has come up with something."

Just as John and Nick reached them, Merrideth's phone rang. She dug it out of her bag.

"Are you all right, Merri?" Nick said as he reached her. "I—we—were worried about you."

"I'm fine, Nick, really." From her phone Brett said, "Who's Nick?"

"Oh, hi, Brett. What's up?"

At her greeting, her three companions' expressions changed: Abby smiled brightly, John rolled his eyes, and Nick Landis' face fell with disappointment.

"So you're not going to answer my question?" Brett said.

Merrideth put her phone to her sleeve and whispered, "Why don't you guys go on to the car. I'll be right there."

"That's all right," Abby said. "We don't mind waiting."

John leaned against a cedar support post and put on his long-suffering expression. Nick stood next to him, hands in his pockets, looking sad.   .

Merri ignored them and put the phone back to her ear.

"Are you there?" Brett said.

"Sort of. Sorry. We're in a restaurant, and it's loud in here. What were you saying?"

"I said don't feel like you have to tell me."

"Tell you what?"

"Who Nick is."

"Good."

"So what's wrong with you?"

"Nothing's wrong. Why?"

"Your Nick said he was worried about you."

"Oh, that. It was nothing. But that's not why you called."

"I need more color advice."

"Okay, shoot."

"I went to the mall to get…something. And while I was there, I thought I might as well look at stuff for my apartment. I found some pillows."

"That's great. But can we talk later?"

"Ah, Nick grows impatient for you to return."

"Nick is not impatient. And even if he were…" She glared at the three shamelessly listening in on her conversation. "And even if he were, well it would be too bad, because I'm talking to you, Brett. So talk. What color of pillows did you decide on?"

"I got blue ones. But then I wondered if maybe green would be better."

"It's not a matter of what color is *better*. You should get the pillows you like."

"But if you took a poll of the average man on the street, do you think he'd prefer blue or green?"

"How should I know?"

"Okay, what about you personally?"

"Blue, I guess. What shade of blue are the pillows?"

"I don't know. Blue."

"Is it more of a cool blue or a warm one?"

"I have absolutely no idea what that even means."

"Is it more like that blue striped tie you wear or your paisley one?"

"Hang on, I'll go get them."

Merrideth heard the sound of doors opening and hangers on clothes rods.

"You sure pay a lot of attention to what the guy wears," John said. "For someone who's not dating him."

Nick Landis straightened his shoulders and lost his glum look. Abby just smiled like a self-satisfied cat. If a cat could smile.

Merrideth shook her head and went back to ignoring them. In her ear Brett said, "Okay, some of the pillows are like my striped tie and some are like the paisley one. That's good, right?"

"Not really, Brett. I'd stick with one or the other and take the rest back."

"That's what I was thinking. I got too many anyway."

"How many did you buy?"

"Ten."

Merrideth laughed. "That's a lot of pillows, Professor

Garrison."

"As I found out. So which do you like better, my striped tie or the paisley?"

"I like them both, but the paisley one is my favorite. I mean since you ask. It's not like I pay much attention." She liked everything he wore, much more than was good for her.

"Oh? If it doesn't matter to you, then I guess I'll go with paisley blue. Since the throw I bought is more that shade. I think."

An image of the two of them snuggled together on his couch in a throw the color of his blue tie popped into her head. She banished it and said, "Okay, then. I have to go now."

"Thanks for the color advice. Have fun, Merri."

Merrideth put her phone back in her bag.

"All done, Merri?" John said.

"Quite finished."

"I wouldn't want you to cut your pillow discussion short," he said, looking at his watch.

"There's no hurry, surely." Abby sent John a speaking glance while Nick was distracted with a passing busboy.

"No, we really must hurry along."

On the front porch of the restaurant they said their goodbyes to Nick Landis for the second time. And for the second time, he stood sadly watching them leave.

In the car, John said, "Everyone wave bye-bye to Nick."

"John, we can't leave," Merrideth said. "I think I've found the Fraileys."

"I have no intention of leaving. Just wave, will you?"

John pulled the car into the street, and they all waved at Nick as they drove past.

"Cluck. Cluck," John said. "He is desperate to have your phone number, Merri, but he stands there like a big chicken, too scared to ask for it. At least Garrison has enough guts to get it."

"Be nice," Abby said.

"I'll drive around the block until he leaves, while Merri tells us what she found out. While she was, you know, time-surfing without us."

Merrideth cleared her throat. "Well...I saw lots of people coming into the Ferry House. For one, Alexander Buel, the famous pumpkin man that Nick told us about. Buel was a tanner by trade, and I heard him talking about leather he was tanning for someone.

More importantly, I heard someone else mention the name *Frailey*. They're bound to come into the Ferry House sooner or later. I just need more time. You know how long it can take to fast-forward through the mundane stuff in people's lives to get to what you need."

"Yes, Merri," John said. "We do know. I can't believe you didn't tell us."

Merrideth turned her eyes away from her friends and studied the view out her window. "When it stopped working that summer, you said it was all for the best. That it was too dangerous to use. If the wrong people got a hold of the program, everyone's privacy would be a thing of the past."

"It *is* dangerous," John said.

"Don't you agree, Merri?" Abby said.

"I do. But, I couldn't resist using it. Don't you see the potential for historians?"

John frowned at Merrideth in the mirror. "And that's how you did the genealogy for Garrison and his aunt?"

"Yes."

"And Fort Piggot!" Abby said. "You used *Beautiful Houses* to find Fort Piggot, didn't you?"

"Yes."

"You should have told us," John said. "You had to know how much we would have enjoyed being in on the find."

Merrideth quailed at the hurt in his voice. "I'm sorry. But I couldn't risk that you'd tell me not to use it."

"I've been thinking about it, John," Abby said. "Your laptop has been up there all this time, and we never got the blue-light special. But Merri did. And so I think she should use it."

"I suppose you're right," John said. "Only do you think sometimes we could come along, Merri?"

"Of course you can, John. It will be like old times."

"Good. We'll get started as soon as Landis clears out."

"But where can we set up?" Merrideth said. "Abby and I might be able to hide out in the ladies' room, but you can't. Besides, sitting on the edge of a toilet seat is not the most comfortable way to time-surf—although it beats sitting on a rock at night in a snowstorm."

John turned to glance at her. "What?"

"Never mind." Mentioning her ordeal to find Fort Piggot would only make him mad again.

"Never fear. That won't be necessary. I already have a spot in mind—a most comfy spot," he said, smiling smugly. "Abby, you might as well call Patty and tell her we're going to be late."

Abby patted John's arm. "You're looking all adventurous. What do you have up your sleeve?"

"You'll see."

When they got back to the Ferry House there was no sign of Nick. John led them past the busy wait staff to the back staircase, Abby hanging on his arm and nearly squeaking with excitement.

"Shhh," he said, smiling fondly down at his wife. "You'll give us away."

Merrideth felt the usual touch of envy at the diabetes-inducing sweetness of her friends' relationship. And as usual, she covered over the feeling with a joke. "Hey, James Bond. You might want to hurry before someone sees us."

"Follow me," John said.

They tiptoed up the stairs. The hall at the top was illuminated by the last of the daylight coming in through two dirty windows, one on either end of it. There were two doors, presumably to the two apartments Nick had mentioned. John went directly to the door on their right and bent as if he were intent on studying the door knob. After a moment he rose and the door swung open.

"Did you just pick that lock?" Merrideth asked in shock.

"Of course not," John said. "It didn't lock properly when Nick and I left, which was due to the piece of cardboard I stuck in the door jam. I saw the trick on TV. Cool, huh?"

"John Roberts!" Abby said.

He grinned at her outrage. "Don't worry, my dear. I haven't gone to the dark side. Landis had me do it. Mr. Starnes is leaving the apartment open for him until he gets the new lock. Landis wants to take measurements and such."

John waved them inside and shut and locked the door. The apartment was tiny but clean, and the walls had been recently painted. Other than the usual appliances, including an ancient microwave, the only furnishings in the combination living room/kitchen was a small dinette table and chairs. In the bedroom a bed with a sagging mattress stood against one wall. Otherwise, the apartment was completely empty, bare of anything of value. If they were discovered, no one could possibly accuse them of theft.

Even so, Merrideth felt like a felon.

From the look on her face, Abby felt the same way.

John put an arm around her shoulders. "Don't worry, Abby. Landis won't mind if we borrow the apartment for a while."

"And you know this because of your ESP?" Abby said.

"What can I say. He's a nice guy."

"Is the electricity even on?" Abby said.

"It is. See the microwave clock?" John said.

"It wouldn't matter," Merrideth said. "I have a military-grade battery for my laptop."

"Good, but I was thinking about heat," Abby said. "We might as well be comfortable if we're going to do this. We'll have years of sitting around in cold jail cells later."

"Don't be such a worrywart." John went to the thermostat on the wall and moved the dial up. After a moment, they heard the furnace kick on, and heat began pumping into the room.

"But what about an Internet connection?" Abby said.

Smiling, Merrideth set her backpack on the kitchen table and started unpacking her equipment. "No worries. Timmy Tech made me another gizmo. It's even better than the one he gave John back in the day. This puppy can pick up a Wi-Fi signal a quarter of a mile away."

"And no pesky passwords, I presume?" John said hopefully.

"You presume correctly."

They positioned their chairs to watch *Beautiful Houses* load. The familiar logo filled the screen, inviting them to *Take a Virtual Tour*. "There it is," Abby said wistfully. "It's been such a long time,"

"Let's just hope it will go into miracle mode again for me," Merrideth said.

After what seemed like an eternity of flickering color-filled screens alternating with black ones, the interior view of the Ferry House taproom, still paused at the moment in time that Merrideth had left it, popped into view.

"And there we are," Merrideth said.

John leaned in to look closer. "It doesn't look much like the restaurant downstairs. But I suppose that's to be expected."

"No wonder," Abby said, pointing to the time indicator at the bottom. "We're in 1840."

"That man holding the mug of beer is Alexander Buel," Merrideth said. "The tanner-slash-pumpkin man."

"Can you un-pause it?" John said.

"Sure."

Buel lifted the beer mug to his lips and drank deeply.

"Cool," John said.

"I forgot how fun it was to see all the details on their clothes," Abby said. "Zoom in a little, Merri."

She did, but even so it was difficult to make out everything. The room was lit only by candles and oil lanterns. Merrideth counted five other men besides Buel, including the barkeeper. Then the door opened and a group of boisterous young men came in, clapping each other's backs and shouting for drinks.

Merrideth stopped the action "Did you notice that clattering sound? They're stacking their weapons on the porch as they come in. They've just come from Muster Day."

"Mustard Day?" Abby said. "That can't be good."

John laughed and pinched her cheek. "You're so cute. It's *Muster*, not *mustard*, Abby."

She turned red. "Explain, please."

Grinning, Merrideth went into professor mode. "For more than a century Muster Day was an important event in every town and village across the country. At least once a year every able-bodied man was *mustered* to drill under the command of the local ranking officer. These local militias were the forerunner of today's National Guard. Mostly Muster Day was a time for the men to swagger, brag, and get into fights. At the end of the day, they drank themselves silly. After the Civil War, the tradition came to an end. It was not, after all, a very effective way to train soldiers."

John turned back to study the paused scene. "So you think we might find Matthias Frailey in this roomful of men."

"As I said, every able-bodied man was required to muster."

"But not necessarily to go to the bar afterward," Abby said.

"True," Merrideth said. "But this is where I heard someone mention the Frailey name. My speakers aren't the best, and with all the barroom noise I couldn't tell who said it."

"Okay," John said. "Let it run and we'll try to pick it out."

Merrideth un-paused and they watched and listened in on the men for several minutes. Most of what they said was good-natured boasting about their prowess with their weapons, overlaid with not-so-subtle innuendos about their prowess in bed.

"Oh, for crying out loud," Abby said. "That is such a cliché."

"The equivalent of the modern-day locker room," John said. "I hope Patty Ann's ancestor isn't one of these jokers."

"Keep listening," Merrideth said. "I know I heard it."

The men continued laughing and talking. Some of them played cards. All of them seemed to put away an incredible amount of beer in a short time.

"I heard it," John said. "Someone said *Frailey.*"

"Which one?" Merrideth said.

"That big dark-haired guy in the corner. I think."

Merrideth zoomed in then rewound and let it play again.

"No," John said. "The man next to him. The one with the brown shirt."

Merrideth zoomed in even closer and rewound again. This time when it played, they saw that the man in the brown shirt was talking to the man on his right. And calling him *Frailey.*

Merrideth paused again. "Okay, I'm going to lock onto this Frailey guy and go virtual."

John exhaled and looked at Abby. "Are you ready?"

"I hope so."

"Hang on to your hats," Merrideth said and set the scene to *Play.*

CHAPTER 5

***

SUMMER 1839

It was one thing to get a little drunk once a year on Muster Day, but enough was enough. Duncan Frailey hauled himself from the bench he sat on and smiled down at his friends' blurry faces. "You lazy lack-wits can stay the night here for all I care." He drained the last of the beer in his tankard, slammed it on the scarred oak table, and then belched loudly. "But I've honest work to do in the morning'."

Their responses were a variety of cheery, but slurred insults that he failed to fully understand. Yes, he had best find his brothers and get out of there—and not just because of the work. If they didn't get home soon, Pa would come after them. Even though he and his brothers had surpassed their father's six-foot height long ago—and had families of their own, for pity's sake—Lachlan Frailey still maintained a substantial degree of authority over them. He fancied himself laird of the Frailey clan, small that it was, as his father had been before him back in Scotland. None of his sons had ever seriously considered disputing that claim.

Leaving his friends to their drinking, Duncan turned and squinted at the smoky room. He spied Angus and Simon at a table in the opposite corner. They were sleeping like babies—very large babies with shaggy dark hair—their heads resting on spilled beer and scattered playing cards. There should have been another shaggy head there, but he pushed that sad thought away before he started blubbering like a baby himself.

But at least that meant he only had to get two dunderheads home this year. Duncan took a handful of Angus' shirt in one hand and one of Simon's in his other and hauled the sluggards to their feet. "Come on, little brothers. Before Pa comes after us—or worse, our wives do."

Duncan stepped into the street with his brothers stumbling along after him. The distance between the Ferry House and the livery stable seemed to have doubled or tripled since they had left their horses there that morning. It came to Duncan that he no longer heard footsteps behind him. He turned, cautiously. Simon and Angus had stopped and were leaning against Cyrus Ellsworth's Emporium. He went back and hauled them upright, and then they continued on their way. The moment they got inside the stable, Angus and Simon slithered down against the plank wall, asleep before they hit the floor. Duncan saddled all three horses and then woke his brothers, hoisted them onto their horses, hauled himself into his own saddle, and led the way down the path toward the Frailey homestead. His brothers groaned as they bobbed along behind him.

The distance to home seemed to have tripled as well, but at last, the four cabins appeared in the moonlight. Only three were inhabited. His parents' cabin, the original one that Lachlan had built in '97, was first in the row, and then came the two built later as he and Angus married. The fourth cabin was to have been Simon and Lizbeth's, but it had been taken out from under their noses by Runt. He couldn't help it, of course. He'd had a desperate need for it. But now he was gone, and the cabin sat empty.

Pa said they had just as well let Simon have the cabin. Runt had made his bed, and now he had to lie in it. Ma said he was like the dove Noah had released from the ark. If he could find solid ground to land on he would. But if he couldn't, he would return to them. And so Simon and his wife still lived with Pa and Ma, while everyone waited to see if Runt would return to the roost.

There was a thump and then a yelp. Duncan yawned and rubbed his eyes. Finally he turned in his saddle. Angus had fallen off his horse right in front of Ma and Pa's cabin. He wasn't surprised. It was a miracle either of the lads had stayed in their saddles that long.

Simon put a finger to his lips to shush Angus, then shouted, "Be quiet, you lack-wit, before Pa hears you."

"Yes, do be quiet before you wake your ma," Lachlan said softly from the door of his cabin. "It's bad enough you stay out late drinking. The least you can do is not wake your poor lasses and babes with your carrying on. You ought to know better, Duncan. And you, Angus Frailey, should be ashamed of yourself—leaving your poor lass home alone with the babe nearly here."

"Is Jewel well, Pa?" Angus said contritely. He sounded sober but made no effort to rise from the ground.

"Yes, no thanks to you, you big galoot. Your mother kept her company most of the evening. I suggest the three of you beg pardon of your dear wives first thing tomorrow."

"Yes, Pa." Duncan rolled his eyes, secure in knowing it was too dark for his father to see. As if Lachlan hadn't lifted his own beer tankard right alongside the other men until three years ago when he passed the age limit for the militia. Ever since, he had been crankier than a bear each time Muster Day came around.

"And I expect you to be outside ready to work come sunup."

"Ah, Pa," Simon groaned. "We're all tuckered out from marching about all day."

Duncan punched his brother's arm and sent him a warning look, which of course he didn't see in the dark. It wasn't a good idea to remind their father of his past glories on Muster Day.

"What was that for?" Simon asked querulously.

Lachlan grunted. "Then you'd best get some sleep, lads." He opened the cabin door quietly and went inside.

Simon dismounted and held out a hand to help Angus up.

"I'll take care of the horses," Duncan said. "You little sleepy heads go on and let your wives tuck you into your beds."

Simon's teeth shown white in the darkness as he grinned. "Are you stalling, big brother? Too scared to face Anne?"

Duncan swatted at his brother, but Simon danced out of reach. Angus laughed, but then put a hand to his head and groaned.

The cabin door opened again, and Ma appeared at the threshold, wrapping a shawl around her shoulders. The white nightgown she wore glowed in the moonlight.

"Is there any word, Duncan?"

"No, Ma."

Simon stepped up on the porch and put an arm around her shoulders. "Maybe next time, Ma."

She nodded. After a look toward the empty cabin, she turned and went back inside. Simon glanced back at Duncan and Angus and then followed her, shutting the door behind him. Angus turned away and shuffled down the lane toward his own cabin, and Duncan led the horses to the barn.

***

THE PRESENT

Pausing the action, Merrideth pulled herself out of 1839 and back to the present.

"Wow. Wow. Wow," Abby said.

"I know," John said, hugging her. "I forgot how intense it is to go virtual."

Merrideth shook her head and laughed. "You think that was intense? You should have seen Frances Ballew do frontier surgery at Fort Piggot. There was this man, I forget his name, who got scalped by the Indians and—"

"Can you take me to see Fort Piggot?" John said.

"Sure," Merrideth said. "Assuming we can get down into the woods to the ruins without Nelda or Brett seeing us. We could go tomorrow if you like."

"Me, too," Abby said. "Only no surgery, please."

Merrideth laughed. "No surgery. Okay, back to the topic at hand. The good news is now we know for sure that Simon and his wife Lizbeth are the two twenty-somethings in Lachlan's household in the 1840 census. Unfortunately, that doesn't help us find Matthias."

"Surely he's the one Duncan thought of as Runt," John said.

"Maybe," Merrideth answered. "Probably even, because if he weren't a son, why would Lachlan give him the cabin he built for Simon and Lisbeth? But I've learned not to jump to conclusions in this business."

"If only Duncan had been thinking a little clearer," Abby said.

John nodded. "But even if he hadn't been tipsy, I don't think we would have necessarily picked up every thought in his head."

"That has occurred to me before," Merrideth said. "Our brains have lots of nooks and crannies—dark corners even we don't visit. I believe that even in virtual mode we probably only pick up a fraction of the person's thoughts. So if we want to know with certainty who Runt is, we'll have to re-wind until we see him in person."

"Why not fast-forward until they come out of the cabins again? Since they all went to bed thinking about Runt, maybe they'll say something more about him in the morning."

"And more about what his *desperate need* was," Abby said.

"All right," Merrideth said and set the controls. "Let's try that for a while."

The Frailey brothers came outside the next morning, looking miserably hung over. Their father Lachlan was all chipper and smiling. Abby wanted to see the women and the inside of the cabins, but they decided not to take the time.

Instead they followed Duncan as he and the other men began the arduous work of lumbermen. Lachlan may have been deemed too old for the militia, but he still had the stamina and strength of a much younger man. His sons' endurance went beyond amazing. They hitched a team of oxen and used them to pull logs out of the woods to the edge of Lusk Creek. There they bound the logs together into bundles, and the oxen pulled them down into the water. In 1839 Lusk Creek was much larger than what they had seen out their car windows, with enough volume to be called a river, actually. The bundles of logs became barges, waiting to be floated down to the Ohio River, then to the Mississippi and on to New Orleans, just as Nick Landis had explained earlier. The whole process had taken hours of back-breaking work, and that wasn't even counting the time it had taken the men to cut down the trees in the first place.

"Man, that makes me tired watching," John said. "But weren't they ingenious? All done without power saws or gas engines.

"Or electricity," Merrideth said. "I can't imagine living without it. Think of all the things we would miss in their world."

Abby stretched and yawned hugely. "But as Thoreau said, 'simplify, simplify, simplify.' Not that I'd want to go without vacuum sweepers, electric can openers, hair dryers—"

"Or Starbucks, ATMs, and cell phones," John said.

"Not to mention the computer we are supposed to be using," Merrideth said. "Might I remind you that we still have no clue why Matthias left? And while we're in the Fraileys' time, our own time is ticking away."

"Yes, Merri, you should up the speed," Abby said. "Or we'll use up our whole lives waiting around for someone to mention Matthias Frailey."

"What good will that do if the whole screen is a blur?" John said. "You can't see them or hear what they say."

"He's right," Merrideth said.

John looked at his watch. "I've been keeping track of the time we've spent in virtual mode, and something weird is happening. Have you noticed?"

Merrideth cleared her throat. "Oh, yes. About that. I may have forgotten to mention the time warp phenomenon."

"Time warp?" John perked up at the term.

"What are you talking about?" Abby said.

"I discovered it when I was time-surfing at the fort back in November. I began to notice that there was a discrepancy between my time and the pioneers' time. Apparently, there's not a one-to-one correlation between our hours and their hours. A time warp. Or at least it seems like it from here. So actually, I figure we'd be better off going virtual most of the time. Because the longer we time-surf—"

"The more time we have to do so," John said with amazement.

"How is that possible?" Abby said.

John snorted. "How is any of this possible? We should just be grateful it happens or we'd never get anywhere."

"Then why didn't we ever notice it back in the day?" Abby said.

"Maybe because we didn't get the chance to time-surf for extended periods of time," Merrideth said. "And thus there wasn't enough of a time disparity to be noticeable."

"You remember how it was," John said. "Always furtively trying to catch a few stolen moments here or there when no one was looking."

"Yes," Abby said. "Unlike here, we didn't have the luxury of doing it all night in the privacy of our own apartment."

John laughed. "You naughty girl!"

"I didn't mean—"

Now Merrideth snorted. "As if you two ever had furtive

shenanigans before you got hitched."

"I wonder what your physics professor would have to say about the possibility of time warping," John said. "You haven't told him, have you?"

"Of course not. He'd feel obligated to reveal *Beautiful Houses* to the scientific world."

Abby was still looking thoughtful. "Even with time warp, I suppose you have to take into consideration other factors. Like our rule about not following people into their bedrooms and bathrooms."

"And the boredom factor," John said. "I have no interest in sitting here watching someone sew buttons on his shirt or clip his toenails or—"

"I think we get the idea, John," Merrideth said.

"Okay, then," Abby said. "It seems to me that the best course is to set it to a moderate rate, then slow down and listen in from time to time to see what's going on. Then if anything interesting pops up we can go virtual without worrying too much about wasting time."

"Sounds reasonable to me," Merrideth said.

They settled in to watch and listen, keeping their ears tuned to any mention of *Runt*, a younger brother, and especially the name *Matthias*. But other than a few grunted instructions, the sweating men had no time or energy for conversation.

Merrideth sped past the night hours, and on the second day, a three-man crew of river men took charge of the load of timber at the creek. Lachlan instructed his sons to escort them as far as the Ohio to make sure the barge was stable. Duncan and his brothers mounted their horses to comply with their father's order. At the last minute Lachlan handed Duncan some coins and asked him to stop in Golconda to get a cone of sugar. His ma was planning a birthday cake for him, and he had jolly well better be surprised when she brought it out.

Laughing, he doffed his hat and then trotted with Angus and Simon down the path along the creek bank. Lachlan stood watching his handsome sons go. Fatherly pride was written all over his face.

Merrideth paused the scene. "Well, we've expended nearly an hour of our time watching two days in the Fraileys' lives, the *Reader's Digest* condensed version, anyway, but I didn't hear anything useful. Did you?"

"Let's go a little longer," Abby said. "Duncan told Angus and Simon that they'd stop off at the Ferry House to eat when they were finished. Maybe when they're not working they'll finally get around to discussing the elusive Runt."

"Good idea," John said.

Merrideth sped up the action until the monitor was a mere blur. When she slowed to real time, Duncan and his brothers were just stepping into the crowded Ferry House inn late in the afternoon.

"Perfect timing, Merri," John said.

"You always had the knack," Abby said.

"Just luck," Merrideth said. "Okay, I'm going to go virtual now, or we'll never hear what they say in the noise of the inn."

"All right," Abby said. "But if it turns into another drunken scene, feel free to speed past it."

"Don't worry. I will."

※ ※ ※

OCTOBER 1839

Duncan put the letter safely in his shirt pocket, then removed his hat and wiped his face with his shirt sleeve. Replacing his hat, he sauntered into the Ferry House, a brother on each side. The inn was already crowded.

"Whew!" he said to the room at large. "It is hot out there. You'd think 'twere August, not October."

Samuel Landis responded from behind the bar. "Indeed it is, Duncan. Why, it's so hot the catfish jumped out of the river into my stew pot just to get away from the heat." Other than the merest flicker of a smile, Sam wore his usual bland expression.

Duncan laughed. "Good. We were just saying how we were hungry for your catfish stew."

"And bring us some beer to wash it down with," Simon said. Duncan gave his brothers a warning look and Angus added, "Just a pint for each of us."

Sam nodded his assent.

They found a table and lowered themselves onto the chairs. The sugar cone poked his hip, so Duncan dug it out of his pocket and plunked it down in the center of the table. "Don't let me forget that. I don't want to disappoint Ma."

Simon grinned and poked his arm. "You're the one that would be disappointed if she couldn't make your cake."

A burst of laughter came from across the room. Then Herman Stodges got up from the table where he sat with his usual cronies and made his way over to them, carrying his beer tankard with him. "You boys mind if I join you? I reckon you've got the room, seein' as how your little brother ain't here."

Having Stodges sit with them was bound to give him dyspepsia, but Duncan couldn't think of a polite way to say no. He nodded and Herman took the remaining chair at their table. Angus and Simon didn't say anything, but Duncan knew they weren't any happier about it than he was. A more intelligent man would have realized he was intruding. But Herman Stodges was not known for his brains.

"Guess you done shipped off another load of timber," Herman said.

"You guessed right," Simon said. "It's on its way to New Orleans."

"Guess your pa's glad ain't no one around to steal his trees no more."

Duncan glanced at Angus. He was the hothead of the family, and with Stodge's stupid words, his eyes had already turned wintery and his cheeks blood red. Duncan put a calming hand on his brother's forearm, and Angus blew out a breath as he struggled to keep his temper.

"You guessed wrong on that one, Herman," Duncan said. "They never took a single tree the whole time they were here, and you know it."

"Well, anyway, we was just wondering," Herman said, gesturing to his friends across the room, "if your brother and his...*wife*...are coming back. Or are they gone for good?"

Angus started to rise, but Duncan held his arm until he settled down.

"Funny you should ask that, Stodges," Sam said, setting bowls of catfish stew on the table in front of them. "Ironic, you might say."

Herman's face turned a shade redder than normal. "What's that supposed to mean?"

"I'll leave you to figure it out," Sam said, turning to go back to the bar.

"Don't forget the beer," Simon said to his back. Sam didn't bother to answer.

"What's that word he said?" Stodges demanded. His breath nearly knocked Duncan to the floor.

"He means, Herman," Duncan said patiently, "that it's odd you should be asking so politely after our little brother and his wife when you and your friends over there are some of the ones who made them feel unwelcome."

"I never did him no wrong, and that's a fact," Herman said with righteous indignation. His friends sent sideways looks their way. "I always liked your little brother. But I won't lie. I wasn't sad to see his...*wife*...go somewheres else to throw her litters."

Duncan and his brothers bolted from their chairs, nearly bumping into Sam who had arrived with a tray of beer tankards. Angus lunged for Stodges, but Duncan was the first to get his hands on the man's neck.

Mayor Lusk bolted out of his office shouting, "What in tarnation is going on in here?"

Duncan couldn't answer. A red haze filled his eyes, and a roaring sound filled his ears. After a while he realized someone was shouting for him to let go and that Mayor Lusk would arrest him if he murdered the man. Duncan managed, with effort, to loosen his fingers enough to let Stodges take a breath.

"There's a good lad," Sam said. "Now, let him go, Duncan."

It occurred to Duncan that it was the most riled up he'd ever seen Sam. With effort, he released his hold on Herman Stodges' scrawny neck and the fool fell away, gasping and holding his throat. Angus shoved Stodges back across the room toward his cronies, who had risen from their table but were apparently too cowardly to come to his defense. They took him into their bosom, thumping him on the back and sending dire mutterings and scowls toward Duncan and his brothers.

"I'm glad I won't have to arrest you for murder, Duncan Frailey," Mayor Lusk said. "That would have ruined my day. Stodges, hateful viper that he is, isn't worth spending even a single day in jail for." With the mayor's encouragement, they sat back down to their meal. But Duncan pushed his away with an apologetic look at Sam, and then drained his tankard. He would have ordered more beer if Angus and Simon hadn't been there.

"Have you had any word from your little brother?" Mayor Lusk said.

He probably meant to take his mind off Stodges, but the subject of his brother's whereabouts was equally upsetting.

Duncan pulled the letter out of his shirt pocket and laid it on the table. "A letter came today."

"What's it say?" Sam said.

"Ma would get mad if we opened it before she saw it," Simon said.

"And you don't want to see Ma mad," Angus added. "I get my temper from her, you know."

"The postmark reads *Eagle Creek.*" Duncan put the letter back in his pocket. "Cyrus says that's in Gallatin County north of the salt springs."

"You think he'll ever come home?"

"Ma's about given up on it, Mayor," Simon said.

"Well, at least you and Lizbeth will finally get a cabin of your own," Angus said.

"I'd rather have Runt back," Simon said.

Duncan shook his head at Angus' daft words and patted Simon on the back. "I know you would, Simon. We all would."

CHAPTER 6

***

THE PRESENT

Merrideth paused the action and blew out a rush of air. Stodges should have had those hateful words choked right out of him! She shook her head. No, those were Duncan's thoughts, not hers. She took a few deep breaths to clear the rage from her chest. Sorting through the tangle of other people's emotions and her own was not her favorite part of the time-surfing experience. But it was clear that Duncan's anger at Herman Stodges was connected somehow to a deep sadness for his brother, although how or why she hadn't been able to pick up.

Abby and John looked as if they were a little shell-shocked. But no wonder. It had been fifteen years since they had last rummaged around in other people's minds, and it would take them more time to get back to normal than it did her.

"Runt," Abby gasped. "He...is definitely their little brother."

"You're white as a ghost," Merrideth said.

"I think... I may vomit... from that Stodges guy. And not...just from his breath. Duncan was disgusted by the awful man."

John, who was struggling to breathe himself, put a comforting arm around his wife and studied her face. "Abby you'd better not...talk yet. Just breathe." He left her and went to the kitchen sink. "Does this work?" He answered his own question by turning on the tap. "The water is still on. Come get a drink, honey."

Abby went to him and put her mouth under the faucet's flow. After a moment, she straightened and wiped her face on her sleeve.

"Are you all right?" Merrideth said.

"I'm fine." Abby came back and sat down at the table. After a few more deep breaths she said, "Now, I'm just annoyed. We still don't know the brother's name. Isn't anyone ever going to say it out loud?"

"It's right there on the table," John said. "Zoom in on the letter, Merri."

"Right! I didn't think of that." Merrideth rewound carefully to the point when Duncan laid the letter on the table, then she paused and zoomed in. The ink was a little smeared and the style of writing was elaborate, so it was difficult to decipher.

Abby was the first to do so and nearly squealed with excitement. "It's from Matthias Frailey!"

John clapped a hand to her mouth in alarm. Fortunately, there was no indication anyone had heard her outburst. The apartment was quiet. Only faint sounds and smells from the restaurant below drifted in.

When he removed his hand, Abby whispered, "Sorry."

"It will take a lot of rewinding," Merrideth said. "Matthias has been gone a while."

John looked at his watch. "Even with the time warp factor— assuming that's really happening—it's getting late."

"Why don't we…" Merrideth stopped when she heard noises coming from the hall. Abby and John's eyes went wide, and she felt her own do the same. "What's that?"

"The tenants in the other apartment coming home?" John said. He didn't sound confident in his statement.

"Or Nick Landis here ready to move in?" Abby squeaked.

"Surely he wouldn't until the lock is changed," John said.

Merrideth's phone chose that moment to ring. It sounded incredibly loud, even from inside her shoulder bag. They froze, staring at each other in alarm. She scrambled to silence the phone and then hurried to get her backpack to start loading the laptop.

John went to the door and looked out the peephole. "It's all right, Merri," he said softly. "I don't think they heard."

"Who?"

"It's a young couple. They just went into the other apartment."

"We'll have to be even quieter now that they're home," Abby said.

Merrideth sat back down in front of her computer. "Okay, we got a reprieve, but we'd better hurry in case someone else comes along."

"First, you'd better call Brett back," Abby said.

"He can wait," Merrideth said. "And what makes you think it was Brett, anyway?"

Abby gave her a sly smile. "Are you saying it wasn't?"

"Okay, I'll call him. But only so he won't call back at a bad time." She could take her phone into the bathroom away from Abby's nosiness, but that would only make the call into something more than it was. Friends didn't need to hide away to talk to each other. So she remained where she was and called Brett's number. She was thinking up a message to leave when he finally answered.

"Sorry to bother you, Merri, but since I'm an epic fail when it comes to color, and you're an expert…well anyway, the wise man knows when to seek advice."

Merrideth chuckled. "You're still worried about the pillows?"

"In a way."

"What's wrong with them?"

"The dang things are all shiny and new—show-offs, that's what they are. They're making the walls look really crummy. I'm going to have to paint after all."

Merrideth laughed. "Well, you can't have your walls feeling insecure around the pillows."

Brett laughed softly in her ear. "I knew you'd understand. So I went to Home Depot and asked the clerk at the paint desk to give me five gallons of white paint. The man laughed in my face. Then he asked me if my wife knew I was picking out the paint, and when I explained that I'm not married, he took me over to the paint samples and said, 'Here, have at it. Let me know when you decide.' Merri, did you know they have 459 shades of white paint to choose from? White, for crying out loud. So help me figure out which one to get."

"You counted?"

"Of course I counted."

"Okay, since you went with your paisley-tie shade of blue for your pillows that tells me you prefer warmer colors. So naturally, you should get a warm shade of white."

"So how do I know which ones are warm?"

"Tell me some names."

"All right. Here's one called *Arizona Tan*, but don't let the name fool you. It's white. And so is *Almond Toast* and the one next to it called *Bagel*. Then there's *Mayonnaise, Wild Mushroom,* and *Banana Split*. They're all white."

"Are you sure you're at the paint store and not the diner?"

"Oh, if you're tired of the food theme, try these on for size: *Puppy Paws, Baby Turtle, White Rabbit,* and *Kitten Whiskers*. And they're all white. I swear it."

Merrideth laughed. "I'm sorry, I'm not going to be able to help without seeing them. I could go with you tomorrow, if you like."

"I'd like to get it now, so I can start painting first thing tomorrow when the light's good."

"Then just pick one you like, Brett. I'm sure it will be fine."

"Then I'm going with *Arizona Tan*, because it's the least ridiculous name. Are you going to be home with the door knob soon? I could come over and put it on."

"I'm not sure when I'll be home."

"They must have a lot of antiques there."

"You wouldn't believe how many. And there are tons more we want to see."

"You and Nick."

"Me and John and Abby. Nick's gone."

"Really? How interesting. Well, have fun."

"Oh, I will." When she got off the phone, John and Abby were staring at her.

"It's about time," he said, looking pointedly at his watch.

"Oh, shush," Abby said. "It's only natural that Merri would want to keep in touch with her—"

"If you say *boyfriend* I will smack you, Abby. Brett just needed help with colors, that's all. He's not color blind exactly, but apparently, he can't distinguish between shades very well. Who would have thought?"

"Not everyone has your eye for it," Abby said.

John harrumphed. "Most people learn their colors in kindergarten."

Merrideth harrumphed back at him. "When Brett was in kindergarten he was thinking about more important things than the color of his crayons. The little genius could spot patterns and number sequences that no one else noticed. His teacher, Miss Nelson was amazed by his ability to—" Merrideth shut her mouth. "Never mind. We should get back to work."

"We were only waiting for you, Merri," Abby said, grinning. "And waiting and waiting.

"You realize the restaurant closes at nine o'clock?" John said. "If we don't find the answers by then, we'll be locked in until they re-open tomorrow."

"What about the back service entry by the stairs?" Merrideth said.

John leaned back in his chair. "I'm sure that stays locked. The tenants have keys. We don't."

"You can't be serious," Abby said. "We can't spend the night here!"

"It's our only option, Abby," John said. "If we want to find Matthias Frailey."

Merrideth blew out a breath and studied her friends. "I've never been good at all-nighters, but I guess I can manage one for a good cause."

"I don't like it," Abby said. "But I'm game if you guys are."

"Good," John said. "But let's go downstairs and get something to eat first. The smell of food cooking is driving me crazy."

Just as they reached the halfway point on the stairs, they heard the couple from the other apartment come into the hall. They hurried down the remaining stairs ahead of them, barely making it in time to avoid being seen, then slipped out the back service door and went around to the front of the restaurant.

They took a few calming breaths. And then grinning conspiratorially, John opened the door for her and Abby, and they went in. It was early enough that there were still plenty of tables available. When the waitress came they ordered hamburgers and coleslaw, figuring that would be the quickest to get and easiest to take upstairs in to-go boxes. While they waited for the food, Abby and John went outside to make two phone calls: one to Patty, to let her know they wouldn't be back that night and one to check in with the girls at Abby's parents' house.

Merrideth sat at the table, thinking of Duncan and all the others who had once hung out at the original Ferry House so long ago. She was filled with a sense of poignancy—or some emotion impossible to name—to think that the Fraileys she had seen, so young and full of life, had grown old and eventually died. But they wouldn't be forgotten—not if she could help it. Patty would put them in Toad's baby book, and the memory of them would be passed on to the next generation or two. Then, hopefully someone else would take up the duty of preserving and passing on the family's history.

Merrideth's stomach growled. She scanned the room, hoping to see the waitress coming. The Frailey brothers would have been eating their catfish stew—ugh!—somewhere just to the right of where she sat.

Right where the hostess was seating Nick Landis.

She turned away and pretended an intense interest in the view out the window.

"Merrideth!"

Too late. She put on a smile and turned to watch Nick coming toward her. He stumbled over a chair leg, nearly dropping his satchel on a man eating spaghetti, but after a mumbled apology continued on his way. It was obvious Abby was right about Nick's crush on her.

She ought to find him attractive. He was intelligent, nice looking, and a little nerdy in a cute way—just the type of man she had always dated in high school and college. But for some reason he just didn't add up for her.

At last Nick arrived happy—and uninjured—at her table. Too polite to presume, he stood waiting to be asked to sit. He looked somewhat like a puppy quivering to be petted. Had all the men she'd dated been as tame? An image of herself holding out a dog biscuit to Nick popped into her head, and she scolded herself for the uncharitable thought. Nevertheless, she allowed herself a small smile and said, "Sit."

"Thanks." Nick sat down in the chair across from her. "I thought you were long gone back to Marion." He looked like he was envisioning a romantic candle-lit dinner with her.

"Abby and John will be back in a minute," she said quickly. "We decided to hang around a while and see the sights. We always like to soak in as much history and local color as possible wherever we travel."

"Did you go to Buel House?"

"No, but we want to."

"I suppose you saw the mural down on the levee wall."

"No. Not yet."

"It commemorates the crossing of the Cherokee during the Trail of Tears. I could show you after...no, I guess it's too late for that. The sun set when I wasn't looking."

"Maybe some other time."

Over his shoulder Merrideth saw Abby and John come through the front door. They stopped when they saw Nick. Abby pointed a finger at the ceiling and mouthed something that she didn't understand. Merrideth squinted back at her and gave her head a tiny shake.

"What do you think of our Sarah Lusk?" Nick said. "Quite a woman for her time."

"Sarah who?" Merrideth said.

"You know. The woman who founded the town."

Next to Abby, John took up the communication challenge, pointing and mouthing as she had. Merrideth got the message right away, but then John had always been better at charades than Abby. They wanted her to keep Nick occupied while they went upstairs to time-surf. As if that were going to happen.

"There's a monument in Sarah Lusk's honor with a brass plaque that tells about her," Nick said.

He glanced down at his phone, and Merrideth took the opportunity to shake her head more vigorously at Abby and John. After a few more weird gesticulations, they finally gave up trying to convince her of their plan and started toward her table.

When Nick looked up from his phone Merrideth smiled and said, "A monument? Where? We haven't come across it yet. You know, in our sightseeing and all."

"By the courthouse. Next to the front door. You walked right past it."

"Oh, that one," Merrideth said. "Yes, we saw it."

"Nick," John said and sat down. "Who knew we'd run into you again?"

A small frown appeared on Nick's handsome face and then disappeared. "Hi, again. You must think I eat every meal here. Actually, I'm considered a good cook."

"I'm sure you are," Abby said.

"Yeah," John said. "I bet."

The waitress brought their drinks and another menu for Nick.

"I hear the steaks are excellent," Abby said. Merrideth suppressed a smile. It was good thinking. A steak would keep him at the table long after they were gone.

"Yes, I think that sounds good right about now," Nick said, smiling at Merrideth as if it had been her suggestion. Nick told the waitress what he wanted and she jotted it down on her pad. "And you all's orders are coming right up," she said before hurrying away.

"Nick was just telling me about Sarah Lusk," Merrideth said.

"It's quite an interesting story," Nick said.

He went on to tell them about the founder of Golconda, adding details not included on the brass plaque. His description meshed closely with what Merrideth had seen of the woman. His excruciatingly detailed account might have been interesting if Merrideth hadn't been counting the minutes until they could get back upstairs to continue hunting for Matthias Frailey.

When the waitress brought their hamburgers in Styrofoam to-go boxes, Nick looked at them in surprise. And then he trained puppy-dog eyes on Merrideth. "But I thought..."

"Thanks again, Nick, for all the history," John said, rising quickly from the table. "Enjoy your steak."

"Yes," Merrideth said. "It was fascinating."

"Well, goodbye, then," Nick said.

John led Abby away, and Merrideth followed them, trying to forget the disappointment in Nick's eyes. She felt him staring at her all the way to the door.

When they got to the back stairs, John stopped them. "I'm going to the store to pick up a few things before they close. I've got to move the car somewhere, anyway."

"Then buy me a toothbrush," Merrideth said. "I don't want to end up with breath like Herman Stodges'."

Abby gave John a quick kiss. "Me, too. But hurry back."

"I'll be back in a jiffy. Make that a half a jiffy. Just give me my hamburger. I'm starving."

After he'd gone quietly out, Merrideth and Abby went back upstairs and ate their own burgers while watching Duncan's life go by on the computer screen. If only they knew a specific date and time to plug into the program, Merrideth would be able to find his brother Matthias within seconds. But all they had was the impression that he had moved away from home a few weeks or months before the scene they'd just observed in the Ferry House on October 9, 1839. But as she well knew, searching through only a few weeks of a person's life required a substantial amount of time. All she could do was run in reverse at fast speed, then stop to check—rinse and repeat—until they reached a time when Matthias still lived in Golconda.

"It's so tedious," Abby said. "I'd forgotten that part."

Merrideth raised her eyebrows and gave her a look. "You're complaining? Really?"

"Sorry. You're right. I'm the worst sort of ingrate—like the Children of Israel carping about their miraculous manna in the wilderness. Besides, this tedious part gives us a chance to talk woman-to-woman."

"About what?" As if she didn't already know.

"It's time you tell me more about him."

"Him who?"

"Don't play dumb, Merri."

Merrideth sighed. "You already know all you need to know about Brett Garrison. He's a fellow professor at McKendree. We're friends. The end."

Abby opened her mouth to speak and then seemed to change her mind about which tack would be the most effective for prying information out of her. After a pause, she said, "He seems like a nice guy."

"He is a nice guy."

"And he sure is nice to look at."

"Hmph. Just like I said. You were ogling him."

"I just have eyes that work really well, praise the Lord. Brett seemed very comfortable in your apartment this morning."

"Yes, I guess so. As small as it is, there's not much…." And then what Abby was hinting at sank in. Merrideth smiled brightly and said, "Oh, didn't I tell you?"

"What?" Abby said.

"Brett moved in with me. That's why he is so familiar with my apartment. And he's fixing our doors to shut properly because we do love our privacy."

"Oh." Abby blinked at her like a baby owl. "I was hoping you'd find someone, but I didn't think…"

Rolling her eyes, Merrideth relented. "Abby, you're such an idiot. We are not living together. We are not even dating. When will you believe me when I say I don't date colleagues? Everyone knows that's career suicide. Brett is just a friend."

Abby let out a relieved breath. "Okay, then let's get on with the manhunt—for Matthias, I mean," she said with a grin. "Here let me try. I used to be pretty good at this."

Abby set it to rewind at a faster rate than Merrideth thought prudent, but she held her tongue. Abby deserved a turn at the fun. The seasons changed as they continued to sift back through Duncan's life. Although there was still no sign of Matthias, they did get a good look at the Frailey family's lumber business.

Faint noises came from the hall. Someone was coming. She and Abby looked at each other, eyes wide. The someone tapped softly on the door, and a smile bloomed on Abby's face. "It's our secret knock," she explained.

"Of course you and John have a secret knock," Merrideth said, rolling her eyes. "Doesn't everyone?"

He came in loaded down with plastic shopping bags. How he had managed to lug it all up without being seen was a mystery they didn't take time to discuss.

"Boy, it's dark in here," he said, setting the bags on the kitchen counter. "I forgot to warn you about not turning on lights until I got something to cover the window."

"And yet the little women managed to think of it themselves," Merrideth said. "Amazing."

John grinned and tugged at her hair. "Oh, stop, Merri Christmas. You know I respect your ginormous brain."

"What's all this?" Abby, said eyeing the bags. "You must have bought out the store."

"It's amazing what you can find at a Dollar Store. Did you know they have blankets there?" Out of the largest bag he removed a green blanket in a zippered vinyl case and held it for them to see. "It's thin and wimpy, but it should work to cover said window."

"What else?" Merrideth said, unable to curb her curiosity.

"These," John said, handing Abby three flashlights. "Even with the blanket, we should keep the light to a minimum. Toothpaste and brushes, as requested, and soap and paper towels as an added bonus."

"I'm all in favor of good hygiene," Abby said.

"That's one thing I've always admired about you," he said. "And here are mixed nuts and cheese crackers in case we get hungry later. And coffee so we can stay awake."

Grinning, Abby took the coffee from him. "My hero."

"Instant?" Merrideth said with disgust.

"What was I thinking? I'll go back and buy a coffee maker. And a waffle iron would be nice—maybe a bread maker, too. Oh, and one of those turkey deep fryers."

"Don't get your knickers in a twist," Merrideth said.

"But what about cups?" Abby said.

"Never fear, my love," he said, pulling three ceramic mugs out of a bag. "And last, but certainly not least, breakfast." He opened a white paper bag, and Merrideth got a glimpse of three jelly donuts. "Unless you think we should eat them now before they get any staler."

Abby took the bag from him, closed it firmly, and put it on the counter.

"Now," John said, rubbing his hands together in anticipation. "Tell me what I missed while I was out foraging."

"Not much," Merrideth said. "Right now, we're in the summer of 1838."

"We got to see their steam-powered sawmill in operation," Abby said.

"Cool," John said. "Show me."

"I thought you'd want to see it."

Before Abby could restart the scene, the apartment doorknob rattled and then rattled again. Someone was trying to get in.

John walked carefully to the door and looked out the fish eye. "It's Nick," he mouthed. "He's muttering something about the lock."

Merrideth tiptoed over to John. If they remained quiet, would Nick decide that he had accidentally locked the door earlier when he showed John the apartment? Or would he come to the conclusion that someone had locked it from the inside? He might get it in his head to call the landlord. Or even the police. Merrideth pushed John aside and opened the door a crack.

"Nick." She couldn't tell if his wrinkled brow was from confusion or anger.

"Merrideth?"

"I suppose you're wondering why we're in here."

"You could say that, yes."

Merrideth tried to think of what to say. Everything that came to mind was a big, fat lie. She couldn't tell him the truth without endangering the program, and even if she did tell him, he wouldn't believe it. Who would without seeing it firsthand?

Nick's face lit up. "Don't tell me you decided to rent the apartment?" It didn't even make sense, of course, especially for someone as intelligent as Nick. Was he so smitten with her that he was actually happy she'd rented the apartment out from under him?

"Not exactly," she said.

As she was furiously thinking what to say next, John reeled her back into the room by the tail of her shirt and poked his head out the door.

"Merrideth didn't have your phone number, Landis," John whispered.

"She wants my phone number?"

"Heck yes, she wants it, man. But she's sort of shy. So anyway, when we decided to stay in town—so we could take you up on your offer to give us a tour of Golconda—we didn't have any way to contact you. And since there are no motels around, I thought, hey, what about the vacant apartment?"

"Now see here—"

"Abby said we shouldn't without asking you, but I told her you wouldn't mind."

"I suppose it's all right, but—"

"I'll pay you, of course."

"But there's no furniture in there."

"There's a bed."

Merrideth pictured the look Nick must be wearing as he contemplated where the three of them would sleep. John must have realized how kinky that sounded, because he quickly added, "Not that we'll be sleeping. We're pulling an all-nighter so Merrideth can work on her new book. Did she tell you she decided to write about the Trail of Tears? Abby and I are helping her with the research."

"Really? I'm sorry. I guess I was blabbing so much about my own book at lunch that she didn't get a chance to mention hers. Is there anything I can do to help?"

"There sure is. Take us on that tour tomorrow morning."

"I'd be glad to."

John stopped talking, and there was a long silence.

Finally Nick said, "Well, I'll leave you to your work, then."

"Bye," John said and closed the door. He turned the lock and leaned against the door. "I told you he wouldn't mind, Abby. I hope you know you're writing a new book, Merri."

Merrideth shook her head. "Don't hold your breath, John. It's not my responsibility to turn that line you just fed Nick into reality."

"It would be a good topic," Abby said.

"I'll think about it."

John went to the table and wrote something on Merrideth's yellow tablet. He tore off the page, folded it, and then went to stand by the door.

"What on earth are you doing, John?" Abby said.

He grinned. "Wait for it. Wait for it."

Someone knocked on the door. John opened it and Nick stood there looking sheepish. "I forgot Merrideth's—"

"Here you go, Landis," John said, handing him the paper. He shut the door before Nick could respond.

"What do you know?" Abby said, laughing. "He finally got the courage."

Merrideth huffed. "Oh, that's just great. Now he'll really be a pest."

"I think you had better try to keep him happy, Merri," John said.

"Said the pimp to the streetwalker," Merrideth said, glaring at him

He laughed. "Think of it as a sacrifice for the cause of history. Seriously, Merri, if Landis loses hope, he might decide to get mad about us being here."

"I guess you're right."

John patted her back. "Okay, then, back to the past.

Show me the steam mill you were talking about. I do love old timey technology."

"For a little while," Abby said.

The Fraileys' work days were long and arduous. After they felled trees with axes and crosscut saws, the oxen dragged the logs to the mill pond where the men poled the logs into position and secured them on a steel carriage that guided them to the saw's whirring blade. Out the other side came boards which they loaded onto a huge wagon. Powerful draft horses pulled it to a large shed, and finally the men unloaded the cut lumber and carefully stacked it for drying.

When Merrideth slowed the action down so they could listen in, there was much good-natured teasing and camaraderie among the men. But there was also a lot of sweat, fatigue, and minor injuries—mashed fingers, splinters, aching muscles—all accompanied by humorous grousing. But still only three of Lachlan's sons were there. Matthias was nowhere to be seen.

When they followed the men home they finally met the Frailey women and spent a little time watching their days. The women were hard workers, too. The wives—Lachlan's Eileen, Duncan's Anne, Angus' Jewel, and Simon's Lizbeth—seemed to get along together as well as their men did. They didn't chop down trees, but they did do an amazing amount of hard physical labor managing their households. And they appeared to spend even more hours working on a typical day than the men did.

"Okay," Merrideth said. "That's enough of that. The goal is to—"

"Find Matthias Frailey. I know," John said.

"Before morning if possible," Abby said, suppressing a yawn. "Matthias still isn't there, so obviously we'll have to keep rewinding."

Merrideth continued the process of rewinding, stopping to check, then rewinding some more. Each time the men were working industriously as usual, but there was still no sign of Matthias. She started to rewind once again, but Abby grabbed her hand to stop her.

"Wait, Merri," she said. "Zoom out, would you? I think I saw something."

CHAPTER 7

The something turned out to be a *someone*. At the far right edge of the screen a man sat on a fallen tree watching the men work. She zoomed in more to see his face. He was quite a bit younger than the other men, but he had the same dark, wavy hair and gray eyes as the three Frailey brothers and was every bit as handsome as they were.

Merrideth smiled at her friends. "I think we just found Matthias Frailey."

"He looks so young," Abby said, studying the screen.

John chuckled. "Especially when you think of him as Patty Ann's great, great—however many— great grandfather."

Merrideth checked the time indicator. She had gone back much farther than she thought. The date was November 6, 1838. "Matthias was born about 1818, so that makes him about twenty here."

"He looks a little like Brett, don't you think, Merri?" Abby said.

"Maybe. But Brett's eyes are green. Emerald green. I thought at first that he wore contacts, but my friend Marla said…" Abby was grinning at her, so she shut her mouth. No doubt she'd just sounded like a besotted fool.

"I hate to rain on your parade, ladies, but we don't know for sure that he's Matthias," John said. "He might be a hired hand or maybe just a friend."

"Are you kidding?" Abby said. "He looks almost identical to Duncan, only younger and not quite as muscular."

"There's one surefire way to prove it," John said. "Switch the

74

lock from Duncan to this man and go virtual. We'll find out who he is soon enough."

"Can't," Merrideth said. "Or we'll end up right back at the Ferry House. Remember, the only reason we're at the sawmill is because we're locked onto to Duncan, and he took us there."

"Sure you can change the lock to Matthias," Abby said. "I don't remember which setting you use, but it's on the program menu. Somewhere."

"You're kidding!" Merrideth said. "Do you realize what that means?"

"Shh!" John said.

"Sorry." Merrideth lowered her voice. "But if Abby's right, it means we can trace Patty's ancestors as far back as we want—to Scotland and beyond."

"Can't we already do that?" John said.

"No. Think about it," Merrideth said. "Say we locked onto Lachlan, which we wouldn't even be able to do without spending hours searching for a time when he comes into the Ferry House. But say we did get a lock on him and rewound his whole life—all the way back to Scotland to when Lachlan was a mere fertilized egg—then what?"

"Then it would get extremely weird," Abby said. "Talk about invasion of privacy."

John frowned. "I think what Merri is saying it that there would be no way to get from Lachlan, the zygote, to either of his parents, the previous generation."

"Exactly," Merrideth said. "But even if we could—even using the fastest speed we have available—it would take forever to rewind a single person's life, and then that of his parents, and then his grandparents and so on. But if we can switch the lock—"

"And we can," Abby said, smiling. "I just found the setting."

In her excitement Merrideth could barely keep seated. "Then we'll only have to rewind Lachlan until he's back in Scotland. Once there, we can switch the lock to his father, and then his father's father, and on into antiquity. Sure, it would still take a huge amount of time and perseverance, but think of the possibilities!"

John grinned. "Then show us how to make the switch, Abby, and we'll see what's on Matthias Frailey's mind."

***

NOVEMBER 6, 1838

"I said it's dinner," Matthias shouted over the roar of the mill. He held up the burlap tow sack for his brothers to see.

"What?" Angus shouted.

"I. Said. It's. Dinner."

"What?" Simon said.

All three of his brothers were snickering at him like the noonday heat had baked their brains. Matthias shook his head in disgust, and then, smiling evilly, pretended to drop the sack on the ground. Buttermilk, cold from the spring house, was a particular favorite of his brothers, and Ma had promised to send a Mason jar of it to go with their lunch.

Matthias smiled at Duncan's expression of alarm.

Angus pulled the lever, silencing the mill at last. "Dang it, Matthias. Why'd you go and do a thing like that?"

"I would have done it if it wasn't for having to explain to Ma about the broken jar."

Normally, Matthias would have laughed off their teasing. But then if things were normal, he would be working alongside the men instead of playing errand boy for the women. The situation made him as cranky as an old sow with two dozen piglets. He had the urge to heave a few chunks of wood at his brothers' thick heads to knock some sense into them. Grimacing, he lowered himself to the log to rest his stiff leg. It had been five weeks since he'd broken it felling a tree, and it still screamed like a banshee when he tried to put it to use.

His brothers came to him, wiping the sweat from their faces and swatting away the sawdust coating their clothes.

"What do you say, lads?" Duncan took the burlap sack from Matthias. "Should we throw Runt into a pit and sell him to the Egyptians?"

Angus sat down beside Matthias and took his head in an armlock against his sweaty chest. Matthias didn't mind too much. It was just one of Angus' ways of expressing affection, most of which involved a certain degree of pain. But he was always the first of his brothers to know when a fellow needed cheering up.

"I guess not this time," Angus said, releasing him with a

brotherly punch to the shoulder that nearly sent Matthias tumbling off the log. "Him being a poor, crippled child and all. Not unless Ma goes and makes him a fancy coat of many colors."

"Besides," Simon piped up. "Pa loves me best."

Matthias hauled himself up. "I'll tell him you said so," he said, limping to his horse. Thankfully, none of them tried to help him onto it as if he really were a poor, crippled child. And he made it into the saddle without too much trouble, and his dignity still intact.

Then Duncan called, "Hey, Runt?"

"Yeah?"

"Be sure to wear an apron when you wash those dishes for Ma."

Matthias didn't bother to respond, just shook his head in disgust and continued on his way. But he was grinning when he went around the bend and lost sight of the big oafs.

***

THE PRESENT

When Abby paused the action, Merrideth came back to the present with the sound of John's laughter in her right ear.

"That was funny," he said. "Some things never change. They sounded just like my brothers and me."

"I felt sorry for Matthias," Abby said. "They shouldn't have been so mean to him. Especially since he was hurt."

"Your soft heart is one of the things I love most about you, Abbikins," John said. "But see, we males bond together best when—"

"Could you two focus, please?" Merrideth said. "The key point here that we now know that man is, in fact, Matthias."

"Yes. At last," Abby said.

Merrideth stretched a kink in her neck. "Sometime between now—I mean *then*—and October 1839, something happened to cause Matthias to move away from his family. His rough, but obviously loving, family."

"And away from a lucrative lumber business," John said.

"It had to be something awful for Lachlan to leave him out of his will," Abby said.

"Maybe Matthias did the prodigal son thing," John said. "Demanded his inheritance and split."

"Matthias isn't like that," Merrideth said. "It's that Herman Stodges guy's fault. He did something horrible to Matthias, and then—"

"I object, Your Honor. That's hear-say evidence," John said. "Do you hear yourself, Merri?"

"What?" Merrideth mentally replayed her words. "You're right. I'm basing my assumptions on the feelings I picked up from Duncan. I suppose I need to do a better job of untangling his from mine."

"So we'll just have to keep searching," Abby said, reaching for the mouse.

Merrideth's phone chirped. "I'm getting a text from Nick."

"He's not coming back, is he?" John said. "If he does, someone else can think of what to tell him. Not lying is hard work."

"*Not lying*, John?" Abby said.

"Just a teeny stretching of the truth."

Merrideth wasn't sure whose side she should take. John was a straight-arrow in all his personal and professional affairs, so if he thought what they were doing was ethical, then it probably was. And it wasn't as if everyone didn't lie once in a while anyway. Maybe Abby was just being too persnickety about it. Merrideth sighed. Or maybe she herself was a little too eager to time-surf to be entirely objective about the ethics of the whole thing.

"If I may interrupt this Aristotelian splitting of philosophical hairs, Nick wants to know if we're going to eat breakfast in the restaurant, and if so, can he join us."

"He is getting to be a pest, isn't he?" Abby said.

John grinned. "But as I said, Merri, you've got to keep the man happy."

Merrideth gave John's ear a twist. To the sound of his pained laugh, she texted Nick a "yes," adding a smiley face for good measure. "There, that ought to keep him happy." Before she could set her phone down, it chirped again. She sighed. "Now he wants to know what time."

"For crying out loud," John said. "Tell him you'll call him in the morning."

Merrideth texted that along with another smiley face. "Okay, back to work. Abby, I'd fast-forward slowly—if that makes any sense. Then if we see anything odd, and you can set it back to real time."

At the speed she had set, Matthias' leg seemed to heal overnight, although as John pointed it out, it probably hadn't seemed like it to him at the time. Soon Matthias was back to the lumber business alongside his father and brothers. Their days were spent either felling trees or finishing lumber at the mill. It was hard, back-breaking labor, but the men laughed often and continued to enjoy each other's company. There was nothing to indicate ill feelings among them. They always stopped their work when dusk approached and spent the evenings with their families inside the snug cabins. On Sundays, they took time to rest, although the women's work never entirely ended. After everyone got home from services at the little church in town, the men played with the children in the yard or sat on their porches with the women.

"The Fraileys' lives are obviously happy and content," Abby said. "I saw absolutely nothing to indicate any trouble that would cause Matthias to leave."

Yawning, Merrideth stood and stretched her stiff neck and back. "No, but carry on, Musketeers. I need to use the bathroom."

When she returned, John was at the controls, and Abby was at the microwave making coffee.

Abby smiled dubiously. "You want a cup?"

"No, but I'll take one."

"Come see this," John said. "I think I found something. Maybe. Anyway, it's weird."

"What is it?"

"I skipped ahead," he said. "Or rather, I skipped back. Whatever."

"You sure did," Merrideth said. The time indicator read January 1839. "If we don't do this systematically, John, we'll miss something."

"Sorry. I got impatient. Don't worry. I jotted down the date and time where we left off in case we need to go back. Anyway, see how unhappy Matthias looks. I got the impression someone was sick."

"Time to go virtual, I think," Merrideth said, sitting down next to him.

.

CHAPTER 8

As Matthias rode along, he repeated Susan's instructions to himself lest he forget what he must tell Prudence Wilson. It was a bitter cold morning, and his words came out in white clouds. The dried mullein leaves were for tea. The pleurisy roots were for hot compresses to put on the baby's chest. Prudence was to get the baby to take as much tea as possible and renew the compresses every hour until the coughing stopped.

At last, the Wilsons' homestead came into view. He trotted into the clearing in front of their cabin, expecting to find Obadiah working, maybe chopping firewood. But no one was in sight. Even though he had made plenty of noise to alert them to his presence, there was no indication, not even a face at the cabin window, to show that anyone had noticed his arrival.

He dismounted and tied Champ to the hitching post. "Obadiah? You in there?" No one answered. He lifted down his saddlebag with the precious medicines and went to the door. He knocked, but no one answered that either.

Then the sound of singing came to him from somewhere behind the cabin. When he reached the back, he found Obadiah with his hat in his hands and Prudence holding little Sarah in her arms. They were singing *Morning Hymn*, the sweet words coming from their mouths in the same frosty white clouds. They smiled a little when they saw him. Matthias wanted to ask them why they were singing in the cold. Then he saw the mound of stones at their feet.

He was too late with Susan's remedies. The pain of it brought tears to his eyes, but it was nothing compared to how she and the others would suffer when he told them that another child had fallen victim to the harsh world of Golconda. How blessed he was to know that his own babe lay snug in his new cradle, warm and well-fed!

He let his saddlebag slide to the ground and took off his hat. His throat was too knotted from holding back the tears to join in the singing, but the Wilsons carried on steadfastly to the end of the hymn:

All Praise to Thee, who safe hast kept,
And hast refresh'd me whilst I slept,
Grant, Lord, when I from Death shall wake,
I may of endless Light partake.

Praise God from whom all Blessings flow,
Praise him all Creatures here below,
Praise him above, ye Heavenly Host.
Praise Father, Son, and Holy Ghost.

When they finished, Matthias put his hat back on and shook hands with Obadiah. Prudence wiped her eyes with the tail of her shawl. Her cheeks were red from the cold and her eyes from weeping. "The baby died yesterday about sundown, Matthias. We cared for her as best we could, but—"

"I know you did, Prudence."

Little Sarah fussed, and Obadiah took her from Prudence and held her close to his chest. "I couldn't dig the baby a proper grave. The ground's frozen solid."

"Anyway, they wouldn't let us bury her in the churchyard," Prudence said.

"Who wouldn't?" Matthias said.

Obadiah's eyes turned to shards of ice. "The preacher said it wasn't proper. Sam Landis told me Herman Stodges and his friends put him up to saying it."

Matthias exhaled in disgust. Stodges' attitude was no surprise, but that Reverend Miller had gone along with the hatefulness sickened him. The fact that the child's grave was a pile of cold stones in the Wilsons' back yard next to their woodpile and washing cauldron—well, *that* was what wasn't proper. And he would go and tell Reverend Miller so to his face. Undoubtedly, trying to convince him to do the right thing would be a futile endeavor, but he would speak his mind. He could do no less. And come spring, when his own child was strong enough for the journey—

Obadiah clapped a hand on his shoulder. "We never said thank you for bringing the medicine."

"If only I'd been here sooner."

"You're a good man, Matthias Frailey, but you *are* only a man," Obadiah said. "If the Lord was here, he'd tell us that the child is only sleeping. Then he'd raise her up, like he did the little girl in the Bible."

"I know it." Matthias picked up his saddlebag and slung it over his shoulder.

Prudence sniffed and gave him a watery smile. "I've got coffee. Come inside and warm up before you go, Matthias."

"Thank you kindly, ma'am, but I have a stop to make before I go home."

***

THE PRESENT

John reached for the mouse to pause the action, and in doing so, jarred Merrideth into the present. Don't stop, John! I have to see him!" Her face heated when she realized how weird her outburst must have sounded—obsessive almost. Why had she been so reluctant to leave Matthias?

"Matthias?" John said.

Merrideth rubbed her temples. "Who else?"

"The poor little thing," Abby said. "The baby, I mean. Why on earth wouldn't they let it have a proper burial?"

"I can think of only one reason for that in southern Illinois, 1839," John said. "She wasn't white."

Merrideth snorted. "And how did you come up with that brilliant conclusion. You saw her parents."

"It wasn't the Wilsons' baby," Abby said. "I think they adopted her. Recently, I'd say. They hadn't even had time to name her."

"That doesn't necessarily mean the baby was adopted," Merrideth said. "With the high infant mortality rate back then, some parents waited to come up with a name until they were confident the baby would live. But still, you may be right." Merrideth leaned back in her chair and contemplated the ceiling. "The parents could be slaves working the salt mine at Equality. It's not that far away. Although how the Wilsons ended up with their baby is beyond me. The children of slaves belonged to the master."

John stood and slowly paced across the room and back. "What if...what if the father were white? What if he married a black woman, and they had a child together? What if she died—or was taken away—and the father found that he couldn't raise the child on his own? What if his own family refused to step up to the plate and help? What if he asked the Wilsons to foster the baby for him?"

"That's a lot of what-ifs," Abby said.

"Sorry, John. Your theory won't fly," Merrideth said. "Interracial marriage was illegal."

John stopped pacing. "I know that. I meant a common-law, hush-hush marriage."

"I suppose it's possible," Merrideth said. "But we're getting completely off track."

He lifted one eyebrow. "Not if Matthias Frailey is the white man in question."

"Wow. That's pretty far-fetched," Merrideth said.

"I agree," Abby said.

John put up a hand in protest. "It fits much of the information we have. Fact one: Matthias seemed unusually concerned about the death of the Wilson's baby."

"Because he's a nice guy," Merrideth said.

"Hear me out, please. Fact two: Herman Stodges didn't consider Matthias' wife a true wife and made disparaging remarks about her offspring. Fact three: His own father said that Matthias had made his bed, and now he must lie in it."

"I don't think Lachlan meant that in a condemning way," Merrideth said. "More that he was resigned to the consequences of his son's actions. At least that was the way Duncan seemed to interpret it."

"Well, maybe, but you cannot dispute fact four: In 1839 having a black child would certainly constitute a scandal for Matthias Frailey, one big enough that he felt he had to leave home."

"And maybe even big enough to disinherit him," Abby said

thoughtfully.

"But you're forgetting the most important fact," Merrideth said. "At the time of the baby's death, Matthias already had a wife and baby at home."

"Susan," Abby said.

"No, he married a woman named Emmaline," Merrideth said. "I'm thinking maybe Susan was a local herbalist."

"True," John said. "But that wouldn't necessarily preclude having a secret wife."

Merrideth let out a disgusted snort. "Let me get this straight. You're saying Matthias was a bigamist. And his family—his very nice and loving family—were such sanctimonious toads that they refused to care for the baby. But the Wilsons—fine Christians that they are—agreed to help Matthias with his little problem. And so while his wife Emmaline is home rocking the baby in the new cradle—his white baby—Matthias is taking medicine out to the Wilsons for his sick black baby."

"That's just not possible," Abby said. "The whole time I was inside Matthias' head, I never picked up anything like that. I think he's a good guy."

"I *know* he is," Merrideth said.

"You're right. You're right," John said. "The jury will please disregard the attorney's crazy theory." Yawning hugely, he stood and stretched. "I think it's time to make coffee."

Abby chuckled. "I have a feeling we're going to wish we *had* sent you out for a coffee maker, John. An espresso machine, to be specific. We're going to need lots of caffeine before this night is over." She got up and followed him to the counter. "And where are those cheese crackers?"

After a moment of staring unseeing at the monitor, Merrideth straightened in her chair and grabbed the mouse. "What is wrong with me?"

"Sleep deprivation?" Abby said.

It took Google only a few seconds to tell Merrideth what she wanted to know. And then she felt like slapping herself. "All right. I have a new theory about the baby. If I weren't so bad with dates I'd have realized it at once."

"You're a historian," John said. "You're not allowed to be bad with dates."

"Nevertheless, I am," Merrideth said with disgust. "It's a

number thing. I feel stupid enough around ordinary people. But around Brett, I really feel dumb. He can remember dates and addresses—any number—after only a glance. Apparently forever."

"You are not dumb, Merri," Abby said.

John nodded wisely. "But if Garrison makes you feel like you are, then that's a good reason not to hang around the guy."

Merrideth laughed. "Good one, John. Anyway, back to what I realized."

"Yes, what did you realize?" John said.

"Hurry up and get over here, and I'll show you," Merrideth said. The microwave dinged and a weird smell wafted into the room. "What is that?"

"That, my dear Merri," John said. "Is the smell of desperation."

Abby laughed. "It's coffee, kiddo. Really bad coffee."

"It smells like you boiled your sneakers in it," Merrideth said. "Bring me a cup, will you?"

"You can have this one," John said. "I haven't worked up the courage yet anyway." He set it down beside her. Merrideth picked up the cup and studied it suspiciously then took a cautious sip. "Not as bad as it smells."

"Go on," John said. "What's your theory?"

"I've set the time to the morning of December 3, 1838. Now if Matthias will cooperate with me..." Merrideth un-paused the action, and the image on the screen scrambled as the program adjusted to the date setting. "Keep your fingers crossed. If he happens to go to the Ferry House on December third, I think I can prove—Hey, watch it, John. You're getting cracker crumbs on my keyboard."

"Oh. Sorry." He stepped back and brushed crumbs from his shirt.

Merrideth stopped the action, and there Matthias stood on the boardwalk, just ready to walk into the Ferry House. She smiled in satisfaction. "Can you believe it? Okay, Matthias, help me prove my theory."

"What theory?" Abby said plaintively.

"Just watch," Merrideth said, setting the program to go virtual.

CHAPTER 9

Matthias stepped into the blessed warmth and wrestled the door shut. He set his rifle against the wall and nodded a greeting to the six or so men there. Angus waved to him from the back table.

"Whew!" Matthias said, rubbing his hands together. "It's colder than a pump handle in January!"

Sam Landis looked up from the bar where he was drying beer mugs. "Or an iron commode," he said without cracking a smile.

"I can never out do you, Sam," Matthias said with a laugh. "Bring me coffee, would you?"

When he reached the table where his brother sat, Angus said, "Did you get Champ shod?"

Matthias settled into the chair across from him. "Yep. How about you?"

"They're out of black thread," he said, "Otherwise, I got everything Ma wanted."

Sam brought the coffee and Matthias stripped off his gloves and held the hot mug in his cold hands.

"Drink it fast, Runt," Angus said, sipping from his own mug. "Snow's coming, and we'd best be on our way."

"Good thing we shipped that last timber when we did, brother. The channel's getting a might narrow for my taste. The ice must be four or five feet out from the shore. Except near the docks. The ferry's keeping it broken up there pretty good."

"But for how long? With this cold, I reckon the ice will build up faster than the ferry can break it up. Not enough traffic."

The door opened and a blast of cold air came in. "You gotta

come see this!" Isaac Frederick said from the doorway.

"Dang it," Sam said. "Shut the door."

Isaac glared at Sam, but stepped inside and pushed the door closed. "Come see," he said again. "The Injuns are here, coming across on the ferry. Can't count how many."

"Now?" Angus said. "In winter?"

"Now," Isaac said.

Angus pounded his fist on the table, making their coffee mugs jump. "Then Old Hickory's given the Cherokee a death sentence."

Matthias stood and hurried to the side window. He scraped away the frost. Sure enough, the ferry was docked, and people were coming off.

Angus joined him at the window. Herman Stodges and Pleasant Lyman left their table and came to look out, too.

Sam Landis wiped the bar thoughtfully. "I thought sure when they didn't come before, they were waiting for spring."

Mayor Lusk came out from his office to see what the commotion was. "What's going on, Sam?"

"It's the Indians, sir," he said. "They're finally here."

"Nothing stops Old Hickory from getting his way," Lusk said bitterly. "No matter that the Supreme Court ruled against him."

Sam raised an empty tankard in a mocking salute. "To King Jackson."

Mayor Lusk went back into his office and then came out again, putting on his coat. He opened the door and stepped out into the cold. Matthias went with the mayor, and then Angus, Sam, and some of the other men followed them. They stood on the boardwalk in front of the Ferry House and looked down the embankment at the dock twenty-five yards or so below them.

The ferry was full to bursting with people, wagons, and horses. One of the ferrymen opened the gate, and three men on horses trotted off onto the dock and then up onto the landing. Matthias was surprised to see that only one wore a U.S. Army uniform. The other two were Indians, although not like any he'd ever seen or heard tell of. Their faces were bare of war paint, and there was no sign anywhere of tomahawks or feathers, much less human scalps. They wore sheepskin coats, much like the one he himself wore, and each had a rifle among the other gear hanging from his saddle. The only things strange about their appearance were the calico turbans they wore on their heads and the shirts of the same bright fabric showing at their throats.

The three horsemen shouted commands, and the Cherokee began pouring out of the ferry. The dock became a drum, the wooden planks amplifying their footsteps as they crossed, carrying bundles, baskets, and babies on their backs or hauling their belongings in over-laden handcarts with creaking wheels.

A gust of wind came around the side of the inn, and Matthias pulled his hat down over his ears. While he'd been gawking, news of the arrival had apparently already begun spreading through town in the mysterious way such things always did. Next door, shoppers came out of Ellsworth Emporium where they had likely been stocking up ahead of the snow and gawked at the newcomers just as he had. And then all along the way, people began to come out of the other business establishments to watch.

The first of the Cherokee to walk down Main Street ranged from very young to very old. Some looked around curiously, but most kept their eyes down as if they didn't notice the crowd of white people that had gathered on the boardwalks to watch them being herded like cattle down the street.

Matthias felt ashamed and turned his eyes away.

Next to him, Pleasant chuckled and said, "Little early for a Fourth of July parade, ain't it, Mayor?"

"Shut up, Pleasant," Lusk said.

Pleasant's expression turned distinctly unpleasant. "Just funnin'," he said sourly. "That's all."

The last passenger on the ferry was a gray-haired old man driving a covered wagon. He whistled and slapped the reins on his horses' rumps but didn't make much progress. From where he stood, Matthias couldn't tell what the problem was.

John Berry, the ferry operator apparently thought he wasn't trying hard enough. "Hurry up, you old fool!" he shouted. "Can't you see there's people waitin' on the other side for the ferry?"

Matthias turned his eyes to the Kentucky shore. With the gray sky of the impending snow, visibility was poor, but he made out the canvas top of another wagon and several ghostly figures walking about on the shoreline.

The wagon came off at last. Berry closed the ferry's gate, and the ferrymen and dock hands grabbed their tow ropes and began to pull. The pulleys creaked, and the ferry moved away from the dock to begin its trip back to Kentucky. Matthias was surprised to see

Berry running the ferry in person. He usually stayed on the Kentucky side, leaving the actual work of manning the ferry to his workers.

Mayor Lusk heaved a disgusted sigh. "I do so regret selling the ferry to him. My mother would turn over in her grave if she knew."

The old man's covered wagon started up the embankment, but the three mounted men passed it, their horses' iron shoes striking sharply on the stone paving. When they drew abreast of the inn, the men reined in.

Matthias could not keep himself from staring at the two Indians. They didn't make eye contact with any of the people on the boardwalk, just faced the street as if bored by the whole situation. Their skin, what he could see of it, wasn't red after all, but a burnished shade of brown not much darker than his own got in the summer.

The uniformed soldier tipped his hat to Lusk. Matthias wasn't surprised that the soldier knew he was the one in charge. Lusk was the kind of man who wore authority and responsibility as easily as he wore his hat.

"Good day, sir. I am Robert Lusk, the mayor here," he said, stepping forward.

"Private Burnett, sir, out of Captain Abraham McCall's Tennessee Company, 2nd Regiment, 2nd Brigade, Mounted Infantry. I am charged to escort these souls to the Oklahoma country. Please tell your folks they don't have anything to worry about. We'll pass through as soon as may be and set up camp west of town."

"I expect you'll be following Lusk Road, then?"

"All the way to the Cape Girardeau ferry on the Mississippi."

Herman Stodges turned his head to the side and spat into the street. "Nothin' to worry about, you say?"

Mayor Lusk shot him a stern look, and Stodges settled for mumbling under his breath. Lusk turned back to Private Burnett, his face solemn. "You have to follow your orders, soldier. But it is a sad charge you have."

One of the Cherokee turned and looked briefly at Mayor Lusk. His face remained impassive, but a flicker of emotion glimmered in his dark eyes. He soon turned back to study the street, but his horse and that of his companion twitched their tails and became suddenly restive, as if it were up to them to display the emotions their riders refused to let show on their faces.

"It is a sad task indeed, sir," Private Burnett said.

The old man's covered wagon finally made it up the hill. The tired horses pulling it continued slowly down Main Street, following the people who had gone ahead on foot. The canvas was laced up tight in back, so Matthias couldn't see those who rode inside. But their shadows played over the canvas, and a few mysterious Cherokee words drifted his way.

Then the wind came rushing around the building again, and Matthias and the others stepped back for what protection the inn could provide. In the street, the wagon's canvas top flapped like sheets on a clothes line, and the people's tattered cloaks whipped against their legs.

"Why are you traveling so late in the year?" Mayor Lusk said. "I suppose that's some Washington bureaucrat's fool idea."

"They are fools. That they are," Burnett said wryly. "But they weren't fool enough to suggest traveling in winter. We started in June. Should have been in Oklahoma country by now, or at least to Arkansas, but everything went wrong. First a terrible drought came and dried up most of the creeks and ponds thereabouts. Then the gripe and ague hit, and many of the people died in the stockades."

"Stockades?" Angus said. "You put them in stockades?"

"It was not my idea to do so, sir," Burnett said. "But the army had to have somewhere to put them while we rounded them up. But as I said, the drought came. It was bad for the people in the stockades, but the chiefs figured it would be even worse to be on the road not knowing whether they'd be able to find water along the way. They asked to be allowed to wait until fall, and the government said they could. Finally, the drought broke, and we left the first of October. But you can have too much of a good thing, as I'm sure you know. The rain just wouldn't let up, and the roads turned into swamps. And then winter came early. I must say y'all's winter is brutal. Back in southern Georgia where these Indians are from, they say the temperature rarely falls below forty all winter. And snow, if they get any, doesn't 'mount to a hill of beans."

"Well, Private," Mayor Lusk said, "I reckon they are unlucky all around, because this is the coldest winter we have had in Illinois for a long while."

Cyrus Ellsworth came out of the Emporium, elbowed his way to the front, and stood shivering in his shirtsleeves. "Soldier, I have an idea you might need supplies. Salt and coffee perhaps? If you'd like to step into my store just yonder."

"Thank you." Burnett turned and spoke to his companions.

Matthias couldn't make out what he said and thought at first that the wind had garbled the words, until he realized in astonishment that he was speaking in Cherokee.

"We are getting low on a few things," Burnett said. "Running Dog will get them while Black Feather and I go on ahead to lay out the camp for the others."

The man he indicated as Running Dog dismounted and tied his horse to the rail. Cyrus' eyes grew wide and he sputtered, "But he's an Injun."

Private Burnett's eyes narrowed, but he smiled calmly and said, "That he is, sir. He is Chief Hiawassee's eldest son, a member of the Cherokee Lighthorse Patrol, and the leader of this contingent. Don't worry, sir. He's carrying legal tender, courtesy of the U.S. government."

Isaac Fredericks muttered, "Make sure he don't steal you blind, Cyrus."

"That's right," Pleasant Lyman said angrily.

Beside Matthias, Angus shifted. "And, Cyrus, you make sure your prices don't take a sudden notion to rise. I'd not like to think you'd take advantage of the situation."

Matthias cleared his throat and hid a smile. Undoubtedly his brother was remembering the time sugar went scarce and Cyrus kept jacking the price until it was so high no one but Mayor Lusk could afford to sweeten his coffee.

Cyrus' brows rose and he looked down his nose at Angus, which with his short stature was no mean feat. "Of course not," he said indignantly.

Running Dog stepped up onto the boardwalk and bowed to Cyrus. "After you," he said politely—in perfect English.

Cyrus' eyes widened, and then he walked stiffly down the boardwalk to the Emporium, looking nervously over his shoulder every few steps.

A smile flickered across Private Burnett's face. "Thank you, Mayor Lusk. We'll be on our way." Then he tipped his hat, and he and Black Feather trotted down Main Street.

Herman Stodges spat into the street again. "They'll be wanting firewood."

"Of course they will, Herman," Obadiah Wilson said. Beside him, his wife Prudence put her handkerchief to her eyes. "Oh, Obadiah, how will they survive in this cold?"

"Well they're not cutting my trees," Stodges said, stepping down to the street. "I'll see to that. Yes, sir." He hurried down to where his spotted horse was hitched. Then, after checking his rifle in its scabbard, he mounted and rode off to the north toward his homestead.

"There must be something we can do to help," Prudence said.

"Pray, ma'am. Pray," Mayor Lusk said.

"How many do you reckon there will be?" Matthias said.

"I don't know," Lusk said. "I should have asked Private Burnett."

"Who cares?" Isaac Frederick said. "One Injun is one too many. They'll rob you then scalp you while you sleep."

"You all can stand around here watching," Pleasant said. "I'm going home before they steal my livestock. And you'd best call up the militia, Captain Lusk."

"Don't be a fool," Lusk said. "Look at them. Did they seem like troublemakers?"

"There's the ferry coming back already," Angus said.

A snowflake landed on Matthias' eyelashes and then another on his cheek. The clouds were gray and looked full to bursting. There was sure to be several inches of snow before morning.

"Come on, Prudence, I'm taking you home," Obadiah Wilson said. "We can do our praying from there."

They hurried down the street to their wagon. Other people on the boardwalk began to leave ahead of the snow. Those that remained stood hugging themselves in the cold as they watched the ferry's approach. At last it bumped into the dock, and Berry's men secured it. Another workman unlatched the gate and swung it open. Then more Cherokee, bent with the loads they carried, stepped onto the dock.

The embankment was always slick under the best of conditions. How would they make it to the top once the snow came in earnest? Already a woman had slipped on the stones and fallen to her hands and knees. Struggling to rise under the burden on her back, she slipped again. Several people went past her, but a tiny old woman stopped and took her by the hand.

She would never be able to raise her. Matthias stepped off the boardwalk and went down the embankment, nearly falling himself in his haste.

Both women looked up at him, blinking at the snowflakes that fell into eyes wide with either surprise or fear. "Here, take my hand," he said, not knowing if they understood English. The old woman stepped aside and Matthias lifted the fallen woman to her feet. A mewling sound came from her pack, and Matthias realized it was a baby. She lifted the child down from her back and began suckling it. Embarrassed, he wanted to turn away but knew that if she slipped again he wouldn't be able to help her if he did.

The old woman patted the mother's arm and spoke words he couldn't understand. It sounded reassuring. They gave Matthias shy glances and quick smiles, ghostly glimmers of smiles anyway, and continued with the others up the embankment.

Angus threaded his way through the flow of people and came to where Matthias stood. "Lord have mercy on them! How will they make it?"

"I don't know. The snow's coming faster every minute."

After the last of the foot passengers left the ferry, several men disembarked, pulling handcarts loaded impossibly high with all manner of goods. Behind them, men on foot led six or seven horses carrying women and children. Last of all, another covered wagon lumbered off the ferry and started up the embankment. The driver whipped the horses, but still the wagon slipped on the snow-slick stones. Matthias and Angus went to the rear of the wagon and pushed. It didn't go forward, but at least it didn't slip backward onto them either.

Still straining to hold the wagon, Matthias found himself inches away from a small serious face with curious brown eyes peeking out through the canvas lacing. He looked about five or six.

Matthias turned to look up at the inn. With the snow, he couldn't identify the men who stood watching from the boardwalk. He called for them to come down and help, but they turned away as if they hadn't heard him. Maybe they hadn't; the wind was kicking up more. But wasn't it clear that help was needed?

The little boy still stared at him from the back of the wagon. He and Angus renewed their efforts, and the wagon finally surged ahead. The face disappeared, replaced by a little brown hand that waved at him.

Chest heaving from the exertion, Matthias waved back, smiling in spite of the grim circumstances. He and Angus watched the retreating ferry. When they had their breath back, they climbed back up to the inn.

Some of the bystanders on the boardwalk were calling out mocking comments, pointing and laughing at the helpless sojourners passing by. Rage rose in Matthias' throat. It was overlaid with shock at discovering the meanness hidden away in so many of his neighbors' hearts and now revealed unashamedly for all to see. There was a tussle of some sort down the street, and then Mayor Lusk shouted that everyone should stop gawking and go on home while they still could. Then he hauled Pleasant Lyman away by his collar. Good, Matthias thought with considerable satisfaction.

The Cherokee just kept their faces straight ahead and trudged down Main Street heading west.

CHAPTER 10

***

THE PRESENT

Merrideth closed her eyes and blindly grabbed the mouse to stop the action. Her stomach roiled, and her brain was a roller coaster of conflicting thoughts and feelings. Matthias' primary emotions had been shock, anger, compassion—and shame. The Cherokee felt the same anger and shame, all the while some of the spectators harbored a nasty mix of hatred toward them and almost a sense of satisfaction at their plight. Or at least Matthias thought they did. She would try to keep an open mind about it.

All that, together with her own feelings, resulted in an emotional overload to her system that was almost painful. She took one deep cleansing breath, and then another. After what seemed like an hour, but which was surely only a minute or two, her confusion began to diminish, and she opened her eyes.

Abby and John shivered and their faces were chalk white. Abby held her hand to her mouth and looked like she might be sick any moment.

"Take deep breaths, honey," John said, putting an arm around her shoulders.

"It helps if you keep your eyes closed, Abby." Merrideth realized she was shivering, too. She willed her body to stop, reminding herself that she was in a comfortably heated room, not outside on that cold December day in 1838.

Abby followed their suggestions, and after a minute, the color began to come back into her face.

"The Trail of Tears," Merrideth said in wonder. "We just saw the Trail of Tears."

Abby shook her head as if trying to dispel the painful images. "Dear God, what they went through."

Merrideth put a hand over Abby's. "I know. And we're just getting started. That was only a few minutes of their trip. I forget how long it took them to reach Oklahoma. I'll have to look it up."

"So that's why they traveled in the winter," John said. "I've always laid all the blame on Andrew Jackson. I didn't realize they had so many delays."

"Like the Jews," Abby said. "When I read the *Diary of Anne Frank* in school, I kept wondering why they didn't all run away from the Nazis before the war while they had the chance. It wasn't until college that I learned about some of the political factors that prevented them from doing so."

"It's a good analogy. In many ways," Merrideth said. "Hindsight is always 20/20. If the Indians had known to what lengths the government would go to get the land, they could have unified and protected themselves. They were beginning to do so, but they ran out of time. And as for Jackson, don't worry about assigning him too much blame for the tragedy, John. To be fair, though, you can trace the idea of Indian removal all the way back to George Washington's policies. And Jefferson cited it as one of his reasons for the Louisiana Purchase."

John grunted in disapproval.

"Sorry," Merrideth said. "I know he's is your favorite president. Here's a better topic. Remember that soldier on the horse? Private Burnett?"

"Yes. He seemed like a decent guy in the midst of all the horrors."

"He was. He wrote about his experiences with the Removal. His eyewitness account is one of only a handful. Without it, we would not know much about what went on."

Abby wiped at her eyes. "The magnitude of the injustice hit me when that Cherokee man spoke perfect English. Not that it should matter, of course, but I have to be honest and admit that it seemed so much worse knowing they were so...so...civilized."

"The Cherokee were one of the five so-called civilized tribes in the East," Merrideth said. "Before Jackson's removal policy, the government's goal had been assimilation of the Indians into the white culture. Various efforts to facilitate that had been going on for years. They sent Christian missionaries to convert the Indians, and they sent government agents to teach them modern agricultural practices. Part of it may have been altruistic, but the policy was also in the government's best interest, because they knew that an agrarian society required much less land than a hunter-gatherer one did, thus freeing up more acres for the white settlers."

"Then came Andrew Jackson," John said.

"Yes," Merrideth said. "Good old Andrew Jackson. He had no interest in assimilation. All he wanted was for the Indians to be gone post haste. He began bribing the chiefs to sell their tribal lands, or if that didn't work, he outright stole them. Whatever your attitude about assimilation, and I have mixed feelings, his removal policy effectively halted the progress of it and changed the course of history."

"I can't get the picture out of my head of that one woman lugging a baby on her back and carrying another in her arms," Abby said.

Merrideth wiped at her eyes. "I know. I've read that some Cherokee parents begged white families along the way to take their children because they feared they wouldn't survive otherwise. Which brings us back to my theory about Obadiah and Prudence Wilson's baby. It was obvious that they were sympathetic to the Indians' plight. It's not a stretch to think they agreed to take in a child."

"We could lock onto Prudence or Obadiah and easily find out," John said.

"I don't think I could bear to watch a mother give away her child," Abby said, her voice choked with emotion.

"I know. It's another horrible similarity to the Jewish Holocaust." John brushed away a strand of her hair and kissed her cheek. "Are you ready to go again, honey? We'd better speed up because—" he rubbed his eyes. "Man, that sounded incredibly callous. Sure, just fast-forward past their suffering, as if it didn't matter."

Abby patted his cheek. "We know very well that you're not callous, John Roberts."

"Okay, we'll stick to Matthias, then." Merrideth switched off virtual, un-paused the scene, and then set the speed several ticks faster than real time. At that rate, the snow came so fast it looked like Golconda was experiencing a blizzard. It was difficult to see much of what was happening.

But it was clear enough to know that Matthias and Angus stayed there hour after hour, helping people up the bank onto Main Street. For a while, Mayor Lusk, Alexander Buel, and two other men came to help. But by mid-afternoon, only the Frailey brothers remained to assist the Cherokee pouring into Golconda.

Merrideth increased the speed again, and the December day wore on. On some trips the ferry brought only people, mounted or on foot, including more soldiers here and there. Other times it carried covered wagons, up to four per trip, or cattle and other livestock, which men on horses herded down Main Street as well.

The condition of the Cherokee appeared to decline with each subsequent group that came off the ferry. Some shivered in light clothing that might have been suitable for Georgia, but was definitely inadequate for an Illinois winter, even a normal one. And with each group it got more and more difficult for them to watch. When a woman went by shepherding four crying children, Abby wept along with them.

"Don't cry, honey," John said. "They'll have a chance to warm up when they get to camp."

"Oh, I hope so," she sobbed.

But then John nearly lost it, too, when a man came up the embankment wearing only rags on his feet, each foot print in the snow tinged with pink.

Merrideth went to the bathroom to cry. When she had composed herself enough to watch more, the miserable day was finally over, the sky so dark they could barely see Matthias and his brother. The ferry stopped running. Matthias stood at the riverbank looking across to Kentucky where campfires dotted the shoreline, indicating there were many, many more people waiting to cross. At last, Matthias and Angus climbed the embankment themselves and headed home.

"What wonderful men they were," Abby said, wiping her eyes. "I keep thinking of that parable Jesus told."

"'Whatever you did for one of the least of these brothers and sisters of mine, you did for me,'" John said.

Abby was certainly right about them being wonderful men. At least Matthias was for sure. The strong connection she felt with him came, she knew, from the intimacy of being inside his head for such an extended period. She hadn't been privy to every thought, to every shadowy corner of his brain, but she felt certain that he was genuinely kind. There had been only concern for others, not one hint of guile in him. Kindness was a surprisingly attractive character trait, one that didn't show up at the top of most women's lists when they were shopping for men. Yes, he was attractive, all right. But she wouldn't let herself think about it. Falling in love with a dead man was as stupid—and pointless—as falling in love with a fictional character in a book.

If only she could use the software on the men of her own time. There would be no question about a guy's thoughts and motives. She'd know in a flash what he was really like—if he were safe. Like a prescreening program. Now that was an online dating service she would be interested in!

How would Brett measure up? Not that she planned to date *him*. But it would be interesting to get inside his head. Would she find he was truly as nice as he seemed, or would she discover that he had only fixed her doors because he hoped to manipulate her into dating him?

No, it was probably best not to know Brett's or anyone else's thoughts—any living person's anyway, because knowing for sure that a few people actually, genuinely liked her would be offset with the proof that most didn't. It was better to only suspect, not know that for a fact.

Merrideth snapped out of her weird thoughts and focused on the screen in front of her. She increased the program's speed until Matthias and Angus became dark blurs of incomprehensible pixels on the screen.

When the screen lightened with the new morning, she slowed again and found Matthias and Angus back at the ferry helping another group of travelers just stepping onto the dock. The snow had stopped, leaving a beautiful three-inch deep white blanket glinting in the morning light. The path, however, was already churned up, meaning a group of Cherokee had already passed by.

All day, the ferry made trip after trip, disgorging hundreds more passengers, and livestock, wagons, and carts.

"Kiddo, you're going to have to speed up more," John said.

"That is if we're ever going to find out what happened to Matthias. Let me remind you two teachers that I don't get the holiday off. I have a big case waiting for me bright and early Monday morning."

Abby smiled encouragingly at her. "Maybe I could come back down here with you some time to study this more, Merri."

"I know. You're right," Merrideth said, reaching for the mouse. "I'll just steel myself and fast-forward through this."

"Hold on," John said, pointing to the screen. "What's up with that?"

The ferry was just docking. A man on horseback was the only passenger.

"It can't be the last of them," Merrideth said. "You can see more people still waiting on the Kentucky side."

"Okay," John said, sighing. "Let's watch for a little longer. You might as well go virtual while you're at it."

Merrideth laughed. "Addictive, isn't it?"

CHAPTER 11

***

DECEMBER 4, 1838

Matthias watched with amazement as the ferry pulled up to the dock. The Lusk Ferry—well, it was Berry's Ferry now—could carry up to four covered wagons or a whole crowd of people. And hundreds and hundreds of Cherokee on the Kentucky side still waited in freezing weather to cross the river and get to the camp.

And there sat Cornelius Smothers on his sorry-looking horse all alone, right smack dab in the middle of the ferry.

Angus called to him, "Hey, Cornelius. What are you, the King of England, or what?"

Berry's man opened the gate just then, making enough racket that Cornelius apparently did not hear him. Cornelius clucked, and his horse carried him off the ferry. The dock worker shut the gate and the ferry started back for Kentucky.

"Have they gone on?" Cornelius said looking nervously around.

"Who?" Matthias said.

"The Injuns. I don't want any of them following me home to Elizabeth and the girls. Injuns love blond-haired scalps, you know."

"I reckon you're safe, Cornelius."

Angus stuck a thumb over his shoulder toward the river. "You know a lot of those cold people waiting over there could have shared the ferry with you."

"Don't look at me, Angus Frailey. It was Berry. Made them wait. Said I was to go to the head of the line. He said he wasn't about to start lettin' dirty redskins ride alongside of white folk."

"I should have known," Angus said in disgust.

"You'd think he'd want to crowd as many as he could on before the river freezes up," Matthias said. "He's got to be making a fortune at twelve cents a head."

Cornelius laughed. "Oh, he's making a fortune all right, the lucky dog. He's chargin' them Injuns a dollar each. They're scrambling to come up with the fare, too."

Matthias shook his head in wonder at mankind's greediness. "Mayor Lusk's mother will really be turning over in her grave." He remembered the feisty old woman fondly. "If she was here, she'd probably take her gun over to Kentucky and shoot him."

"You'd best be getting on home, Cornelius," Angus said.

"See you, boys," he said and turned his horse toward the embankment. When he got to the top, Angus called out, "Hey, Cornelius."

"Yes?"

"Keep your eyes open for scalpers."

His eyes went wide and his horse danced nervously. "Thanks, I will." He spurred his horse into a trot.

Matthias laughed until he snorted. "You're a devil, Angus, you know that?"

Angus grinned back at him. "Come on, little brother, let's go warm up before the ferry gets back."

The street was empty except for Cyrus, who was sweeping the snow away from the Emporium's door. Apparently folks had obeyed Mayor Lusk's order and gone home. Or they'd gotten their fill of the sights. Or maybe, like Cornelius, they were holing up at home, guns to the ready in case any bloodthirsty savages happened by looking for scalps.

Cyrus stopped sweeping when he saw them and leaned on his broom. "Do you think there will be more soldiers today?"

"Why?" Angus said.

Cyrus smiled went wide with satisfaction. "They've got money in their pockets, that's why."

"You're bound to have more customers," Matthias said. "If the soldiers are not too busy with their herding."

"Glad business is good for you." Angus said, smiling tightly.

Cyrus, apparently not hearing the sarcasm in their voices, smiled wider. "Indeed, it is."

Angus looked like he was about to punch the man's smiling face, so Matthias opened the door of the Ferry House and shoved his brother inside. The room was empty except for Sam at the counter, who looked up and said, "You're wanting coffee I expect."

"Right you are, Sam," Angus said. "We're nearly froze, although I'm embarrassed to even mention it in view of the situation."

"I was just telling Mr. Landis the same thing." The voice belonged to a middle-aged stranger who sat at the window table, a plate of bacon and eggs in front of him. "I slept upstairs in a fine featherbed while my Cherokee brothers and sisters slept in the cold. Your Illinois winters are a frightful thing, but, even so, my wife didn't want to stay here. I had to insist. She's with child, you see."

"I assure you, we think it's frightful weather, too, but I take your meaning," Angus said.

"Won't you join me? I'll buy you breakfast."

Matthias wondered at the man's generosity toward strangers. Angus looked as confused as he was. "No thanks, mister," Angus said. "We already ate breakfast."

"I would have finished mine long before now," the man said, "but I was attempting to repair our wagon." He rose from the table and extended a hand first to Angus and then to Matthias. "Please allow me to introduce myself. I am Reverend Daniel Butrick, missionary to the Cherokee at the behest of the American Mission Board in Boston. Clara and I are traveling with our flock. We'll settle with them in the Oklahoma country, God willing."

Angus gave him their names and then grinned, "The way you talk, I didn't reckon you were from around here."

Butrick smiled. "No, we are strangers to these parts. Perhaps you didn't notice us yesterday for all the chaos, but Clara and I most certainly saw you. We praised God for the way you were assisting the people in their hour of need." He gestured to the table again. "Please, at least let me purchase your coffee."

"We thank you kindly," Angus said, sitting down across from Reverend Butrick.

Out the window Matthias saw that the ferry was still at the

Kentucky shore, so he sat, too. "Just for a short while, Reverend."

Sam brought the coffee. "The preacher says he needs lumber to fix his wagon. I told him the Frailey boys might be able to find a board or two." Sam's voice remained deadpan as usual, but his eyes held a hint of humor.

"A few," Angus said drily.

"That's wonderful," Reverend Butrick said. "Just tell me where I should go to purchase them."

"There's plenty at our place," Matthias said. "But that's a ways out there and we don't plan on going home 'til dark."

"I could go get what you need, Reverend," Angus said. "If you're going to be here a while."

"We'll be here, Clara and I, as long as it takes for the people to cross the river. It will likely take two more days."

"Then we can bring the lumber tomorrow," Matthias said.

"How many Indians are coming across?" Angus said.

"When we left Georgia there were nearly a thousand," Reverend Butrick said. "Sadly, we have lost nineteen souls, and the journey is far from over. Lieutenant Wheeler reckons Golconda is about the halfway mark."

Matthias glanced out the window. "The ferry's back." He stood and put his gloves on. Angus gulped the last of his coffee and got up, too.

Reverend Butrick quickly donned his coat. "Then it's time for me to get back to leading my flock."

The Fraileys' own preacher had surely heard about the situation by now. Matthias thought about going to the church to find out for sure, but it seemed like a waste of time when there was so much he could do to help at the ferry. Anyway, Reverend Miller was probably already busy gathering food and clothes for the needy.

On the way down to the dock, Matthias struggled to find a way to ask Reverend Butrick about the Indians. "Reverend, you called them your flock, but surely you're not saying that…I mean they're heathens, not Christians, right?"

Smiling, Reverend Butrick put his hand on his shoulder. "Let me tell you about the Cherokee, Mr. Frailey. Over the past fifty years, the tribe has made tremendous social and educational progress, of which they are rightfully proud. They set aside their age-old blood feud laws and now have a democratic government similar to our own—with a system of judges to enforce the new laws, too. They have built schools and libraries."

"Schools? Like with desks and books?" Angus said.

"Yes, like that. A growing number of Cherokee have acquired the skills of reading and writing, thanks to Sequoyah's fine syllabary and translation work. Their newspaper the *Cherokee Phoenix* is published once a month in both Cherokee and English. Before we left, there were plans for a museum."

Matthias studied the preacher. He did not appear to be jesting. "A museum?"

"Certainly."

Matthias turned back to watch the newest group of tired people coming off the dock. They had left behind more in Georgia than he had reckoned.

"Many of the people live—lived anyway—in houses much like their white neighbors, some of them every bit as fine. Yes, by anyone's standards, the Cherokee are a civilized nation. And on that basis some call them Christian. Of course, that's not really what it means to be a Christian. But I assure you that many Cherokee *have* joyfully accepted Christ and are now my true brothers and sisters and I their temporal shepherd. As for the others, I keep preaching the Gospel and offering a cup of cool water where I can."

"'Unto the least of these my brothers,'" Matthias said softly.

"Ah, you know the Scriptures," Reverend Butrick said with a delighted smile. "Might I deduce that you and Angus are in the fold as well?"

Matthias looked at his brother and smiled. "You might. And should."

"Let us get on with it then, Runt." Angus grinned. "Although it will be a helping hand and not a cup of cool water we'll be giving on this winter's day."

"Pray the ferry continues to run swiftly, Reverend Butrick," Matthias said. "It looks like more snow is coming."

CHAPTER 12

***

THE PRESENT

When Merrideth's brain shifted back to the present, she realized that Abby and John had made the transition from 1838 quicker than she had and apparently with none of the unwelcome physical side effects of before. They were discussing the degree of the Cherokee's social and political advancements. She, however, was not up to intelligent discourse. For one thing her skull felt like someone had stuffed it with fiberglass insulation. For another thing, she was angry—or at least annoyed.

It wasn't her friends' chattering, although that, too, was starting to get on her nerves. And it wasn't that Matthias had started quoting Bible verses, which she normally found irritating. It was the same verse John had quoted earlier, and like John, he had managed to pull it out of his head at a moment's notice and not be sanctimonious about it, unlike her college roommate, who had rained endless verses down on everyone's heads without suitable deeds to match the words.

The words of the Scripture passage resonated with Merrideth, and she found herself yearning to help the *least of these* as Matthias and Angus had done. Maybe that was what was missing from her religion. When was the last time she had helped a needy person? When she got home she should find some. Surely even a small town like Lebanon had poor people. Maybe Brett or Marla knew where to find them.

No, it wasn't the quoting of Bible verses that had disturbed her. After another moment, her thoughts sorted themselves out. "She was pregnant."

"Who?" Abby said.

"The missionary's wife. That is so annoying."

"What's so annoying about that?" Abby looked at her warily. "People do tend to have babies."

"It's annoying that some people are so obsessed with foisting their white religion on the Indians that they are willing to risk their lives to do it. I saw the same thing when I was following Brett's ancestor James Garretson when he went as a missionary to the Indian tribes. In this case, Butrick is—was—even willing to endanger his family, too."

Abby glanced momentarily at John and then said, "What makes you think he plans to *foist* his religion on them?"

"It's what they did, Abby. All part of the government's assimilation program. Surely you've read about the mission schools with their harsh programs to exterminate Indian culture? The forced conversions to Christianity? The teachers used to beat the children if they spoke in their own language. And they—"

"I know, Merri," Abby said. "I've read accounts of horrible things. But we have no reason to think this Reverend Butrick was like that."

"Maybe not," Merrideth said, rubbing her tired eyes. "I should reserve judgment until we have the chance to see more of his interactions with the Cherokee. Maybe we'll have time to switch the lock to him and get inside his head for a while. That would show his motives quick enough."

"Don't you think his actions already give us evidence of his motives?" Abby said. "I think he should be commended for leaving the comforts of home to travel the Trail of Tears with the Cherokee."

"At the risk of his wife and baby's lives? Did he think the Indians didn't have their own religion?"

"So you think all religions are interchangeable?" John said. "We'll all get to Heaven one way or another?"

"Yes, some of the greatest, most moral, most sincere people in the world have been non-Christians. Hindus, Muslims…whatever."

"But Jesus said—" Abby said.

"Shouldn't we get back to work? I don't want to waste a single minute when I have the chance to see the Trail of Tears firsthand. You said we could come back to Golconda another day, but we all know there are no guarantees we could ever find our way back to the same moment in time. *Beautiful Houses* has always had a mind of its own. It allows us see what it wants us to and closes down when it decides to."

John chuckled softly. "You should try to remember never to voice that theory, or the guys in white coats will come take you away for an extended vacation."

"But first," Merrideth said, "I need to take a few notes. Why don't you guys grab a couple of minutes of shut-eye?"

"Good idea." John put his head down on his arms in front of him on the table. "I think I'm going blind."

"Maybe I'll rest my eyes, too, if you're sure you don't mind." Abby put her head against John's shoulder and closed her eyes.

"Go ahead and sleep if you can. I'll wake you in a minute."

Merrideth got a legal pad out of her backpack and began to write. Her brain being mush, the thoughts came slowly at first, but then the names and scenes began to rewind in her mind, and she hurried to get descriptions down before they were gone. Hopefully, she would be able to find substantiation elsewhere for some of what she'd seen and heard. Her students would love the specifics. They were what made history come alive for them. And maybe she would write a book about the Trail of Tears after all. The Fort Piggot book she had begun writing was coming along nicely. Assuming she could get a publisher for it, maybe they would agree to a whole series on southern Illinois history.

Merrideth tamped down that exciting thought and concentrated on her note-taking. She was confused by some of what they had seen, with all the jumping back and forth in time. Putting it all down in chronological order would be helpful. When she had written all she could remember, she set aside her pad and pen. Abby and John appeared to be thoroughly conked out, so she donned her ear buds. Clicking off *Virtual*, she un-paused the action and set it to run a few ticks faster than real time.

The people coming off the ferry obviously knew Reverend Butrick, some giving him respectful nods as they passed by. Others paused to speak to him, although at the speed she had set, it was impossible to understand what they said even if she knew Cherokee. She wished she had time to slow down and really listen to them speak. It would be an awesome way to learn the language. Merrideth had to admit that there was nothing about Reverend Butrick to indicate his motives were less than sterling. It was obvious that he genuinely loved his flock. He stood there hour after hour laying kind hands on as many shoulders as he could reach. Once, she slowed briefly and realized that he was speaking in English, pronouncing blessings on the people and encouraging them to endure. They would be at the camp soon, he told them. There they could rest, eat, and be warm.

Meanwhile, Matthias and Angus helped the soldiers and the Cherokee Lighthorse Patrol keep the process of disembarkation going smoothly. Even without being in virtual mode, Merrideth sensed their worry as they raced against the clock to get everyone ashore before the river got too dangerous for the ferry to run. When they weren't assisting people or putting their backs into helping wagons up the hill, they watched the river anxiously.

A odd, garbled noise began. Their sky was dark as if another snowstorm threatened, so maybe the wind was distorting the sound. She slowed to real time, and the noise turned into singing. The music swelled, echoing off the embankment back to the river where it mixed with the sound of the Ohio flowing by. They were singing *My Faith Looks Up to Thee*, only in Cherokee. She had sung the hymn at one of the churches she had recently visited. She couldn't remember which one.

Shaking her head in wonder, she upped the speed again. A tall man carrying an impossibly large bundle on his back stumbled coming out of the ferry onto the dock, but Matthias was there to steady him. The man's expression remained stoic. Later, when a toothless, gray-haired old woman fell going up the embankment, Angus hailed a passing wagon and helped her into it.

Butrick made several trips up to the inn, and Merrideth wondered if he were checking on his pregnant wife. He wasn't gone long enough to have eaten a meal, and neither did she see Matthias or Angus stop to eat as the day wore on.

A freezing rain came in the late afternoon, making everything slick and slowing down the process even more. The soldiers shouted louder, their horses pivoting here and there as they tried to hurry miserable people who couldn't possibly comply.

A young, hugely pregnant woman slipped on the icy embankment in spite of assistance by a woman holding her arm. Matthias went to help her up, then spoke to her for quite some time. Merrideth slowed to real time. Even so, it was not possible to hear what he was saying without going virtual. His words were lost on the wind, but he appeared to be trying to convince the pregnant woman to get into one of the wagons. She didn't speak, but her body language said, "No way, José." Her friend spoke enough for two, and although Merrideth couldn't understand her either, it sounded like she was giving Matthias a piece of her mind. But then again, maybe she was just expressing her concern for the mother-to-be.

Shaking his head, Matthias took the pregnant woman's other arm. Before he could help her the rest of the way to the top, he released her suddenly and hurried back down the embankment. Merrideth wondered at his sudden abandonment, but then she saw what he had seen: a mounted soldier was whipping an old man who lay curled in on himself on the icy ground. Matthias shouted at the soldier, but he only continued the abuse. Then Angus came running. He slid the last few feet, actually colliding with the horse, then reached up and pulled the soldier from it.

Merrideth sat up straighter in her chair. "Whoa!" she said softly and took out her ear buds.

Next to her, Abby lifted her head from John's shoulder and stared at her blearily. "How's it going?" she said, wiping a bit of drool from her mouth.

"You might want to see this," Merrideth said. "It's getting interesting."

Abby woke John, who insisted on making more so-called coffee before they proceeded. When they each had steaming mugs in hand, John went to the counter and brought over the bag of donuts he had bought. "Fuel up. We've got a long way to go before breakfast."

"Can't we go down and get something a little healthier?"

"At five in the morning? And if I, the original Hungry Man, can hold off eating a real breakfast, I know you can."

"Okay, if everyone's ready…" Merrideth rewound a few minutes of time, switched to virtual, and then un-paused the drama frozen on the screen.

CHAPTER 13

***

DECEMBER 4, 1838

The pregnant woman shook off Matthias' hand. "Ma'am, I just want to help you into the wagon," he said. "That's all." She remained silent, except for the sound of her panting, and stared straight ahead as if she thought she could finish the journey—all the way to China if need be—if only she didn't stop walking. The rain had frozen on her head covering, forming a hard shell of ice, but her black eyes shone with a hot fire that belied the cold day.

"Listen, ma'am, it's sleeting pitchforks and hammer handles out here. Let me help you."

She remained mute. Her friend, however, continued squawking like a Cherokee banshee. Some of her anger was directed toward her friend, like maybe she was also trying to convince her to get in the wagon. The rest was aimed squarely at Matthias, obviously warning him to back off. He wished he knew how to soothe the woman's fears.

Before he knew whether the pregnant woman would comply with his request or not, the driver shouted something, and the wagon jerked and continued on its way, leaving them standing there halfway up the embankment. The wagon didn't get far before its wheels started to slip on the ice. Matthias resolutely took the woman's arm, her friend took the other, and they moved her out of the wagon's path should it come sliding back down the embankment. She slipped on the stones and would have fallen, but Matthias held her upright.

Behind him, the soldiers shouted for the people to go faster. Then came the unmistakable sound of a leather whip biting into flesh. Matthias turned and saw that a mounted soldier was striking an old man who lay on the ground at the horse's feet.

"Wait for me," Matthias said to the banshee friend. Then without stopping to see if she understood him, he released the pregnant woman and ran, half sliding, back down the slope toward the soldier.

"You heard the lieutenant," the soldier screamed. "Get moving, old man."

Before Matthias could reach them, Angus came barreling up like an angry bull, and pulled the soldier out of his saddle, whip and all, then drew back his huge fist and punched him in the face.

Blood streaming down his face, the soldier pulled out of the grip Angus had on his coat and brought the whip up to lash at him. He didn't have much room to maneuver, yet still he managed to land a blow. Just as the tail of the whip cut into Angus' cheek, he grabbed it and wrested it from the soldier's hand, angrily hurling it away. Matthias ducked in time, or it would have hit him.

Angus wasn't bleeding too badly, and he most assuredly would not appreciate his runt brother interfering in his fight, so Matthias left him to it and went to tend to the old man. He extended his hand to help him up, but the old man looked at him in bewilderment, refusing to take his hand. Then Matthias saw that he was blind, his eyes milky with cataracts. Speaking soothingly, Matthias reached down and grasped him under his arms and pulled him to his feet.

Angus crouched in a fighter's stance and smiled at the soldier with devilish anticipation. "Come on, fight *me*, why don't you?"

The soldier backed up into his horse, and it danced away, leaving him standing in the open holding his bleeding nose. The people had stopped walking and stood watching. Their faces remained expressionless for the most part, although Matthias caught a hint of laughter and satisfaction in one young man's eyes.

"What's the matter, yellow dog? You only fight blind men?" Angus spat out.

The soldier pulled a gun from the holster on his hip and aimed it at Angus.

"Private, lower your weapon!" The command came from another soldier who came trotting up to maneuver his horse between the two men. "That's an order." His beard and brows were white with ice, giving him the appearance at first glance of a much older man than he actually was.

The private heaved an angry breath and reluctantly lowered his gun. "Lieutenant Wheeler, this civilian was interfering with the Removal."

"I saw what he was interfering with, Private McDonal. Put that gun away before someone gets hurt."

McDonal glared at Angus, then holstered his gun.

"Now go make yourself useful to that wagon," Lieutenant Wheeler said. "With the ice, it will need several men pushing if it's ever going to make it up that hill." When McDonal turned to comply, the lieutenant waved his hands at the people who stood watching the dispute. "Move!" he shouted. "Go, go." The Cherokee turned their faces away and resumed trudging up the slope. Two Cherokee girls came forward shyly and took the old blind man by the hand. They spoke softly to him and led him away.

Lieutenant Wheeler reined his horse around and faced Matthias and Angus. "I apologize for Private McDonal. He took my orders to an extreme I did not intend. We're all under pressure to get the Indians across the Ohio before it becomes impassable. I do appreciate your assistance in that task."

"You're welcome, Lieutenant Wheeler, but I assure you that my brother and I are assisting the Cherokee, not you." Angus stood, hands on his hips, his face still blazing red. Matthias put a restraining hand on his arm before his brother's temper got him arrested.

"Nevertheless," the lieutenant said mildly, "I do thank you." He turned his horse and started back toward the ferry.

"Lieutenant," Matthias called. "How many are still on the other side?"

"About thirty people and a few handcarts. Should need only one more trip after this."

"That is welcome news, sir." Matthias suddenly remembered the pregnant woman. She and her friend had not obeyed him, but had gone on, somehow making it to the top of the embankment. They huddled together staring down at the activity on the dock.

When she saw him looking at her, she tossed her head.

Matthias huffed. "That woman's stubbornness knows no bounds. But I am not going to squander any more time arguing with her."

The freezing rain turned suddenly to sleet and began to ping on their hats and coats. "Can you believe this weather?" Angus said. "What next? Whirlwinds?"

"It would not come as a surprise," Matthias said. "At least it has cooled your temper."

"Yes, I believe I have vented my spleen."

"Then you should go help that fool McDonal with the wagons like the lieutenant said."

Angus mumbled something under his breath and turned to go.

Matthias laughed. "And don't hit him."

Matthias went back down to the ferry to help Reverend Butrick. A woman was cautiously trying to cross the icy dock with a sleeping child in her arms and four little girls clinging to her skirts like rust on iron.

Butrick extended his hands to the youngest girl, who looked about three. But she shook her head at him and, eyes wide with fear, buried her face in her mother's skirt.

"River crossings are always hard for the people, even in the best weather," Butrick explained. "Many still believe that evil spirits enter our world by way of rivers and streams. It is why their Cherokee leaders balked at traveling by flatboat as the government originally planned. The journey would have been much swifter and easier for them. But alas, the old ideas persist."

Buttrick spoke encouragingly in Cherokee, and at last the little girl lifted her arms and allowed him to pick her up. He handed her to Matthias and then reached to get the next, whom Matthias took with his other arm. Butrick took the last two girls by the hand and helped them step down from the icy dock. He spoke again and they went and stood beside Matthias. Matthias set the little girls down and reached both hands out to help the woman. She slipped and cried out, fearful she would drop the little one she carried, but by grabbing her coat, Matthias managed to keep her on her feet.

In spite of all the jostling, the child didn't make a peep. His mother, however, began to cry. Butrick put his arms around her, and she said something that made him look like he would commence crying himself.

"What's she saying?" Matthias asked.

Butrick sighed and spoke over the woman's head. "Awinita's children are hungry. They didn't have time to cook their food before they came on the ferry."

"Tell her the camp isn't much farther. They can eat there."

"Distance is relative, son," Reverend Butrick said. "It will be a long time before they eat again." He called out in Cherokee, and one of the men coming off the ferry stopped to talk with him. After a disgruntled look, the man took Awinita's baby into his arms even though he already carried a huge burden on his back. Then he took the hand of the littlest girl and started for the embankment. Awinita followed with her other children in tow.

"He is not the father?" Matthias said.

"No," Butrick said sadly. "He is a man with many problems of his own. But he will help Awinita get to the camp."

Others came off the ferry after them, but Butrick stood in a daze watching Awinita and her family climb the embankment. Her baby finally awoke and began to wail in the man's arms.

"Our Lord warned of the last days. 'Woe unto them that are with child, and to them that give suck in those days! But pray you that your flight be not in the winter, neither on the Sabbath day: For then shall be great tribulation, such as was not since the beginning of the world to this time, no, nor ever shall be.' But the Lord knows our sorrows. Did he not also walk his own Via Dolorosa?"

Matthias nodded his head in agreement. The Scripture was apt, although he didn't know what that last part meant, and the preacher looked so sad that he didn't like to ask. "If it was summer time, I'd go catch fish for them, Reverend," Matthias said. "She could make fish stew for the children."

The preacher started out of his sad musings. "You're a good man, Matthias Frailey," he said, patting him on his back. "If our Lord were here, I am quite certain that you would give him your fishes and loaves. And he would feed these people. Indeed he would. I told Awinita the Lord will provide. And He will. Somehow."

Matthias watched Awinita and her children go until they were lost to view in the crowd of travelers. And then he saw that the pregnant woman was still sitting at the top of the hill. Apparently, her friend had had the sense to go on to the camp, but there she sat, the stubborn woman. Well, if she wanted to sit on a rock until she turned into a block of ice, it was her own choice. He heaved a sigh and turned back to the ferry.

A handcart was stuck on the ramp and blocked the way for the last of the people on the ferry trying to disembark. The man to whom it belonged was tall and strong, but the cart, piled as it was with his family's belongings, was heavy and unwieldy. Somehow, the cart had gotten turned and one wheel was stuck in the space between the ramp and the dock.

The owner was trying to lift it out while a woman, presumably his wife, held the cart's handle, ready to pull it the moment it was free. The two dock workers stood idly by watching. The men still on the ferry were loaded down with their own possessions in huge packs on their back. They would have to remove their packs in order to help. And that would take precious time.

Matthias went to the cart and, together with its owner, lifted it by its side. It rose a little, but not enough to free it from the crack. They continued to strain, but could not raise it any higher. They set the cart down and stood up, panting.

John Berry shoved his way through the waiting people, shouting, "What in Hades is taking so long?"

When he got to the ramp, his red face turned nearly purple. "Get that dung heap out of my way! I got another load of Injuns to get."

"The cart is stuck," Reverend Butrick said. "He cannot help it."

"Pete! George!" Berry called to ferrymen. "What you waiting for? Help them get it out of there."

They scowled at Berry. One of them said, "You help him if you're so all-fired in a hurry. We ain't paid to do it."

Lieutenant Wheeler and Private McDonal trotted over. "He'll have to throw out most of that stuff of his or you'll never get it out," the lieutenant said. "Private, cut the binding ropes." The soldier dismounted and came forward, unsheathing a buck knife at his side.

Next to Matthias, the owner of the cart groaned low in his throat.

"But, Lieutenant," Reverend Butrick said. "Everything he owns is on this cart."

"Do you want all of them to freeze for one man's sake?" Lieutenant Wheeler said.

Private McDonal shoved the Cherokee aside. "Out of the way."

"Wait just a dad-blasted minute, would you?" Matthias said. "My brother can get this thing unstuck." Where was Angus, anyway? He looked around and finally saw him coming back down the embankment. "Hey, Angus, get your lazy self over here," he shouted. "We could use those big muscles of yours." His brother grinned and hurried toward him.

Private McDonal put his knife to the rope.

"Hold on, Private," Lieutenant Wheeler said. "I've seen this man work. He just might be able to do it."

The private looked disappointed that he wouldn't be allowed to cut into the Cherokee's possessions, but he stepped away when Angus got there.

Angus took the time to smile sweetly at Private McDonal, who looked like he was gnashing his teeth, and then turned his attention to the problem at hand. He saw immediately what needed to be done and went to help the owner lift the cart. "Pull when I tell you, Runt."

Matthias went to the front of the cart. "Excuse me, ma'am. Let me take that." The woman looked ready to drop from exhaustion. A flicker of relief passed over her face and she stepped back out of his way.

He gripped the cart's handles, but before Angus' command came, a loud crack sounded. While it still reverberated in the air, a cry rose from the people on the ferry. Matthias thought first that the ice had broken a tree branch, maybe downed a whole tree, except that there surely wasn't enough ice for that yet. Besides, there were no trees close enough for a sound of that magnitude. Angus and the man had turned loose of the cart and stood looking toward the river, as did the people on the ferry.

"What was that?" Matthias shouted.

"I don't know. I can't see," Angus said. "But we'd best get this thing out of here."

Then John Berry shoved his way back onto the ferry. "Let me through, Injuns." After a moment he cried, "Ice!"

The cracking sound came again and someone on the ferry screamed. Remembering what the preacher had said, Matthias wondered if they were worried about river spirits.

Angus grabbed the side of the cart again, and the Cherokee took hold of the other side. "Pull!" Angus shouted. Matthias did, and the cart jumped forward onto the dock.

The man came and took the handle from him. "I am grateful," he said simply, his dark eyes somber. And then he heaved the laden cart off the dock.

The rest of the people came streaming off the ferry then as if spirits truly were after them. Lieutenant Wheeler and Private McDonal trotted off behind them, the lieutenant calling over his shoulder, "Hurry, Berry. Get that last load over here."

The ferryman didn't answer, just stood looking upstream. Matthias followed Angus onto the ferry, and they went forward to stand beside him.

"Here comes another one," Berry said.

Except for the portions kept clear of ice by the ferry's trips back and forth across the river, the Ohio's banks were frozen some fifteen feet out, noticeably farther than when Matthias had checked only two hours before. Chunks of ice continued to float down through the narrowing channel as they had all day. But the chunk Berry pointed at was huge, nearly as large as one of the Frailey log cabins. It crashed into the opposite bank, causing the same loud cracking sound they had heard before. Its impact with the state of Kentucky sent the cabin-sized chunk of ice hurtling toward the state of Illinois.

"Lord have mercy on us," Angus cried. "If that thing hits the ferry it'll shatter it into too many pieces to put back together."

"And we'll all go into the river," Matthias added. He continued to watch its progress, ready to escape if it came close.

At last it became clear that it was not going to hit, and they breathed a collective sigh of relief. Once it was safely past them on its way south, Matthias turned to leave. John Berry would be anxious to get the ferry on its way. But instead Berry brushed by him and hurried across the ferry and onto the dock.

"Where are you going?" Matthias called.

"Up to the inn to get my supper, not that it's any business of yours, Mister."

"You can't leave," Angus roared.

"Can, too." Pete and George followed their boss, looking happy to quit early.

"But, sir," Reverend Butrick cried, "there are people still on the other side. They have no food or bedding. The last supply wagon just went up the hill."

Berry continued walking, saying over his shoulder, "Like Pete said, we ain't gittin' paid enough."

"You're getting paid more than enough, Berry," Angus said.

"Not to git ourselves kilt."

A woman's wail pierced Matthias' ears, and he saw with amazement that the pregnant Cherokee lady was still at the top of the hill. She struggled to her feet and then started down the embankment. She was going to kill herself one way or another. The ice had mostly melted off the stones by the continuous passage of feet, but still they were bound to be difficult for a woman with a huge belly. Surely walking downhill would be even more hazardous for her than going up.

By the time he reached her, she was nearly half way down. She did not seem to notice when he took her arm and helped her the rest of the way. She cried out again, and he recognized the preacher's name among the Cherokee words.

He released her when they got to the bottom, and Reverend Butrick put an arm around her to comfort her. She would not be soothed but spat out another stream of Cherokee.

"I know, I know," Butrick said, patting her back. He sent a sad glance toward Angus and Matthias. "Tsistunagiska's family is still over there. For some reason only known to John Berry, he split them up and made her come ahead on that last trip."

The woman's face was fierce, and hot sparks shot out of her eyes at Matthias, as if it were his fault not Berry's that her family was stranded on the other side. Women.

Matthias turned his attention back to the problem. "The lieutenant said there's only about thirty people left," he said. "Surely they'll take shelter in the ferry hut."

"Berry will have that locked up tight," Angus said. "They'll have to hunker down under the bluffs."

On the Kentucky side, the limestone projected out from the bluffs in one place forming an overhang known as Mantle Rock. Thirty people could maybe fit under it, but it would offer only slight protection from the rain and do nothing at all to provide warmth. Did they even have the means of making a fire?

The woman spoke again, her voice bitter.

Butrick sighed and then interpreted. "Tsistunagiska says the people have been living in white men's houses too long. Now they are soft and don't know how to survive. They'll die of the cold."

Across the river, a man on the Kentucky dock shouted something that was lost in the noise of the sleet and rushing water. Angus shouted back, telling him the ferrymen had left, but the man obviously wasn't able to hear any better than they could on their side of the river. The man kept shouting. Then he threw his hands up in a gesture of surrender and walked away until he was out of their sight. Then several other people appeared on the dock, waving their hands and shouting. Their words were just as jumbled as the first man's. The words didn't matter. Their desperation was clear.

"My poor flock," Butrick said, wiping at his eyes. Whatever optimism he'd had earlier was gone, and now he was beaten and dejected wreck. Matthias was surprised. Weren't men of God supposed to have more faith than ordinary people?

Reverend Butrick spoke to the pregnant woman beside him, but she only tossed her head. Then, pulling her cloak around herself, she sat down on the dock to wait for her family.

"I told her to go on to the camp," Butrick said. "But she says if her family has to sleep on the ice, she will too."

A red rush of anger filled Matthias. He wanted to shake her. "Tell her...I can't say her name...tell her that—"

"White Dove," Reverend Butrick said. "*Tsistunagiska* is translated *White Dove* in English."

"Tell White Dove she must think of her baby, Reverend, even if she's too stupid to think of herself."

Butrick sat down on the dock next to White Dove and bowed his head.

Matthias opened the gate to the ferry and stepped aboard.

"Matthias, don't be a fool," Angus said. "It's too dangerous now, and once the light is gone it will be even worse."

"I can't let them die. You go on home to Jewel and your babies. You've done your part. Wait." He went back onto the dock and held out a hand to Angus. "Give me money. I'm out."

Angus reached into his pocket and pulled out several coins, then dug again until he found another. Matthias smiled. Angus was like that. He would give his last penny without asking why. Matthias took the money from him and went to Reverend Butrick.

"Take her up to the inn and feed her. Give this money to Sam Landis. Tell him if it's not enough, I'll give him more. Or Angus will."

Butrick spoke to White Dove, but she only shook her head and continued sitting there. Matthias reached down and grabbed her under her arms and brought her to her feet. She was as light as a feather, for all her big belly. She glared at him. He gave her a small shake. "Go! Go with the preacher. I'll bring your people to you." Or die trying, he thought but didn't say.

The people on the Kentucky side began to sing that hymn again. He couldn't distinguish the words, and the music was mostly dispersed by the wind, but it was the same hymn all right.

"Oh, my poor, poor flock," Butrick sobbed. "I'll not leave you in your hour of need."

"Reverend Butrick," Matthias said. "Get up and take this woman to the inn. Don't you need to check on your wife anyway?"

Butrick rose shakily, still staring across the river at the raggedy bunch of lost souls.

Matthias shook him as he had White Dove. "They need you alive, Preacher."

Butrick started, as if coming out of a dream. "Yes, and my wife. Poor Clara."

White Dove looked mutinous, but Matthias shoved her at the reverend. He took his hands away in shock. He had just shoved a pregnant lady. What was the matter with him?

"Hurry up, Matthias. The sun's about down."

Matthias turned and saw that Angus already had the ferry untied from the dock and was waving at the people across the river.

"What are you doing?" Matthias said.

"Putting my lazy self to good use," he said with a laugh. "Now grab the other pull rope."

CHAPTER 14

***

THE PRESENT

Merrideth came reluctantly out of Matthias Frailey's time and blinked several times to get the moisture flowing to her dry eyes.

"That was amazing," Abby said. "It's like the time we binge-watched the whole Ken Burns Civil War series that weekend. Remember, John? But let's fast-forward past this part," she said, reaching for the mouse.

Merrideth grabbed her hand. "You can't possibly mean to. We have to see what happens to Matthias."

John patted her back. "Relax, Merri. He's not going to drown."

"But the icebergs!" Merrideth said.

John grinned. "We already know how this movie ends, right? Keep telling yourself that Matthias Frailey lives, marries Emmaline, and goes on to have a family."

"And a descendant named Patty Ann," Abby said.

Merrideth blew out a breath. "I guess I'm getting too caught up in this to think straight."

"We all are," John said. When Abby reached for the mouse again, he stopped her. "But, I want to watch this too. I've always wondered how those ferries operated."

Abby frowned. "We can't keep going at real time, or we'll be here a year."

"Ah, but don't forget our friend Time Warp."

"It only helps so much, John," Merrideth said. Her phone chirped to signal an incoming text.

"Who's awake at this hour?" Abby said.

"Nick," Merrideth said.

John made a face. "Of course he is."

Actually, there were four long texts from Nick, three of which must have come in while they were zoned out. Each had helpful suggestions for places to see around Golconda, which Merrideth could barely read with her fuzzy brain. And John was holding forth about how much time they'd spent in 1838 versus what time it was in their world. Numbers. They made her head hurt. There was no way she could compose even a simple text to Nick, so she put her phone down.

"Let's compromise, John," Merrideth said. "We won't zip past the ferry boat ride since you say you can't live without the experience. But we'll go fast, okay?"

"But then virtual mode won't work."

"I know," Merrideth said. "But it will still be cool. I promise."

John sighed dramatically. "Oh, all right."

Abby laughed at his martyrdom.

Merrideth un-paused the action. Matthias and Angus began pulling on the ferry's ropes, each of which passed through a system of pulleys onboard the craft and at both docks in a continuous loop across the river. As the brothers labored, men on the Kentucky dock lent their muscles to help the ropes continue their circuits. John was suitably impressed by the ingenious man-powered system and the speed with which the ferry made it safely to the Kentucky shore.

They saw that Angus had been right about John Berry's hut being locked. The people huddled around a tiny fire under the rocky overhang Matthias had mentioned. They looked pale, exhausted, and so cold that Merrideth shivered in sympathy.

Matthias and Angus kept watching the river, obviously anxious to get back across to Golconda. But it took time to get everyone on board. The young, elderly, and sick people had to be helped onto the ferry. One young man was coughing so much he had to be nearly carried.

"I wonder which one is White Dove's husband?" Merrideth said.

"The sick one looks about the right age," John said. "But I hope it's not him. If I were a betting man, I'd say he has pneumonia—or maybe even tuberculosis."

"All right. I give in," Abby said. "Let's go virtual. I can't stand not knowing what's going on. But don't blame me if you're late for work Monday morning, John Roberts."

He was saying something about time when Merrideth went virtual.

***

DECEMBER 4, 1838

When the last cart was finally on and Angus was securing the gate, Matthias wound his way through the people to get to the ferry's starboard side. The sleet had stopped, and the sky was clearing in the west. Nevertheless, the light was nearly gone, and the river ran black between its icy white banks. Chunks of ice still bobbed on the dark surface, but none of them looked large enough to be of much concern. Thank the Lord, there were no more cabin-sized chunks to be seen.

Across from Matthias, the young man called Sparrow stood shivering in his thin coat at the port rope, ready to begin pulling. He would warm up soon enough once they began to work the ropes.

Normally, there would be two dock men on each side of the river to help the two workers onboard pull the ferry across the river. But John Berry and his men were long gone. A few of the Cherokee looked able-bodied. But the way the ferry worked, there wasn't room for more than two men at the ropes. Not unless there happened to be a couple of ten-foot-tall giants who could reach the ropes as they went overhead. With none available, getting the ferry to the Illinois shore would be up to Sparrow and him. Since the ferry was at half capacity, it would ride higher in the water, and he prayed that advantage would be enough to make it possible to succeed.

Behind him, the sick man coughed violently, and the people murmured softly. He felt their anxiety, and wished he could speak Cherokee so he could calm their fears. If he knew which ones were White Dove's relatives, he would tell them that she waited safely at the inn. At least he hoped she'd had the sense to do what he told her.

Matthias took hold of his rope and nodded at Sparrow.

"We're ready, Angus," Matthias shouted. "Untether us."

The ferry gave a lurch. Matthias and Sparrow heaved on their ropes, and the ferry came away from the dock. He saw right off that pulling a loaded ferry—even at half capacity—was going to be much harder than pulling an empty one.

Then Angus was there, and Matthias realized that his brother intended to take Sparrow's place at the ropes. Angus was a head taller than Sparrow and probably outweighed him by fifty pounds or more. Angus was in his prime, his well-fed muscles larger than Matthias' own. He'd be able to work the ropes much faster than Sparrow. But a man had his pride and wanted—needed—to be able to protect his family. For the Cherokee men who had been forced to lead their families down the trail at the command of white soldiers on horses, the need would be near to busting out of them.

"Angus," Matthias said. "Lend Sparrow your gloves, will you? These ropes are rough."

Even in the dusk, he could see that Angus looked surprised. Then his face cleared and he smiled, his teeth white in the dusky light. Wordlessly, he tugged off his gloves and handed them to Sparrow.

Smiling his thanks, Sparrow quickly put them on and went back to pulling at an even faster pace, as if determined to make up for the few seconds he had left Matthias alone on the job. Even so, the going was slow and the dock still looked a hundred miles away.

"You're going to split your guts open, Runt," Angus said.

"We can do it."

After a dozen more pulls on the rope, sweat broke out on Matthias' forehead, and he wished he could wipe it before it dripped into his eyes. His muscles were screaming with each pull, and he was beginning to think he had been foolish to be quite so concerned with Sparrow's pride—and his own.

"Ah …Angus? I think perhaps we need your help after all. Can you get the poles?"

Angus laughed. "Sure thing, Runt." He retrieved the ferryman's poles from their rack and gave one of them to a Cherokee man who stood nearby. The man nodded his eagerness help.

Matthias was too occupied with his own task to watch them an instant more, but he knew the minute they put the tips of their poles on the river bed, because the ferry suddenly slipped forward. The dock no longer seemed like an impossible goal.

They were making good progress, but then Angus cried out. "Matthias! The rope! It's frayed nearly through." Matthias could not recall if he had ever heard his big brother sound so overwrought before. Hearing him now sent a jolt of fear to his stomach.

Between pulls Matthias looked at the rope passing by overhead. He couldn't see the frayed spot Angus was concerned about. That portion was long gone on its way to the pulleys on the Kentucky dock. But they would see it again soon enough. That is, if the rope didn't break before it got back to them.

"That fool John Berry was too busy counting his money to tend to his ropes," Angus said bitterly. "And with as much use as they've gotten, it's no wonder they're worn."

"Pray, then," Matthias grunted. "Pray it holds." It was in God's hands. The rope would either break or it wouldn't. His job was to put his back into the pulling. He tried to count his blessings as Ma had taught him. Perhaps Berry's greed had been to the Cherokee's advantage. How many more people would still be waiting on the other side if Berry hadn't run non-stop for the past three days? He would have told Angus that, but he didn't have the breath to spare.

With each pull, Matthias wondered if it would be the last. And with each pull, the pulling got harder. They had surely reached midpoint of the channel where the current was at its fastest and strongest. A woman cried out. Matthias jerked in alarm. Had the rope finally broken? Then he calmed himself. The pullers, not the passengers, would be the first to know if that happened. He glanced over his shoulder and saw that she was pointing at the river, not the rope.

Following her horrified gaze, he saw that fifty yards upstream, another monstrous mountain of ice was coming down the river. Somehow Matthias found added strength to pull harder and faster, as did Sparrow. Still, the ferry slowed against the power of the current that seemed bound and determined to carry them away. The river was queen over everything within her banks. And the chunk of ice, with no will to thwart her sovereignty, was coming straight toward the ferry's flank.

"Angus! Do something."

"I've got it, Runt." Angus removed his pole from the river and held it out over the side of the ferry like a jousting knight determined to unseat his opponent. But before Angus got the chance to do battle with the chunk of ice, it veered away at the queen's whim, and some unseen current sent it eastward toward the Kentucky riverbank.

The impact caused a deafening cracking sound, much louder than what Matthias had heard from the shore earlier. The massive chunk of ice, and the portion of icy riverbank it had sheared off, continued along close to the Kentucky shore. A collective sigh of relief rose from the people, audible over the sound of the water. But then the ice hit a rocky protrusion and recoiled from the bank. Matthias saw with dismay that it was heading right back into the middle of the river channel. Right back in a direct path to the ferry.

Sparrow, his face frantic with fear, turned toward Matthias. Angus dropped the pole onto the deck and pushed Sparrow aside. He took the rope into his bare hands, and the ferry surged ahead. Matthias didn't look to see where the ice chunk was, but from the sound of the people's voices, they weren't out of danger yet. He renewed his efforts, concentrating on keeping up with the impossible pace his brother set.

Someone screamed. Matthias closed his eyes and kept on pulling. Then the rope slipped through his hands as if Jehovah himself had taken over the job for him. He opened his eyes and saw that two men on the Golconda dock were pulling with them. The man in uniform had to be Lieutenant Wheeler. Reverend Butrick labored at the other rope.

Matthias could see the sweat on the lieutenant's face and hear his and the reverend's grunts with each pull. The dock raced toward them. With only a few more pulls from the four of them, the ferry could dock. Then behind him the people cried out again. He risked a glance at the river and saw that the chunk of ice was so close he could have reached out and touched it. Whether it would hit the ferry's stern or not, he couldn't tell. It would be close. He gulped a breath of air and pulled like a team of oxen. The ferry hit the dock, sending tremors through the deck under his feet. The ice floated safely past them, on its way south.

"We did it, Runt," Angus said, grinning happily.

Matthias wiped the sweat from his face and grinned back at his brother.

Then behind him came the sound he had been dreading: first a loud snap as the rope broke and then a whine as it whipped through the pulleys overhead. The people moaned in fear. A moment later, Reverend Butrick fell to his backside on the dock, his rope useless in his hands. Immediately, the ferry slewed violently to the left, held only by the rope that Angus and Lieutenant Wheeler worked. As God willed it, the frayed end of Matthias' rope was caught in the pulley mechanism. It was no longer useful for forward propulsion, but it could serve as an additional tether. Scrambling across the bucking deck, he grabbed the rope just as it was coming untangled from the pulley and tied it to one of the ferry's steel guide rings.

Even in its shallows, the Ohio River was a force to be reckoned with, and Angus and the lieutenant were straining to hold the ferry at the dock with the remaining rope. Clutching the tail of his own rope, Matthias jumped over the rail into the river. The water came half way up his thighs, and the cold shocked the breath out of his lungs. The ferry continued to slew, but he held onto his rope for dear life, his boot heels scraping the rocky river bed.

Reverend Butrick cast aside his useless tow rope and grabbed the tether rope. When he had successfully secured the ferry to the dock, Angus and the lieutenant left their posts and jumped in to help Matthias. With all three of them holding it, the ferry at last stopped trying to follow the river and agreed to go where they wanted it to. They reeled it in until the bow was snugged up to the dock. Reverend Butrick took the end of the rope and tied it securely to the dock.

Chest heaving, Matthias hauled himself up onto the dock and extended a hand first to the lieutenant and then to Angus. The three of them stood there grinning at each other in satisfaction as the people surged off the ferry like evil spirits were indeed after them.

At least for these travelers, the dock wasn't so slippery. The sleet Angus had bewailed earlier had covered the ice, giving them enough traction to make it across the dock and up the embankment.

Two men carried the coughing young man off the ferry. Next came a worried-looking middle-aged woman leading four children of various ages. Calling something in Cherokee, she hurried to

Reverend Butrick.

"Praise God!" he said. "You made it." Butrick switched to Cherokee and told them something that made them smile

"Matthias, Angus," he said, returning to English, "these are White Dove's people. Painted Turtle is her mother, and these are her brother Jacob and sisters Nancy, Eliza, and Amanda. I told them White Dove was up at the inn safe and sound."

Angus smiled and tipped his hat. Matthias reached to do the same but found that his hat was no longer on his head.

Sparrow stepped onto the dock, and Matthias and Angus shook his hand. Sparrow smiled, said something in Cherokee, and tried to give Angus back his gloves. Angus refused to take them, as Matthias had known from the beginning that he would. Sparrow's face turned solemn, and he nodded his gratitude.

Matthias had wondered if perhaps Sparrow were White Dove's husband, but he smiled and went on up the embankment, leaving Painted Turtle and her family standing on the dock.

Matthias smiled. "Reverend, I'm surprised Painted Turtle's stubborn daughter isn't still waiting for you on the top of the hill."

Butrick chuckled with amusement. "She was torn between going on with the people and staying here. She decided that the risk of corrupting her Cherokee soul with white men's luxuries up at the inn was outweighed by her desire to be close when her family got across the river. Besides, my Clara shamelessly appealed to her sympathy for a another pregnant lady."

"And how is your wife?"

"She's fine. No sign of an untimely arrival of our child, praise God."

"And for getting us safely across," Matthias added. "For a while there, I wasn't sure we'd make it."

"You did it, little brother," Angus said, slapping him on the shoulder. "Now we need to get home before Pa comes to town looking for you. He probably won't beat you too hard for skipping out on work."

Matthias wasn't entirely sure whether Angus was jesting, but he smiled in case he was.

Lieutenant Wheeler shook Angus' hand. "We owe you a debt of gratitude, also, Mr. Frailey. I pray the next contingent will find those with equal kindness to help as you did."

"Next contingent?" Angus said.

"You do realize there are eleven more?" the lieutenant said, trying to wring the water out of his pants. "About a thousand each, although God only knows how many will have survived by the time they pass through your inhospitable country."

"God, have mercy!" Matthias said. Angus looked as shocked as he was.

They watched as the last of the people came off the ferry and started up the embankment toward Main Street. A passing woman handed Matthias his hat then smiled and went on with the others. So it hadn't fallen into the river after all. He put it back on his head, grateful for the warmth.

Lieutenant Wheeler mounted his horse. "I'll be off then."

"You ought to dry off up at the inn," Reverend Butrick said.

"Thank you, Reverend. I have a blanket in my saddlebag. Anyway, I have to make sure these folks don't forget to go on to the camp." He nudged his horse's side and followed the Cherokee.

"How about you boys?" Butrick said. "Come along and I'll buy you some coffee to help warm you up."

"That is just what I had in mind, Reverend," Matthias said. "But you need not pay for us."

Angus cleared his throat, and Matthias remembered that they had spent all their money. After a moment he said, "I guess we might take you up on your kind offer after all."

"It would be my pleasure," Butrick said.

Matthias' stomach grumbled, and he remembered he hadn't eaten since breakfast. He wondered if Sam had anything edible left. Then he wondered if the reverend's generosity would extend to a meal to go with the coffee.

"You needn't fear. I have the money," Butrick said, as if he had read his mind. "As a missionary, I don't have much except what the Board sends from time to time. But it's more than my poor flock has, bless them."

"We would be much obliged," Angus said.

"Come then, Painted Turtle," Butrick said. "Let us go up and get your family reunited." He spoke then in Cherokee, and she smiled and began shepherding her children up the embankment. A light shone in one of the inn's first-floor windows, a beacon to Matthias' weary eyes. How wonderful it must look to Painted Turtle's weary family.

When they reached the inn, Angus opened the door and they all tromped in. The warmth and smell of cooking food welcomed him. Sam lifted his head from a table where he had been sleeping, his face creased from lying on his jacket sleeve. He yawned and then got up and went to stir a pot on the wood stove. It smelled like one of his stew concoctions, which he called "stuff." Its contents varied, depending on what was available. Regular Ferry House patrons knew better than to ask what was in it.

Painted Turtle and the children looked at the stove longingly for a moment, and then she gently pushed them to a table in the opposite corner, as if to forestall the children's false expectations of getting any of whatever was cooking in the pot. Matthias felt weak with hunger and wondered when *they* had last eaten.

Reverend Butrick spoke to Painted Turtle, and then he went up the stairs, presumably to fetch White Dove.

Sam brought a stack of bowls and a ladle to the stove, and Matthias went to help him dish up the "stuff." There wasn't much of it left in the pot. Sam gave him a look and handed him a bowl to hold while he ladled more of the stew into a second bowl.

Angus came and peeked into the pot and then looked at the family across the room. "Well, I'll be going on home then. Soon as my pants dry a bit. You ready, Matthias?"

"Directly." Matthias took the second bowl from Sam then carried them to Painted Turtle's table and set them down in front of the two little girls.

They looked up at him in pure amazement. Tears welled at Painted Turtle's eyes and then one fell down her cheek. Matthias looked away, embarrassed, and went back to the stove.

"They'll need spoons," Sam said.

"Right you are." Angus went behind the counter and came back with a handful which he took to the table. He laid one down next to each person.

Sam handed Matthias and Angus three more bowls and then took the empty pot off the burner. They took them to the table and set them before the other children and Painted Turtle. The girls hadn't begun eating yet, just sat waiting patiently. Then, after a look at Matthias and Angus, they all bowed their heads and Painted Turtle spoke what had to be a prayer. He didn't know if it was a Cherokee prayer or a Christian prayer, but it sounded heartfelt.

He and Angus went back to the stove to warm themselves. The heat was wonderful on his wet legs. A sound came from the stairs, and then Reverend Butrick came down smiling widely, White Dove on his heels. Her expression was fierce as before, only this time Matthias rather thought it was due to relief in seeing her family. She went to them at the table, and they all began talking at once in soft Cherokee.

"We'll bring your boards tomorrow, Reverend," Angus said.

"Oh, yes, to fix my wagon. Thank you. I almost forgot."

Matthias glanced at the table. The bowls were empty. White Dove's little brother Jacob was doing his best to lick his clean, but his tongue wouldn't reach. White Dove saw him watching and looked embarrassed. She had no reason to be. Under the circumstances, even his ma would have turned a blind eye at the boy's poor table manners.

"We'll go on then," Matthias said, pulling away from the stove. "Our thanks, Sam."

Sam just waved sleepily to the room at large.

Matthias opened the door, and the cold slapped at his face. Angus followed, shutting the door behind them. They went down the boardwalk toward the livery stable, their feet crunching on the crusty, sleet-covered ice. Main Street was a rutted mess, churned up by the passing of fifty or more wagons and a thousand pair of feet. The slushy surface was sure to refreeze by morning, making it all the more difficult for the next contingent to travel through. There was no telling how bad the street would be by the time the last of the Cherokee passed through town.

The sky, however, was pristine and clear, the stars sparkling now that the storm had passed. Other than the inn, all the other businesses were closed up for the night and the street was dark. Matthias had never been in town so late. It had to be getting nigh onto three in the morning. A yellow cat on the prowl was a spot of relative brightness as it crossed the street ahead of them and padded silently away into the alley.

Like everything else, the livery was dark, but the stable boy came stumbling out with a sleepy hello. He wasn't pleased to learn he would have to wait until the morning to get the money they owed him. Peeved, he didn't stay to help them saddle their horses. They heard him snoring from the back room before they had finished the task themselves.

They mounted and rode down the street. Now the Ferry House was completely dark too. Just past the inn, they would turn onto

Water Street, and it would take them to the trail that led to home and their own beds. Matthias wondered if his horse would be able to see well enough to dodge the gopher holes.

A noise came out of the darkness, causing his gelding and Angus' mare to high-step and snort. Someone was coming out of the inn, and whoever it was did not wish to be seen.

Angus struck a flint, which did little more than light up his own face. "Who's there?" he called gruffly.

A light glimmered in the inn's lower windows. Then the door came open, and Reverend Butrick stood there in his shirt sleeves, holding a candlestick. The light from it revealed White Dove and her family standing on the porch.

A heated Cherokee discussion ensued between White Dove and the preacher.

"What's she saying?" Matthias said. "Wait, don't tell me. She wants to go sit on the embankment to wait for the next detachment to arrive?"

"No," Reverend Butrick said with an exasperated sigh. "She wants to walk to the camp in the middle of the night without a guide to show her the way." White Dove glared at him, Painted Turtle, too, so apparently she was in agreement with the nonsensical idea. The children just looked sleepy.

"Of all the cork-brained ideas!" Angus said.

Matthias watched her face. "White Dove feels like a traitor for not being with her people," he said softly. "Why should she enjoy a soft, warm bed when they sleep out in the cold?"

The fierce look on her face softened, and Matthias had a suspicion that she understood more English than she let on. "And she fears she'll go soft like a white woman and thus not be able to survive the rest of the journey."

Butrick stared at Matthias for a moment and then turned to White Dove and spoke in rapid-fire Cherokee. She didn't answer, just stared at Matthias.

Matthias dismounted and tied his horse to the hitching post. He stepped up onto the boardwalk and went to her. "Tell her I'll take her there." Before Butrick could translate, she sidestepped Matthias and stepped down into the street.

Matthias followed her, grabbing a handful of her cloak to keep her from marching away. "Oh, no you don't," he said, pulling her to a stop. "You're not walking—at least not while I'm around." He went to his horse's side and put his hands together to form a stirrup low enough for her to easily reach. She stared at it for a moment and then put her foot into it. He hoisted her as carefully as he could, and she landed gracefully in his saddle, primly adjusting her full skirt over her legs. It was made of a blue calico fabric much like the dresses his mother favored.

Matthias untied Champ's reins from the rail, but White Dove frowned her disapproval. She held out her hands to the children on the boardwalk, and Angus brought the smallest, a girl of about five or six, and put her on White Dove's lap. Reverend Butrick picked up the other little girl and set her on the horse's rump. Yawning, she put her arms around her big sister and laid her head on her back.

Painted Turtle said something to the boy and oldest girl on the porch. White Dove's brother shifted the large pack on his slender shoulders and looked solemnly up at her.

"Reverend, give me Jacob's pack. I'll carry it," Matthias said.

Butrick went to him, but the boy looked alarmed and backed away into the side of the inn. Butrick bent and spoke quietly in his ear, but whatever he said didn't help. Jacob's expression turned downright mulish.

Apparently, the whole family was as stubborn and prideful as White Dove was. "All right, then," Matthias said. That left the woman's and girls' packs. Painted Turtle was not young and she looked weary. The girl looked to be twelve or thirteen—a younger, skinnier version of White Dove—and was far too frail to be carrying a pack of any size, much less the huge one on her back.

"Then give me *her* pack," Matthias said.

"No thank you," she said in perfect English.

Matthias stumbled in his surprise. "You know English?"

"Yes, sir," she said.

"Nancy's twelve and one of the star pupils in our school," Reverend Butrick said.

White Dove gave a tiny, solemn nod. So she understood at least some English.

Butrick sighed and put a hand on the boy's thin shoulders. "Jacob here was to start last fall, but then…well, that wasn't possible."

"They could ride my horse, Matthias," Angus said, "But if I'm not home soon, Pa's going to go on the warpath." He cleared his throat and looked embarrassed. "What I meant to say is that Pa will be worried and likely come to town looking for us. Who knows what hornet's nest that could stir up? Some of the town fools are just looking for an excuse to go riding around the countryside hunting for Indians to shoot."

"I understand. You go on," Matthias said. "Tell Pa I'll be home as soon as I am able."

"God go with you all," Reverend Butrick said. "Nancy, please tell everyone that Mrs. Butrick and I will be there as soon as our wagon's repaired."

"I will, Reverend."

"All right, then," Angus said, tipping his hat. Then he turned his horse and nudged him into a trot.

Matthias took his horse's bridle and started down Main Street, feeling stupid and guilty that he alone walked unencumbered. He felt even worse when he saw that Painted Turtle and the children intended to walk behind his horse like captives taken in war.

Nancy waved shyly at Butrick. The reverend returned the wave and stood smiling sadly, candlestick in hand, watching them go. Matthias turned back to the road. After a moment, he heard the sound of the inn door closing. White Dove sat tall in the saddle, looking straight ahead into the night.

What had Joseph thought about as he led Mary along the road to Bethlehem? Matthias silently asked for pardon of the Lord in case that was a blasphemous thing to think. But then he decided not to worry about it. Since God already knew his every thought, he surely understood that Matthias recognized that they were just ordinary people walking down an ordinary road in the middle of an ordinary night.

In the quietness, the only sound the crunching of their footsteps, he finally had time to sort his thoughts. He realized that he had been thinking of White Dove as The Pregnant Lady all day, a sort of Cherokee Madonna. It was a word Reverend Miller used, to the dismay of his congregation. Pa, who was staunchly Presbyterian through and through, thought it smacked of Popery.

Madonna or not, White Dove *was* a pregnant lady, soon to be a mother. Only now, images came to him that he had been too busy to pay mind to earlier. The softness of her smooth dusky face. Her flashing black eyes set in a tilt under delicately arched brows. The slimness of her ankles above her shoes. Putting it all together, he suddenly knew that she was very young, probably his own age. He chased that thought away and kept his eyes where they belonged and not where they wanted to go.

Outside of town, Main Street grew narrower and rougher. The wagon ruts grew deeper. White Dove could have followed the tracks easily enough to the camp without a guide. Still, the thought of them alone on the dark road was not something he could abide.

He wondered about the father of White Dove's baby. Had her husband died along the way? There were perils enough, to be sure. Or maybe Indians didn't even marry in the same way white folks did. Then Private McDonal's cruel face came to him. Was it possible that he or other soldiers like him took advantage of the Cherokee women? Was one of them the father of her baby? The thought made him want to choke McDonal. But then, allowing himself to think of the size of her belly—for only a moment, because that seemed really wrong—he realized with relief that she was too far along for that to be the case.

There was a sound behind him, and Painted Turtle said something. He stopped the horse and turned to look. Jacob had tripped on a rut and was on his knees in the road, struggling to stand and glaring at his sister and mother for daring to help him do so. White Dove shook her head, apparently at the foolishness of her brother's masculine dignity.

Matthias grinned at her. "Ha. As if you aren't every bit as prideful."

She tossed her head, but then the moonlight gleamed off the whiteness of her teeth, and he knew that she smiled.

Figuring Jacob's pride would allow him to accept a man's help, Matthias handed the reins to White Dove and went to help the boy up. He dusted himself off, and then they went on. No matter how hard Jacob tried to be a man, he was, after all, only a small boy—a worn out boy at that. Matthias hoped they reached camp before too much longer. Lieutenant Wheeler had said it wasn't far from town, but then he was riding a horse not leading one.

When they came to Alexander Buel's house on the left, Matthias stepped up the pace to get away from the stench of the urine Alexander used to tan his leather. The Buels were a friendly bunch and well-liked. But Matthias had often wondered how the family could stand living with the smell.

About a mile past the Buel's, he saw that the wagons had left

Lusk's Road and turned onto a trail through the woods. Matthias had once traveled it with his father and brothers when they had delivered lumber to Herman Stodges for a barn he was building.

In among the trees, it became harder to see the tracks, even though the branches were winter-bare. The trail began to descend and they came to Sugar Creek. It was frozen, and Matthias wondered where the people would find water. Such untimely weather! They had delayed their journey due to heat and drought, and now they had to deal with frozen rivers and creeks.

Matthias led the horse carefully across the icy creek bed. He looked back, figuring he would have to go help Painted Turtle and the children, but they had already safely crossed behind him. No telling how many creeks they had forded since they left Georgia. When they got to the top of the rise, firelight flickered not far ahead.

After a few moments, they came out of the trees at the edge of a grassy plain where hundreds of Army-issue tents had been erected. They were grouped in an orderly fashion so that six or seven tents shared a common campfire. Across the plain, the hills rose up again, providing some protection from the cold north wind. Sam had said that advance army scouts came ahead of the contingent to map out their stops. They had chosen well. It was as good a site as they were likely to find.

A voice called out on Matthias' left. A mounted Cherokee guard, rifle in hand, rode over to block their way.

White Dove spoke briefly to him. He set his rifle in his lap and turned his horse aside, nodding them permission to enter the camp.

Matthias tied Champ's reins to a small tree. The little girls woke up and rubbed their eyes. Matthias lifted them down from the horse, and then White Dove started to dismount.

"Wait, you'll fall," Matthias said. She frowned but allowed him to lift her down. He set her carefully on the ground, her huge belly between them.

A woman crawled out of one of the closest tents, curious to see what the commotion was. It was the banshee friend who had stayed by White Dove's side at the ferry. She called out, and White Dove answered. The friend, after an askance look at Matthias, came and knelt before the little girls, folding them into her arms. She murmured something soothing, and the girls smiled sleepily. Painted Turtle and White Dove chattered away in Cherokee with their friend.

Matthias stood there wondering what he should do.

Nancy came up beside him and said, "Cousin Talisa is telling them that everyone thought we had died. She says she begged the elders to go back and look for our bodies so they could be buried properly and not left for the white men to throw in the river."

Matthias was indignant. "They'd never do that."

Nancy looked up at him and smiled sadly at his ignorance. "I saw them do it in Kentucky."

He couldn't think what to say.

Painted Turtle spoke to Nancy and then went with White Dove and the little girls into Talisa's tent. Nancy chuckled softly, and Matthias saw that she was looking at Jacob, who sat on the ground leaning against his pack sound asleep.

Matthias pulled Jacob to his feet and propped him up until he stopped wobbling. When he was sure he wouldn't slide back to the ground, he unstrapped the pack and lifted it from his shoulders. Jacob mumbled something, and Nancy smiled. Matthias handed the boy's pack to her and she took it into the tent, Jacob stumbling along after her.

Then the girl was back, yawning sleepily. "I will show you where you may sleep. The young men's tents are always at the outer edge of camp."

"Thank you kindly. But is there a place for my horse?"

She gave him a sly smile. "I doubt there is room in the tent."

He chuckled. "That's all right. He hates to hear me snore."

Nancy giggled. "What is his name?"

"Champ," Matthias said, untying the reins.

Nancy patted the horse's nose. "It is a good name for such a beauty."

He laughed. "He is indeed, but how can you tell with only the firelight to see by?"

"When the morning light comes, perhaps I will find that Champ is an ugly old nag. Even so, he will still be a beauty to me. For, did he not carry my sisters to safety this night? Come, let us put him to bed."

She led the way, and he followed. They traveled along the perimeter of the camp until they came to a makeshift corral where the horses and other livestock were confined. Three men stood nearby guarding them. Nancy said something, and one of them took Champ's reins from him. Matthias stopped him long enough to get his rifle from its scabbard, and then let the man lead his horse away.

"Have no fear, Matthias Frailey," Nancy said. "He will feed your Champ and care for him as best he is able."

She led on into the camp proper, seeming to know exactly where she intended to go. It told him that they used the same formation at every stop. Finally, she stepped close to a tent and called out softly. A young man stuck his head out. His face went from curious to suspicious when he saw Matthias. Nancy spoke to him, and he came out of the tent and stood there, arms on chest, in an aggressive pose obviously meant to intimidate the white intruder.

Matthias ignored him and waited to see what Nancy would do.

She crossed her own arms over her chest, sighed deeply, and spoke again to the young man. At last, rolling his eyes, he opened the tent flap and stepped aside for Matthias to enter.

"Go with Oukonunaka. That means Owl." Nancy explained. "I told him you're a friend."

"Thank you, Miss Nancy."

Owl continued to scowl in a decidedly suspicious and unfriendly manner. Matthias laid his rifle down next to the tent, then edging past Owl, ducked his head and went inside. Light from the campfire shone through the canvas, revealing a row of shadowy lumps, presumably sleeping men. It was warmer than outside due to their accumulated body heat, but not by much. Owl pointed to an empty spot next to the tent wall. Matthias carefully stepped around the lumps and sat down on the canvas floor. The man next to him stirred and mumbled something.

Matthias lay down and pulled his hat down over his ears and his collar up around his neck. He wished mightily for his feather pillow. There was a rustling sound as Owl settled into his own spot near the tent flap. Matthias' eyes were grainy and his brain muzzy with fatigue, but he doubted he would be able to sleep. One of his nameless companions was snoring. In other tents nearby people coughed, and Matthias wondered about the sick man from the ferry. A baby fussed and then quieted. A gust of wind made its way past the sheltering hills to the north, making the tent shiver. Some of it sneaked up under the tent wall and made Matthias shiver, too.

He hoped the sun would come soon.

***

THE PRESENT

Merrideth came to herself long enough to speed past Matthias' well-earned rest. Just as the sun was coming up in his world, she slowed to real time and switched back to virtual mode.

CHAPTER 15

***

DECEMBER 5, 1838

The tent shivered again, and Matthias woke to find it was morning. Owl and the others were gone, and he realized it had been their leaving, not the wind, that had stirred the tent. After so few hours of sleep he felt nearly as tired as before he had lain down. He got up and went to lift the tent flap. His rifle was still where he had left it. Hopefully, Champ was still in the corral.

It was a cold but brilliantly beautiful morning. The trees surrounding the camp were covered in light-dazzled ice, and he had to cover his eyes at the brightness. He expected to see Owl and his friends eating breakfast or at least warming themselves at the campfire. But wherever they were, it wasn't there. The camp appeared deserted, except that the campfire burned steadily, indicating someone had recently tended it. Then nearby someone began to cough. So he wasn't completely abandoned after all.

He walked to the next circle of tents, and then the next. No one sat at any of the campfires, although the coughing of unseen sufferers came from several tents along the way. Did they have medicine to soothe their throats and ease their fevers?

Someone cried out in the distance. And then an eerie wail echoed through the camp, causing the hair on his neck and arms to stand on end. The sound seemed to be coming from the east, and so he walked toward the sun, shading his eyes.

Just beyond the last tents he found them. Hundreds of Cherokee of all ages stood listening to an old man, some kind of priest, who stood on a rocky ledge, his arms raised, speaking to them in solemn tones. At either side of the gathering, the soldiers in blue wool coats sat on their horses watching the proceedings.

He could have gone to ask Lieutenant Wheeler or one of the other soldiers what was happening, and they would probably know. But to the Cherokee it might look as if he were one of them and thus an agent of President Jackson's Removal. And that he was not.

So when he saw Owl and Talisa at the back of the crowd, he went to stand next to them. White Dove must have spoken well of him to her friend, for Talisa gave him a tiny smile. Owl glared a warning at her that needed no translation. She quickly turned her eyes back to the proceedings in front of them. Owl sent a similar bad-tempered look his way and then went back to watching the priest. Did the man blame him for Talisa's friendliness?

Owl's hair was covered in some gray dust, and then Matthias realized that most of the others' ---looked the same. The priest stopped talking, and in the silence, a woman in front of them began to chant. Immediately, Talisa and other women joined her in repeating over and over something that sounded to Matthias like "Yoo-nee-ka-la."

While the chant went on, a man and a woman came and stood on the ledge with the priest. The couple wore only light clothing with no coats or cloaks to keep out the cold. Even worse, they were soaking wet! The priest said something to the shivering man and woman, and they began stripping off their wet clothes even as women came and draped blankets around them. The women carried the couple's wet clothes away, holding them out from their bodies as if they were contaminated. Perhaps it was some sort of purification rite. The chanting ended and the priest placed a necklace over the woman's bowed head and then handed the man something that Matthias couldn't make out. They held the items as if they were of sacred importance to them.

Immediately it called to mind the weddings Matthias had attended in the little church in town. If he *was* witnessing a Cherokee wedding it was more somber than any he had ever seen. But then how could it be otherwise under the circumstances? The couple's faces were difficult to make out, but from where he stood they didn't appear to be young, and so perhaps it was a second marriage. Someone brushed against him and Matthias saw that White Dove stood next to him, Nancy at her other side.

White Dove whispered something to her sister, and then Nancy leaned in and told him, "My sister said to tell you the necklace the priest Attakullakulla gave her is made of sanctified beads for their comfort. To him, he gave tobacco to enlighten their eyes."

"Was White Dove's wedding like this back in Georgia?" Matthias said.

Nancy gasped and her eyes went large. White Dove spat out a burst of angry Cherokee. Nancy shook her head but did not answer, just looked at him with something like horror. White Dove spoke again and then took Nancy by the hand and pulled her away.

Matthias' cheeks went red hot despite the coldness of the morning. He should be thrashed. Why had he not kept his big mouth shut? Husbands and marriage were obviously sore subjects for White Dove. Judging from her reaction, she was having her baby without the benefit of either. Now because of his danged curiosity he'd gone and rubbed salt in her wound.

White Dove and Nancy disappeared into the crowd. A few minutes later, he spotted them next to Painted Turtle near the front. If Jacob and the little girls were with them, they were too short to be visible over the adults. All around him, women started chanting again, repeating the same phrase as many times as possible on a single breath, then gasping and starting all over again.

After a few minutes, two men came and helped the old priest down from the ledge. The chanting trailed away, and the crowd, including Owl and Talisa, began to disperse, the people going back toward the tents. They averted their eyes when they passed him, and Matthias feared they still lumped him in with the white men who sat on their horses watching from the sidelines.

He could not tell where White Dove and her family had gone. But after the crowd thinned out, he could see that he had been all wrong about the ceremony. At the bottom of the priest's ledge where the couple had stood was a mound of stones. There was no mistaking what it was.

With the ground frozen, they had not been able to dig a proper grave. But maybe the Cherokee always buried their dead that way. He would ask Nancy. If he could find her before he left the camp.

And if she would even talk to him after his blunder. Wedding? As if they would even have one in the midst of such sorrow. How had he been so stupid? No wonder Nancy had looked at him with horror.

Lieutenant Wheeler rode up alongside of him. "You needn't stand there with your hat in your hand feeling guilty for being a white boy."

"I don't," Matthias said. "I didn't vote for King Jackson."

The lieutenant leaned on his pommel in a decidedly un-military pose and then laughed. "I daresay you were an infant at the time. But if you had been old enough to cast a ballot, you would have voted for him all right." He put his hand to his forehead in a mocking salute. "Andrew Jackson, the great and glorious general."

"Have you been drinking, sir?"

"I have, indeed." Lieutenant Wheeler belched. "You want a nip?" He drew a small flask from inside his coat and extended it politely toward him.

"No thank you, sir."

"You sure? It'll warm your gizzard and calm your fears. Best thing possible for your miserable winter."

"That's all right, sir."

"Don't say I didn't offer." He pulled on his horse's reins and turned back to the camp.

Matthias retraced his path through the camp. Now everywhere he looked people were bustling about. Women stirred iron pots at campfires or carried water pails. Laughing children raced through clearings and were chided by their elders. Other children, even very small ones, carried branches and twigs for kindling. Young men carried armfuls of larger branches and logs which they stacked near the tents.

Conversations ceased as he approached. Faces turned away, including Owl's, who passed him carrying a load of firewood.

Champ, however, was glad as always to see him and whickered a greeting when he approached the livestock pen. Matthias found his saddle and horse blanket where they lay on the ground nearby. The blanket was stiff with frozen horse sweat. "Sorry, Champ," he said, laying the blanket across the gelding's back.

"He is a beauty, as you said."

He turned and saw that it was Nancy. She looked solemn, although he did not know whether it was from the funeral or because of what he had said. He did not think it was her usual demeanor.

"Thank you."

"Are you leaving?"

He picked up the saddle and settled it on his horse's back. "I'm sorry about being stupid earlier. I meant no disrespect."

"We know you didn't. It was our friend Fox that died. He was in the last group with us on the ferry. You know, the man who could not leave off coughing."

"I remember. I'm sorry," he said again, as if an apology would somehow make up for the injustice being done to her people.

"Fox was sick since we left the stockade in Georgia. We all knew he wouldn't make it to Oklahoma."

"I guess your sister thinks I'm a complete fool."

Nancy's eyes twinkled. "Maybe. But not because of what you said. More on account of you risking your life to help us. My mother is cooking breakfast. She said to bring you."

He glanced at her and then went back to cinching Champ's belly strap. "No, thank you. I'd best get on home."

"You must be hungry."

He was. It felt like the sides of his stomach had stuck together. But they would need all their provisions for the trip to Oklahoma.

"Don't worry. Owl won't glare at you anymore. At least not for the next seven days."

"Why only seven days?"

"It's another funeral custom. For seven days after someone dies, we are not to be angry. And to eat only a little food. As if we had any choice about that." She smiled mischievously. "We are being very righteous. We have eaten lightly for seven weeks, not seven days."

"Why were the man and woman's clothes wet?"

"The relatives of the dead person are to dip themselves in the river seven times."

"But the streams are frozen."

"There's a spring nearby. I heard that it never freezes. They will take their clothes away and burn them. Later, our priest Attakullakulla will purify their tent."

"On account of evil spirits?"

Nancy chuckled. "Maybe in the old days. Now we're more worried about catching fevers and the ague. At least the younger folks who have been educated at the mission school. Some of the old people are angry the lieutenant won't let Attakullakulla burn Fox's tent, like the old ways. But Chief Hiawassee reminded them not to be angry."

"For seven days."

"It's not so long. After all, Reverend Butrick teaches us not to be angry at all. To forgive seventy times seven times as Jesus says."

"What about your sister? Does she forgive me for my rudeness?"

"Come to breakfast and you can ask her for yourself."

When he didn't answer, she said, "Please, Matthias Frailey. It is the only way we have left to thank you."

Put that way, what could he say? He unbuckled Champ's saddle and laid it back on the ground. "All right. Lead the way."

Painted Turtle and women from the neighboring tents were busy at their shared campfire. The smell of frying salt pork made Matthias' stomach clench painfully. Painted Turtle gave him a shy smile and went back to stirring a pot of corn mush.

White Dove and her friend Talisa sat on mats near the fire brushing the little girls' hair. All four looked up at him with interest.

"I cannot remember the names of your little sisters, Nancy," Matthias said. "Are they twins?"

"No, Eliza is six and Amanda is five," Nancy said proudly.

At the sound of their names, the girls put their hands to their mouths and giggled. He smiled at them. Talisa averted her face modestly. Only White Dove continued to look at him. Matthias tipped his hat to her.

Just as he was wondering where Jacob was, the boy came staggering into camp carrying a huge load of firewood in his small arms. Nancy went to help him stack it on the neat pile by their tent. The branches he had gathered were half rotted. It made them light enough for him to carry, but it was the kind of junk wood that burned too fast to produce much heat. With such wood, they would have to gather continuously if they intended to keep the fire burning.

Painted Turtle carried a plate of food to Matthias and indicated with a graceful gesture that he was to sit by the fire and eat. He took the plate and sat where she had pointed. She smiled and patted his shoulder as if genuinely happy to have him there. Other than Nancy's invitation, it was the first hint of welcome he had received. He gulped down several bites before he realized that everyone was watching him. No one else had food. For the second time that morning, his face grew hot with embarrassment, and he put his fork down.

"It is all right," Nancy said, sitting down beside him. "Just smile and say something so Mother knows you like it."

Matthias managed a smile and said, "Thank you, ma'am. This is quite delicious."

Painted Turtle smiled widely and then went to dish up more plates. When everyone had theirs, he resumed eating. He glanced up in time to see Talisa smile a tiny smile before turning her attention to her plate.

He must have been smiling back at her, because Nancy nudged his arm and said softly, "Do not smile at Talisa or there'll be trouble, seven-day rule or not. She is pledged to Owl."

"You need not worry. I will not even look at her."

At the tent across from theirs, a harried-looking woman held a baby on her hip while she dished out food to several small children. It was the crying woman he had helped at the ferry. The little one began squalling, and she paused her dishing up to bounce him on her hip. He continued to cry and she gave up trying to console him and went back to feeding her other children their breakfast.

Once the children had their food, Matthias figured she would suckle the baby, but she did not. Her little girls ate quickly, except for one, who gazed up at her mother piteously. Then her little face crumpled, and she, too, began to cry. Whether in sympathy for the crying baby or for some other reason, Matthias did not know. He just knew he had the impulse to go comfort her as he would any of his nieces or nephews. But not knowing how the mother would feel about that, he stayed where he was.

White Dove set her plate aside and rose, graceful in spite of her condition, and went over to them. She spoke to the woman, but she did not answer, just stood there rocking the crying baby. Matthias could not bear it a moment more. He got up and went over to them. Up close he could see that the woman's hair was gray as the people's had been at the funeral. He realized now it was wood ash. He thought of the Old Testament stories of the prophets wearing sackcloth and ashes as a sign of grief. This mother was surely grieving.

While White Dove attempted to comfort her, Matthias went and squatted down next to the crying girl. He took her onto his knee. She came willingly and put her arms around his neck. She was about the same size as Duncan's littlest girl Sally. He patted her tiny back and said, "Shhh." Apparently that didn't need to be translated. Her crying let up and then turned to hiccups. He picked up her plate and held it in front of her. After another look at him, she picked up her spoon and took a tiny bite of mush. The three other girls, only slightly older than the one on his knee, stared solemnly at him and continued to eat theirs.

But still the baby cried. White Dove continued to speak softly to the woman. Then the woman thrust the baby toward White Dove and said something that made White Dove's eyes turn fierce. Refusing to take the child, she spoke again, but this time her voice wasn't at all soft or comforting. She was fairly shouting at the woman.

Matthias looked across the way to White Dove's family. "Hey there, Nancy, what is she saying?"

Nancy put down the pot she was scrubbing and came over to stand beside him. "White Dove is telling Awinita that now that she no longer has her husband she will have to learn to do what must be done. Back in Georgia, Awinita had a pampered life. She had slaves to do everything for her. Now her children suffer because she waits for someone else to take care of them."

"Slaves?"

Nancy sniffed. "Did you think only white people have them?"

White Dove shook Awinita by her shoulders and then shouted again.

"She's telling her to stop being scared. To be a woman, a mother," Nancy interpreted. "To feed her son."

Awinita began to sob and extended her baby again to White Dove, whimpering something that made the anger leave White Dove's face. After a moment, she took both Awinita and baby into her arms and rocked them. Nancy wiped at her eyes then turned and went to the other side of the campfire and disappeared into the tent.

"Wait!" Matthias said. "Nancy, what did she say?"

White Dove looked at him over the woman's head. "Awinita says the baby cries in hunger."

"You speak English."

"Yes."

"Well, why in tarnation didn't you before?"

White Dove looked at him but did not answer. Then she pulled away from Awinita and spoke to her again, softly this time. The woman sniffed and wiped her nose with her shawl. Then, after a look at the little girls sitting by the fire, she lifted the tent flap and took her squalling son inside.

"I don't know much about babies and...and such." Matthias made a vague gesture toward his chest. "But why doesn't she just...you know...feed it?"

"You mean why doesn't Awinita suckle her son? She says the river spirits have dried up her milk. Personally, I believe it's due to malnourishment. She brought a cow on this journey, but it fell in the Tennessee River just outside of Chattanooga. The cow drowned, as did her husband Elk trying to rescue it. Elk did little to help on this journey. Like his wife, he was used to slaves doing his work. I might be able to talk one of the other nursing mothers into helping feed the boy. If not, he will die."

Matthias swallowed a lump in his throat. "There are bound to be cows around here."

"Even if we knew where to find a cow, there's little money to buy one. Especially with the inflated prices your people charge us for every little thing. I will go talk to some of the other mothers."

White Dove went into her tent, and Matthias heard her speaking with Painted Turtle and Nancy. When White Dove emerged she carried a small oiled leather satchel, which she put over her shoulder. Then with a glance at him, she waddled away. Matthias hurried after her, both to escape the sound of Awinita's crying child and because he didn't like the thought of White Dove going alone.

When she saw him, her eyes opened wide in surprise. "You have no need to come with me. There are no icy hills to climb."

"I know. Do you mind if I go with you?"

"If we were home, Mother would send Nancy to walk with us. But nothing is done properly since we left Georgia. Talisa walks with Owl wherever they like with no one to watch over them. Even our funerals are improper."

It didn't escape his notice that she hadn't answered his question, but since she had not said *no*, he continued to walk by her side. She greeted people as they passed, but continued walking on a determined course through the campground.

"What was improper about Fox's funeral?" he said, adjusting his stride to match her shorter one.

"For one thing, there was no cedar. The young men would have gone into the woods to gather cedar boughs. Some would be used to cover the grave stones. The priest would have burned cedar on a new fire, built especially to honor Fox. And he would have made cedar tea and given it to Fox's family to drink and to sprinkle in their tent to purify it."

"But there's plenty around here. There's a cedar tree just yonder," he said, pointing through a gap in the tents.

"Lieutenant Wheeler says we are not to take it. We are not to cut any of the trees in this place, or the white man will become angry."

He remembered Herman Stodges and wondered if he was patrolling his property on the lookout for poachers. On one hand, Matthias understood his concern. The timber was essential for homesteaders, both for fuel and for buildings, or as a cash crop like his own family's lumber business. Besides, thousands of people passing through a person's property with their wagons and herds of livestock would leave the land damaged for farming. Already, the ruts made by the wagon wheels were deep.

But on the other hand, the Cherokee needed wood for fires to cook their food and to keep them warm. And it was not as if they had a choice in which trail they walked to Oklahoma.

Finally, White Dove stopped at a tent and called out. Matthias wondered how she knew one tent from another.

The tent flap lifted and a man's face appeared. He glanced at Matthias and then turned to White Dove and spoke. She answered. He said more. She took a paper packet out of her satchel and opened it. Inside it were bits of what looked like ground bark. The man held out his hand and White Dove gave him a small pinch of it. Throughout it all the man's face had remained expressionless. With their transaction complete, he gave White Dove a polite nod, almost a bow, and disappeared back into the tent.

White Dove carefully refolded the paper packet and put it back into her satchel then resumed walking.

"What did you give him?" he said, following her.

"Bark from the roots of black raspberries. He will make a tea for his wife. She suffers from loose bowels. It is one reason he said no to my request that she share her milk."

"What's the other reason?"

"He said that even before her illness, his wife struggled to feed their babe. I believe it is the food your government gives us. We are not used to this salt pork and corn mush day in and day out."

"What did you eat in Georgia?"

"The three sisters, of course." She glanced at him and he saw that her eyes twinkled.

So she shared Nancy's sense of humor. That she could joke under such horrible circumstances said much about her character. "Ah," he said, nodding his head wisely. "Cannibalism. Then the Cherokee are not so civilized as I'd heard."

White Dove laughed softly, putting a hand to her mouth to muffle the sound. He wished he could have heard her laugh out loud as she must have in Georgia before her world fell apart.

But at least she continued to smile. "Our people eat corn as yours do," she said. "But with it we have beans and squash. They are our main foods, the three sisters. And we ate many other good things in Georgia—sweet onions, collard greens, okra, peppers. And peaches—juicy sweet peaches. I'm going to miss them most of all."

"Maybe there will be peaches in Oklahoma."

"I doubt they grow there. I have heard it is a dry and barren land."

White Dove stopped at another tent, and this time he asked. "How to you know whose tent it is?"

She smiled slyly. "Can you not read? I thought you were civilized enough for that at least." She pointed to decorations painted on the side of the tent. He had seen them on all the tents. "It says *Lone Wolf.*"

"How do you read it? There are no letters."

She smiled at his perplexity. "We need no letters, only syllables. Chief Sequoyah devised the Cherokee syllabary, and now almost all the young people can read and write it. Many old people, too, although my mother refuses to learn. At the mission school, I learned both Cherokee and English and read every book I could find. When the soldiers came and drove us out of our homes I left many things behind, including my books. And English. I left that behind, too. I vowed never to speak it again."

"Why did you change your mind?"

"I met a kind white man."

Warmth rushed through his chest. Did she mean him? He wanted to ask her, but the tent flap opened and a woman came out holding a baby close to her bosom.

White Dove spoke to her, and the woman shook her head vigorously and clutched the baby so tightly that it began to cry. White Dove spoke again and the woman went back into the tent.

"I don't really blame her," White Dove said sadly. "It is a dangerous journey we're on. A trail of tears. Already so many have died, and we're only half way there. To feed Awinita's babe would put her own little one's life at risk. But there's one more woman to ask. Woya also had a boy child in the spring. But first I must stop at Chief Hiawassee's tent."

"I haven't seen your chief yet."

"He rides in one of the wagons with the old and infirm. He had an apoplexy when the soldiers came to his house."

White Dove waddled on through the camp, passing many tents and people who spoke or nodded their heads politely. Finally, she stopped at a tent and called out. A wrinkled old woman peeked out, and White Dove smiled tenderly at her and spoke softly in Cherokee. The old woman looked cautiously at Matthias then came out of the tent and pulled White Dove down to place a kiss on her cheek. White Dove took a different paper packet from her satchel. When she opened it, he saw that this one contained small dried leaves. White Dove said something, and the old woman helped herself to three of them, then smiled sadly and went back into the tent.

"Pennyroyal is for headaches, among other things," White Dove said. "She will make pennyroyal tea for the chief. Mother said it will not help his headaches, at least not much, but it will be a comfort to her to do something for her husband. Mother reminded me to be careful not to touch the leaves, because pennyroyal can cause a pregnant woman to rid her womb of the babe."

Matthias' eyes widened at the alarming thought.

"Some of the women have begged Mother for pennyroyal, because they do not wish to bring babies into the world on this trail that we follow. She will not give it to them, because it is the Great Father who must decide such things. If only Mother had her medicines she would be able to help ease the people's suffering in many ways. She is *ni sa ho ni*, from the Bear Clan. They are the most powerful of our healers. But she had to leave behind many of her most valuable herbs when we left Georgia. She sorrows greatly for them."

"Are you saying the soldiers wouldn't let her bring her medicines?"

"Yes, but not in the way you mean." She didn't offer an explanation. "Come," White Dove said. "Woya's tent is only a short distance away."

When they reached it White Dove called out the same greeting as before. Woya mumbled an answer but did not come out. White Dove looked at him, defeat in her eyes.

"She said *no*?" he said.

"It was a definite *no*."

"Cannot Awinita give her baby mush? If she cooked it for a long time, and—"

"He is still too young for it. Some mothers have tried, but their little ones get a bloody flux and die all the sooner."

He did not know how long it took for a baby to starve to death. He did not ask White Dove, for he knew he would not be able to bear the answer.

But he would talk to her of other things before they got back to her tent and he had to leave. He was curious to know how old White Dove was, but knowing from experience that white ladies did not like that question, he figured Cherokee ladies didn't either. He wanted to know once and for all whether White Dove had a husband, but still he did not have the courage to ask her. And he would like to know when her baby was supposed to be born. Would she make it to the Oklahoma country before it came? But men were not supposed to notice when women were carrying, much less comment on it. So he did not ask about it or about any of the other things he wished to know.

While he struggled to come up with a question White Dove might agree to answer, there was a commotion ahead of them and three small boys ran past them chattering happily.

"They say Reverend Butrick has returned," White Dove said.

"My brother must have come early with the boards to repair his wagon."

When they came around the next group of tents, Matthias realized they had come full circle and were again at the front of the camp. Reverend Butrick's covered wagon was bumping along on the rutted trail toward them. And behind him came Alexander Buel, driving his farm wagon. As usual, a faint odor of urine hovered about him.

A small crowd had gathered, including Nancy, Owl, and some others Matthias recognized but did not have names for. Reverend Butrick and his wife Clara smiled and called out greetings to the people. The two wagons pulled off the trail and came to a stop. Butrick got down from the seat and then helped his wife. Several people talked all at once, and he put up his hands and said, "Sorry, my little flock. I cannot hear you all at once."

Everyone quieted, and White Dove spoke. Reverend Butrick's face fell.

"What did she say, Daniel?" Clara said.

"I said that Fox died in the night, ma'am," White Dove said. "We buried him a short while ago."

"He was such a brave young man," Butrick said. "His parents must be sorrowing greatly. Still, they know their son has left this sad world for a better one with Jesus."

Matthias was surprised to hear that they were Christians, since the funeral rituals had been conducted by the Cherokee priest.

"Dear White Dove, I'm so happy that you're speaking English again," Clara Butrick said. "I've missed our chats."

White Dove glanced at Matthias before answering. "It was time."

"Matthias, your brother and father repaired our wagon good as new," Butrick said. "The scoundrels refused to charge me a fair price."

Matthias' stomach dropped in shock that Lachlan would stoop to unfairly profiting off the Cherokee's situation. "I'll pay you back, Reverend. I'll go home right now and get the money."

"Whatever do you mean?"

"They shouldn't have acted the pirate like John Berry."

Reverend Butrick chuckled. "You misunderstand me, Matthias. I meant they *under*charged me."

Matthias stomach settled. "I cannot tell you how relieved I am to hear that. Still, they should not have charged you anything."

"I insisted. And now we should be fine for the rest of the journey. In terms of transportation anyway."

"Reverend," Alexander Buel said from the other wagon. "I hate to say it, but I need to unload these pumpkins and get back to town. My work won't wait."

"Pumpkins?" White Dove said. She and Matthias went to Buel's wagon and saw that it was full nearly to the top with pumpkins of all sizes.

"There must be hundreds of them here," Matthias said.

"Yes, the Lord blessed us with a good crop this year," Buel said. "When I saw how hungry some of the Injuns was, I went on home and started hauling them up out of the root cellar. My boys helped."

White Dove smiled happily at the pumpkins.

"I hoped he was bringing leather," Matthias said softly. "The people could use it to make shoes for those that don't have them."

"For now, this is much more valuable," White Dove said. "Do you not see? The Great Father did not send us a cow, but he did give us these pumpkins. We can mash them and feed the little ones."

"Where do you want them, Reverend?" Buel said.

"Here is as good a place as any. The people can come take what they need."

White Dove put up a hand and spoke to the crowd. Instead of coming to get the pumpkins, as Matthias had expected, they fell back, their expressions resigned.

"That is a good plan, White Dove," Butrick said.

She turned to Matthias. "I told them the pumpkins are only for families with little ones. Everyone will want a pumpkin, but they can make do with the salt pork and mush. The youngest children cannot."

Buel got down from the seat and went to the back of the wagon. Matthias helped him lower the end gate and then took two pumpkins out and laid them on the ground next to the trail. Several of the men came and helped carry more.

When they were all in a stack beside the trail, Buel got back on the seat and turned the wagon toward town.

"Thank you, Mr. Buel," Reverend Butrick said. "Your kindness will be remembered."

"Think nothing of it." Buel tipped his hat and whistled to his horses.

White Dove waved and then wasted no time getting back to what needed to be done. She spoke to the men and they picked up as many pumpkins as they could carry and left to distribute them where she had instructed.

"Come, Clara," the reverend said. "Let us go give what comfort we may to Fox's family." They left, discussing which Scriptures would best fit the situation.

Buel stopped his wagon at the trees and called back, "Oh, I almost forgot, Matthias. Your pa said you was to git home lickety split or he's going to jerk a knock in your tail."

"I will, Alexander," Matthias said, grinning at his colorful language. Then he picked up two large pumpkins. "Where do you want these, White Dove?"

It was the first time he had called her by name, and she looked surprised. He quickly added, "*Miss* White Dove."

"There's no need for *Miss*, Matthias. Let us take them to Awinita."

Matthias had liked the sound of her name coming out of his mouth. But the sound of his name on her lips was even more pleasant.

When they got back to the tent, no one was there but Painted Turtle, and it was blessedly quiet. Nancy spoke with her mother and then said, "The baby stopped crying a few minutes ago. Mother doesn't know if he finally got enough milk, or just got tired of crying and went to sleep."

Matthias set one of the pumpkins down by the tent and pulled his folding knife out of his pocket. "Should I cut it in half, or what?"

"Just cut the stem out, please," White Dove said. "Make a small hole, just big enough to get the guts out. Then I'll set it in the ashes to roast."

"We're going to need more firewood soon." He had said *we*. When had he begun to think of it as *his* campfire to tend?

"Joseph and Cousin Talisa should be back with more soon, and then it's my turn," Nancy said. "But, that mean soldier came by and told us we had to let the fires go low." She sniffed disdainfully. "He *claimed* it was Lieutenant Wheeler's orders."

"He probably tells the truth," White Dove said. "We have to make the firewood last until we leave."

"And when will that be?" Matthias said.

White Dove averted her eyes. "The lieutenant says tomorrow maybe."

Matthias flung a handful of the pumpkin's guts away rather

more forcefully than was strictly necessary.

"Stop!" White Dove said. "Do not waste the seeds! I will roast them."

"Really?"

"They are quite good. Probably even civilized people would like them."

He laughed.

CHAPTER 16

***

THE PRESENT

Merrideth paused the action. After drinks and bathroom breaks they decided it was time to go off virtual for a while. They could only take the intensity for so long. The people seemed a bit happier, cheered by the pumpkins Alexander Buel had brought. Matthias roasted one of them, and White Dove and her mother mashed some and took it to Awinita. Her baby boy made faces when she offered him a spoonful of pumpkin, but then he got the idea and began to gulp it down. He stopped crying and he even smiled when Matthias made a funny face at him.

Later White Dove gave Matthias some of the pumpkins seeds she had roasted. Although he refused to take more than a small handful, it was obvious he liked them.

"Isn't that sweet?" Abby said. "He's got to be hungry, too, but he won't take their food."

"I really like Matthias," Merrideth said. "But doesn't it seem a little pervy the way he's so interested in White Dove? For crying out loud. She's pregnant."

John laughed and put his arms around Abby. "Why not? Your friend Abby here was never sexier than when she was pregnant."

"Okay, I'll take your word for it. But please do not ever say the *S* word in my presence again, John," Merrideth said, pretending to plug her ears. "So if Matthias isn't a perv, how about a cheating dog?"

"What do you mean? After all, he's single," Abby said.

"But not for long. I'm sure the marriage registry said December 1838. I don't remember the exact day. I'll have to check my notes. But whatever, in only a few days he will be married to Emmaline. So where is she while Matthias is mooning over White Dove?"

"That's a good question." John leaned in close and peered at the screen. "Something's happening. You'd better go virtual again."

***

DECEMBER 5, 1838

Matthias' muscles were straining and he was sweating inside his coat by the time he got the armful of firewood to the edge of the woods. He'd had to walk a good quarter of a mile before he had been able to find anything to pick up, and it was of such poor quality it hardly seemed worth the trouble of hauling it back to camp. It would burn far too fast to do anyone much good.

The sound of men shouting in English and Cherokee came to him, and he hurried forward. When he got to the clearing he saw Herman Stodges brandishing a rifle at two Cherokee men who held the handles of a cross-cut saw. The saw rested nearly half way through the trunk of a good sized hickory tree. The men had chosen well. The tree appeared to have been dead long enough to be well dried but not so long that it would be difficult to cut. The logs would burn hot in the people's campfires.

"I'll kill you! I swear I will!" Herman Stodges shouted.

Matthias dropped his load of firewood and hurried forward. "Herman, put your gun down, man."

Stodges looked up in surprise. "Matthias Frailey, what in tarnation are you doing here?"

"Trying to help these people survive. They need firewood."

"Well, they're not using my trees for it."

"At least let them finish cutting this one."

"No, sir. That'd just make 'em think they could go on ahead and cut down the rest of my timber."

"Be reasonable."

"Easy for you to say, Matthias. They're not on your land." He lifted his rifle and shot above the men's heads. They dropped the saw handles and stepped away from the tree. "Now git." He waved the rifle to shoo them away. They took a few steps back and then watched to see what would happen.

Shaking his head in disgust at Stodges' meanness, Matthias went to the tree and took the handle of the saw.

"I'll shoot you, too, Matthias. Don't think I won't."

"I'm getting the saw, you fool."

Stodges sniffed. "All right. Be quick about it."

One of the men came and took the other handle, and together they worked the saw out of the tree. Then, after expressionless glances at Matthias, the two Cherokee turned and headed back to camp. He couldn't tell whether they understood whether he had tried to talk sense into Stodges or agreed with him.

Matthias went to gather up the firewood he had dropped. "You going to shoot me, Herman, if I take this?"

"You can take all of the fallen wood you can carry, Frailey. Just don't cut my trees." Stodges holstered his rifle and rode away.

On his way back to camp, Matthias met the lieutenant and two men of the Cherokee Lighthorse Patrol.

"What's going on?" Lieutenant Wheeler said. "We heard a shot."

"Can we walk while we discuss this? I'm getting mighty tired of carrying this wood."

"All right." The lieutenant and the other men turned their horses in alongside Matthias.

"As for the shot you heard, Herman Stodges took exception to people cutting down one of his trees."

Lieutenant Wheeler huffed. "I told them not to cut the trees. Anyone hurt?"

"No just a warning shot. This time." Matthias nodded at the firewood he carried in his arms. "This wood is about as useless as…well, let's just say it's no good. And even this is about gone, Lieutenant. You'll have to either convince Stodges to let the people cut wood or move on until you find a place where they can."

"You don't have to tell me how to do my job, Mr. Frailey." Wheeler ruined the effect of his proud statement by hiccupping. "I've been waiting for my scouts to get back, which they just did. They tell me every creek west of here to the Mississippi is frozen solid. And as for the Mississippi, well, neither the Bainbridge Ferry nor the Green Ferry have been able to run for days. We've got the spring here, so here we'll stay. At least until I hear otherwise. As for firewood, I'll go have a talk with Stodges and see how much money it would take for him to change his mind. I have some discretionary funds. Not much, but some. Which way did he go?"

"That way."

Lieutenant Wheeler nodded, and the three rode off. Matthias hoped Wheeler was sober enough to reason with Herman Stodges.

When Matthias got his armload of firewood back to camp all was quiet. The fires burned low, and the people huddled close to them. At White Dove's tent, he found Painted Turtle stirring mush over a mere scrap of fire. She smiled warmly at him. Across the way, Awinita rocked her baby boy. He wasn't crying, so presumably his belly was still happy with the pumpkin.

Matthias added his firewood to the small stack by the tent. Daylight was about gone, and he hoped Joseph and Nancy would be back soon with their wood. Matthias used hand signs as best as he could to ask Painted Turtle where White Dove and the little girls were.

She seemed to know what he meant and put her hands under her cheek and pointed to the tent to indicate they were sleeping. Good. They needed to rest.

But when Joseph and Nancy came around the tent, their arms loaded down with twigs and small branches, little Eliza and Amanda were behind them, carrying their own tiny loads. He realized then that Painted Turtle had meant only White Dove was sleeping in the tent.

"You will go with me next time," Matthias said. "It's getting to be too far to go on your own, especially with a gun-toting fool riding around."

"We aren't afraid," Nancy said.

Matthias smiled. "I bet you never are." He glanced toward the tent. "I've got to go home now."

"I'll tell her you said goodbye, *Unaka*."

"What is that, or dare I ask?"

"*Unaka* is Cherokee for *white man*."

"Tell her *Unaka* will be back as soon as he can."

***

THE PRESENT

Someone knocked on the apartment door. Merrideth nearly jumped out of her chair, Abby squawked, and John made an odd gurgling sound. Merrideth paused the scene, and the three of them tiptoed to look out the peep hole.

It was Nick, of course. Of course, there was no "of course" about it. It could have been Mr. Starnes coming to check out the strange noises coming from his vacant apartment. It could have been the couple across the hall coming to welcome the new tenants with a hearty chicken casserole.

"What's he doing here?" John said. "Why can't we be left alone for just one minute?"

"Whoa," Merrideth said. "It must be feeding time at the zoo. The bears are getting cranky."

"Ha, ha. Very funny, Merri," John said and then after a pause added, "But true. That donut I ate at five o'clock is long gone."

"It's after nine, and we did promise Nick we'd have breakfast with him," Abby pointed out. She reached for the door knob, but John grabbed her hand. "Wait," he whispered. "I know we're all hungry, but if we go down to breakfast, he'll insist on taking us on his infernal tour of Golconda."

"I'm actually looking forward to it," Abby said. "I keep wanting to go out there and see where it all happened."

"Me too," John said. "But the tour could take all blasted day. We can't stop now. Not until we find out what happened to Matthias. Tell Nick to come back later."

"He's right," Merrideth said. The thought of leaving her laptop—more specifically leaving Matthias—was distressing.

Abby grinned. "Well, don't either of you come crying to me if you faint from hunger."

The knock came again, louder than before. Merrideth opened the door a scant ten inches. Her brain registered the smell of food the same time it did Nick's rather nice smile. He was wearing fresh nerd clothes, which she immediately envied, her own attire being less than pristine at the moment. Her resolve wavered. How wonderful it would be to go downstairs for a nice leisurely Sunday morning breakfast like a normal person.

"Hi," he said. "I was beginning to think you'd all died in there. Maybe carbon monoxide fumes from the restaurant or something."

"No, we're all fine. Just tired."

"Did you get my texts?" Nick said it casually, and she could tell he was trying not to look too eager.

"Sorry. We've been so busy that I haven't looked at my phone in hours." It was the truth, if not the whole truth. "What did you want?"

"I have some ideas for places to show you around the county. You and your friends."

She smiled enough to indicate her appreciation of his thoughtfulness, but not so much that he would be overly encouraged to pursue her, as he so obviously wanted to do.

"You'll want to see them first hand," he continued. "For your book about the Trail of Tears. We can go right after breakfast."

"About that," she said. "We're probably not at the stage where we should leave our work quite yet."

His face registered his disappointment, and she felt like she'd just kicked a puppy. "We could come down later. Make it more like brunch."

"You've got to eat if you're going to keep up your strength for your work."

It sounded like something a nerd's mom would say, and she wondered if he still lived with his parents. "We've got snacks and such."

"I could bring you breakfast."

"You would do that?"

"Of course. Just tell me what you want."

"I'm not picky. Whatever's on the menu." Behind her she heard John whisper, "Bacon." So she said, "I do love bacon."

"All right, then. Room service coming right up."

She smiled. "Thanks, Nick."

When she got back inside, John said, "If he brings bacon, I may fall in love with him myself." Then his eyes widened in alarm. "He knows he's bringing breakfast for all of us, doesn't he?"

"I'm sure he will, John," Merrideth said, even though now that she remembered the look on Nick's face, she wasn't so sure.

"Do you think he's related to the barkeeper at the Ferry House?" Abby said. "I think his last name was Landis."

"Was it?" John said.

"We can ask him about his family later," Merrideth said. "Meanwhile, let's see how much time in Matthias' world we can cover in the half hour it takes for Nick to get back with the bacon."

Merrideth's phone rang before she could sit back down at the computer. "Or not. While I take this call, why don't you guys fast-forward through Matthias' journey back home? Let me know when he gets there."

"Sure," Abby said, looking amused. "Take your time."

"Do not take your time," John said. "Hurry."

Waving away his comment, Merrideth spoke into the phone. "Brett. Good morning."

"Hey, I think I'm going to like *Almond Toast*."

"You will?" And then it sank in that he was not talking about food. "I thought you were going with *Arizona Tan*."

He laughed. "I changed my mind at the last minute. I got hungry and toast started sounding really good about then. Anyway, it looks good. You should come see."

"So how much have you painted so far?"

"My bedroom is done. I think I can finish the rest by nightfall. By the way, we're still on for tomorrow, aren't we? Church, remember?"

It took a minute to sink in. "Oh, yes. Church. She had told him she wanted to try out his church, but with all that had happened, it was the last thing on her mind. Still, she had said she would go. "Ten o'clock, right?"

"Right. Say, I could finish painting later if you want me to come over and put the door knob on now."

"Actually, I didn't make it home last night."

"What happened? Are you all right?"

"Time just got away from us...and then it was so late that we didn't want to drive. And anyway, the antique show continues today and—"

Beside her, John whispered, "Merri, ask him about time warp."

Merrideth put her hand over the phone. "What? Are you kidding?"

"He's a physics expert, isn't he?"

"Yes, but I thought you didn't want him to know."

"You don't have to give it away. Just ask him if time warp is theoretically possible."

Merrideth uncovered her phone. "John wants to know if time

warp is only in sci-fi movies and books or real."

"Why?"

"He's into that sort of thing. I guess looking at all the antiques got him thinking about the passing of time."

"Well, you can tell him that yes, time can warp."

"Really?"

"You sound more excited about that than I would have guessed."

John nudged her and Merrideth nodded her head yes. "Do you mean theoretically, Brett, or has it been proven?"

"Proven. It can actually be measured. The gravity of the sun can cause a shift in radio waves and thus changes the time it takes for them to reach a receiver. It's only about a thousandth of a degree of change."

Nodding her head again at John, she said, "That sounds small."

"It is. Not at all noticeable without scientific measurement. But time can definitely get weird."

"No kidding."

"What's he saying?" John demanded.

Merrideth put a finger up to shush him.

"It's a matter of perception, of course," Brett continued. "With a temporal illusion the person may perceive time slowing down, speeding up—maybe even stopping altogether. Another misperception called the telescoping effect causes a person to think that an event occurred farther back in time than it actually did. Vierodt's Law says that—"

"Hey, Brett. time out. Tell John. My brain is starting to bleed." She handed her phone to John and he took it like she was offering him a plate of liver.

"Yeah?" John said into the phone. "Go on." From the expression on his face, he got over his distaste soon enough and was enjoying whatever physics mumbo jumbo Brett was telling him. From time to time he said "really?" or "right" and even a "cool!" or two.

Merrideth went back and sat down at the table next to Abby while they waited for John.

"So you're going to church with Brett tomorrow?" Abby said casually. Too casually.

"Don't read anything into that. I'm still church-shopping. He's very religious, you know. What I said last night? Brett would never move in with me."

"That's good. When you say religious, you mean he's a Christian?"

"Duh, Abby. He's not a Buddhist, Jew, Taoist—much less an atheist."

"But you know there's more to being a Christian than going to church, don't you, Merri? John and I have tried to tell you—"

"Don't worry. Brett is the real Bible-quoting type of Christian."

"He does that?"

"Yes. But not in a weird way. He's the kind you and John are, I guess."

A huge smile lit up Abby's face. "That's great, kiddo."

"I knew you'd be happy about that. Brett would probably even meet your exacting standards for a husband, not that you need to worry about that." John was still chatting away into her phone with Brett. It felt weird to know the two men were connecting. "Actually, I don't even know why Brett's interested in me. I'm not ever going to be the type to go around saying *praise the Lord.* No offense."

"Pardon me, Merri, but I feel a *praise the Lord* coming on."

Merrideth rolled her eyes. "What for this time?"

"Because I think God sent Brett into your life for a purpose. Maybe—"

"I think he's becoming more John's friend than mine. When are they ever going to get off the phone?"

"How about those churches you've been trying out, Merri? Have any of them come close to meeting *your* exacting standards?" Abby smiled, but there was a tinge of sarcasm in her question that she probably didn't even realize had leaked out. She could not seem to comprehend why Merrideth would want to go to any church but the one she and John attended. It was a nice enough church, even though the sermons were long and everyone lugged Bibles with them every week. But she just wasn't comfortable in a church where at any moment someone near you might have an emotional outburst of *amen* or *hallelujah.* What was wrong with wanting a little more decorum?

"No," Merrideth said. "They all had one thing or another wrong with them. If Brett's church doesn't work out, I was thinking maybe I'd try something more on the High-Church end of the spectrum. You know candles, incense, and art—that sort of thing. So if the inquisition is over, could we get back to work now?"

"I'm sorry, Merri. I didn't mean to come across like that. You know I love you like a sister."

"I know."

"I'm praying you find what you're looking for."

"What's she looking for?" John said, handing Merrideth her phone. "Garrison said to tell you goodbye."

"It sounded like you were having a nice conversation," Abby said.

"I guess he isn't such a bad guy. He really knows his science."

"I should hope so," Merrideth said. "I'll tell President Peterson you approve."

"But he isn't so in love with his science that he doesn't have room for faith."

Merrideth gasped. "Please tell me you didn't quiz him, John. You did, didn't you?"

"Of course I did while I had the opportunity. And he passed with flying colors."

"Oh, well, then, if he has the John Roberts Seal of Approval I'll start planning my wedding," Merrideth said with as much sarcasm as she could muster.

"I wish," Abby said.

John frowned. "I wouldn't go that far."

"Come on, you two," Abby said. "Let's get back to work. I've got it all cued up to where Matthias just reached his home."

"Good. Let's get back to 1838," Merrideth said. "If we stay in our own time much longer I might commit murder."

CHAPTER 17

***

DECEMBER 5, 1838

Smoke curled out of the chimneys of the Frailey family's snug cabins, carrying the smell of roasting meat to Matthias' nose. Home. What would it be like to leave it forever, to go to some faraway place where peaches wouldn't grow? Champ picked up his pace, anxious to get to the barn where he knew he would get corn in his feed box. Would they even be able to grow corn in the Oklahoma country?

His mother twitched back the curtain and smiled at him. He waved, then took Champ to his stall and unsaddled him. He poured a scoop of corn for him, and the cows in the next stall mooed to let him know they'd like some, too. But he knew quite well that they had already been fed and milked. He left Champ to eat his supper while he went to see about his own.

When he opened the cabin door, his mother said, "Hello, stranger. You look nearly frozen."

"I'm fine, Ma." He kissed her cheek and then leaned in to sniff what was cooking on the hearth.

"It's ready. Get your plate."

He took off his coat and hung it on the peg. He took her a plate from the shelf, and she dished up roast pork and potatoes onto it. Then she went to the sideboard and cut two thick slices of bread and gave it to him.

He nearly groaned in happiness. "You made light bread."

"Enjoy it while you can, Matthias. The flour's gone. We'll be back to corn pone until your pa can switch to milling grain for me."

He was so hungry he had to force himself to bow his head to pray. It was a short prayer. When he looked up, his mother put a mug of frothy milk beside his plate. He smiled his thanks. Then, picking up his spoon, he told himself to savor the food, not bolt it down like a starving dog. But in spite of his best efforts, he couldn't quit shoving it into his mouth until it was gone.

"There's plenty more, son."

Guiltily, he pictured White Dove and her people eating their supper of corn mush and salt pork in the cold. "No," he said, sopping up the last of the gravy with his bread. "This is all I need. More than I deserve. I am most grateful, Ma."

Her eyes widened in surprise. It shamed him to know that he had not told her nearly often enough.

"You are most welcome, son. A woman takes joy in seeing her family eat well, now doesn't she?"

"Where's Simon and Lizbeth?"

"They're walking in the orchard."

"In this weather?"

"I suppose they figure a little privacy is worth the cold."

"Pa says we'll finish their cabin soon."

"Lizbeth never complains, but I'm sure she will be pleased to have her own home, especially with the baby coming."

The door opened and his father came in, and with him a gust of cold air. "The prodigal son has returned, I see," Lachlan said with a grin. He hung his coat and came to the table, buzzing Matthias' head with his knuckles as he passed him. "I hope you left some supper for me."

Matthias smiled. "I left you some, Pa, although it was difficult."

"Prodigal son? Don't listen to your father," Ma said, setting a plate before Lachlan. "He's proud of you and Angus for doing your Christian duty to those poor people."

"That I am, son," Lachlan said, taking a bite of food.

Matthias wanted to tell his parents about the people he had met—White Dove, Nancy and the rest of the family. The crying woman who had no joy in seeing her family eat well. He wanted to tell them how the wind whistled in the tents and the old people coughed and the babies cried in hunger.

But his father was happily eating his supper and his mother was humming at the hearth. The cabin was warmed by the fire and also by the love all of them shared. It was home, and it was too perfect to spoil with tragic stories.

"Yes, you two did your Christian duty, Matthias. In truth, Angus will likely carry that whip mark for doing it. So now it's time for you both to get back to your family responsibilities. We've got more work than you can shake a stick at. Isaac Gregory stopped by. Says he wants a barn come spring." Lachlan paused to take another bite of his supper.

Matthias smiled to himself. With the order for barn lumber, Mr. Gregory had redeemed himself in his pa's eyes. Just the week before, Lachlan had been grousing because Gregory decided to break up the flatboat the family had arrived in to build a shed instead of buying new lumber from them. Personally, Matthias thought it was a wise decision.

"I forgot to say that Cyrus wants his lumber now," Lachlan continued. "He cornered me in town last week and nagged like an old hen.

"I suppose it's dry enough, but what's the rush? He can't start on that new house he's planning until spring."

Lachlan sighed. "There's no reasoning with Cyrus. He wants it now. So we'd best get that delivered before he has an apoplexy. And then we'll need to deal with the trees the ice storm took down."

"At least it saved us having to *cut* them down," Matthias said.

"The ice was a blessing in disguise," his mother said.

Not for everyone.

"And it's time to grease the mill pistons," Lachlan said. "I was going to have Simon do it, but he insists you have a rare talent for the task."

Matthias snorted, but held his tongue. There was no use arguing with Pa once he made his mind up, but he would tell Simon what he thought of his perfidy at the earliest opportunity. The rascal knew full well that it was his turn to do the messy job.

"Don't look so glum. We all have our parts to play, son. So get your rest. We'll be up early."

"We always are, Pa. I think I'll go on to bed now." He carried the plates over for his mother and then climbed the ladder to the loft.

It seemed like a fortnight since he had last been in his own bed. It was a new feather bed of blue ticking that his mother had made him for his last birthday. He took off his boots and outer clothes then lay down on the bed and pulled up the quilts. She'd made those for him, too. The bed was soft and wonderful, a far cry from the bare tent floor he'd slept on the night before. He surely had thanked Ma when she gave the bed to him, had he not? In any case, he would thank her again in the morning. The chinking in the logs was tight, but the wind rattled the window panes. It didn't matter, though, because the quilts were warm, and the feather bed hugged his tired body. Even so, he could not fall asleep for the pictures in his head.

***

THE PRESENT

A knock on the door jolted Merrideth back to the present. John was the first to snap out of it enough to realize that it was their breakfast being delivered. He had the door unlocked and opened before Nick could knock a second time.

"Come in, Landis," John said. "What took you so long?"

Nick came in carrying two large plastic bags with the unmistakable bulges of Styrofoam to-go boxes. "What my husband meant to say is *thanks, Nick, that smells wonderful*," Abby said.

"You're welcome." Nick stood there looking curiously around the apartment while John took the bags to the counter. His expression changed when he saw the prodigious amount of debris that had accumulated during their long night. The apartment looked like a pack of 13-year-old junk food addicts had been squatting there for a month.

"Don't worry, Nick. We'll clean it up," Merrideth said. "The place will be immaculate. I promise."

Nick smiled at her and started across the room. She closed the laptop just before he reached the table. He turned his eyes to her yellow legal pad. She wasn't worried about him reading it. Her handwriting was so atrocious she could barely interpret it herself.

"How's your research coming?" Nick said. "You don't seem to

171

have many notes."

"All here," Merrideth said, tapping the laptop. "And here," she added, tapping her temple. "We made a lot of progress, but there's lots still to do." She took the laptop to the bedroom in case he got the idea he'd like to look at her notes.

When she got back, she saw that Abby and John had unloaded the plastic bags. John nearly swooned when he discovered the Styrofoam boxes held a sampling from the Sunday buffet, including tons of bacon.

While they ate, Nick continued to quiz Merrideth about her alleged book as if he were trying to make up for talking too much about his own the day before. John and Abby took turns trying to distract him without much success.

Finally, Merrideth remembered something that would be sure to derail Nick's interest in her book. It was the least she could do for a fellow historian. "Nick, we discovered—in our research—that there was once a barkeeper at the Ferry House named Sam Landis. Interesting, huh? I'm planning on including him in my book."

Merrideth realized her mistake as soon as the words were out of her mouth. If he asked for documentation, she wouldn't be able to give it to him.

"Really?" Nick said.

"Yes," Merrideth said, glancing at Abby and John. "Sam Landis was sympathetic to the Cherokee and fed some of them at the inn. Do you think you might be related to him?"

"I'll ask Mother to see if we have an ancestor named Samuel. She's the family historian."

"So, Landis, what do you do besides write books?" John said.

Merrideth was glad for the distracting comment. From the look on John's face, he had done it on purpose. Hopefully, Nick wouldn't think to ask how she knew about Sam Landis until they had left Golconda.

It worked. Nick spent a solid five minutes describing the insurance agency he ran out of his home—he did not live with his mother—and explaining how he planned to turn the apartment into a more suitable office for his business. He even offered to show them an insurance policy. To get him off that unwanted topic, Abby resorted to asking him questions about the tour. He waxed eloquent about that for another five minutes, apparently ready to drag them out the door the moment they finished eating.

"It sounds great," Merrideth said. "But, we can't…for a while, I mean. Give me another couple of hours to work here, because I have to—"

"If you don't want to go, just say so, Merrideth." From the look on his face, Nick had reached the limit of his patience.

"Well, actually…" John said.

Merrideth stepped on his foot to shut him up and then hurried to say, "Oh, no, Nick. It's not that at all. I'd love to go on the tour." And she really did. It would be wonderful to walk in all the places Matthias had walked. To see the landscape he had looked at.

"We all would," Abby added.

Nick wiped his hands on a napkin and stood. "I understand. The early stages of writing a book are tricky."

"I'll call you," Merrideth said. "I promise."

She couldn't tell if he entirely believed her, but he did get his smile back. When he was gone, Merrideth retrieved her laptop and reloaded the program.

"I feel terrible," Abby said. "I wish we could show Nick his ancestor Sam Landis."

"I know," Merrideth said. "He would enjoy time-surfing so much."

John folded his arms over his chest. "Buck up, ladies. Even if Landis were capable of keeping a secret of this magnitude, and we sure as heck don't know him well enough to make that judgment, it would take too long. By the time we explained *Beautiful Houses* and listened to him ooh and ahh and ask a million questions, we'd be out of time to do what we came here to do."

"You're right. I know that," Abby said.

"Okay," Merrideth said. "Back to 1838."

CHAPTER 18

***

DECEMBER 6, 1838

The sound of the saw mill shrieking in the distance woke Matthias. His brothers were already working, and he was a slugabed. Pa was sure to be peeved. When he got downstairs, he quickly downed the mug of milk and ate the bread and cold meat his mother had left for him and then hurried into his coat.

When he got to the barn, he heard the softer, more pleasant sounds of his mother's humming and milk hitting tin pails. He went to the stall where she and Jewel worked. The family's three cows continued placidly eating hay, but the women looked up and smiled at him.

"You must have been tired," his mother said.

"I guess I was. Sorry I'm late. I'll get started with the feeding."

"Angus already fed," Jewel said with a smile. "He said you'd need your sleep."

Affection for Angus swelled his heart. Angus' generosity was just another reason he was his favorite brother, not that he could admit that out loud.

Although the women fed the cows and chickens, it was his chore to feed and care for the rest of the livestock—their oxen Nell and Bell, the riding horses; and the four big Percheron draft horses, the steers fattening in the pasture, and the hogs fattening in their pen. Even on a good day it took him over an hour to do his chores and another hour to do it all over again in the evening. And then he was needed at the mill. Even a small operation like theirs, was a five-man job at minimum. In the summer, Pa hired extra help some days.

Matthias felt the unwelcome pangs of guilt for all the extra work he had made for Angus and everyone else while he had been gone. Doubtless Pa was growing impatient for him to get back to work. He started to leave, but then Jewel rose from her milking stool to stretch. He took a quick look at her belly but turned away before he could see much.

Jewel laughed. "You do know about the birds and bees, don't you, Matthias? I'm sure Angus would be glad to tell you a thing or two."

He felt his face coloring. "Yes, Jewel," he said with as much dignity as he could muster. "It's just that I've been worried about White Dove."

"Who is this White Dove, son? Angus didn't mention her."

"Just one of the Cherokee I met, Ma." Well, *just* wasn't right, but he wouldn't tell her that. "She's going to have a baby, and I'm not sure she'll make it to Oklahoma before it comes."

Jewel's expression turned from amused to horrified. "Oh, Matthias, I hadn't thought about that. Although I should have realized— as often as the Lord has blessed me and Angus with babies—that naturally, there'd be some coming for the Injuns along the trail."

Jewel pulled her skirts close to her body. "Is she as big as me?"

Matthias took another quick glance. "Bigger."

Jewel and Ma looked at each other. Some silent message passed between them.

"My baby is due to arrive in a month, Matthias. I'm hoping by Angus' birthday on the fifth. "

"Oh." A sick feeling filled his chest. White Dove and her people needed to leave right away, or she would have her baby on some stretch of that cursed trail.

His mother smiled sadly. "You'd better get along to the mill, son."

"Hurry," Jewel added, "or you'll be the butt of your brothers' jokes all day."

They were right. He should hurry. But he stood there for a long moment watching the milk foaming in their buckets. It took a lot of milk for all of them. Even so, two cows were sufficient to provide plenty for everyone. But his mother liked to keep a spare cow. The frontier was an unforgiving place, and survival was not a sure thing. Ma said you never knew if one of the cows would get sick and stop giving milk, or even die. But Ma took good care of them, and there was always fresh milk for all his nieces and nephews at every meal. And the women made butter and cheese. Whatever milk wasn't used for those purposes was poured out to the hogs so it didn't go to waste. Yes, a cow was a wonderful thing, another blessing he usually took for granted.

His mother looked up again, no doubt surprised to find he was still standing there. Finally, he turned and left the barn. He had done his Christian duty, and now his family had need of him. The thing to do was to get to work and stop worrying about things he could do nothing about.

He followed the path behind the barn to the sawmill. Along the way, he pulled rags out of his pocket and stuffed his ears with them. Turning logs into usable lumber was loud work.

Normally, they were able to keep the steam engine running all winter with little trouble. But with the unusually cold weather, the mill pond kept freezing over, and they spent the first hour every morning chopping through the ice with sledgehammers. It was essential to keep the area near the engine's water intake pipe open, for without water, there would be no steam to run the saw. Furthermore, without water there was no way to float the logs into position for the saw blades.

If the ice got thick enough on the pond to be safe, they'd be able to slide the logs to the saw instead of floating them to it. But until then, the danger of breaking through was too great for that, and so they continued to contend with the ice.

All that had already been done, and Duncan and Simon were man-handling logs with their ringdogs into the saw mill's hungry maw. The saw blade sliced away the outer layer of bark. On the other side, Angus took the bark and flung it onto a growing pile a short distance away. After all the bark was removed, they would run the log through the saw again. On each pass, an inch-thick oak plank would come out.

The ten-foot planks were heavy. Angus was quite capable of carrying them alone, but it was much less tiring and quicker with two men, so Matthias put on his gloves and hurried to take his place across from him.

Angus grinned when he saw him. "About time you got here, Runt," he shouted. Matthias was relieved to see that the wound on his cheek from McDonal's whip didn't look too bad. Even if Pa was right about it scarring, it wouldn't make his brother any less handsome. They each took an end of the plank and heaved it into the waiting wagon. He and Angus prided themselves on getting them perfectly aligned.

Just as there was an art to stacking lumber, there was a science to keeping the boiler stoked and the engine roaring. And that was their father's job. Pa had strict rules concerning every phase of the business. He was determined to keep everyone safe, or as safe as a man could be in the lumber business. Matthias enjoyed the work, even the lowliest jobs, like shoveling up the sawdust and stub ends of oak, hickory, and walnut littering the ground. No part of the tree was wasted. The sawdust fueled the boiler. And they all took armloads of the stubs up to the cabins to be used for firewood.

Matthias lost track of how many foot of plank he and Angus had loaded on the wagon. The saw shrieked, a board came out, and they stacked it. Usually, the rhythm kept him from thinking overmuch. Sometimes he liked to imagine what would be built from the fine lumber he cut. But today he saw no new barns, houses, or stores in his mind's eye. The only pictures in his head were of the people camped west of town burning rotted wood to try to stay warm.

Midmorning came, and abruptly Matthias found that he could not continue the work. His breath was coming out all wrong, and his heart throbbed in his chest as though he had just run all the way from the house. He left his place and went to sit on one of the upright logs they kept around for that purpose.

Angus shouted and Duncan pulled the switch on the mill. "You hurt?" Angus said into the silence.

His father came from behind the boiler looking worried. "Are you, lad?"

"No, Pa."

"Then what in tarnation are we stopping for?"

"Sorry, Pa." He told himself to stand right this minute, to stop being lazy and get back to work, but his legs refused to obey.

His pa studied him in puzzlement. "You rest a bit more, lad, and then go on and grease the pistons. I want 'em slicker'n deer guts on a door knob, you hear?"

"I will, Pa," he said.

"While we're stopped, I might as well file the blades." His father started to walk away, but when he realized that Matthias wasn't moving, he came back and sat down on the log next to him. "I dinnae understand what the problem is, lad."

"Begging your pardon, Pa. I cannot mind what you told me to do."

His father's face grew dangerously red. "Are you defying me, son?"

"Oh, no, Pa. I'd never do that."

"You're acting daft, lad. A nod's as good as a wink to a blind horse. Explain yourself."

"I cannot explain it," Matthias said. His father said nothing, just kept waiting for him to get out what was on his mind. At last, he gathered his courage and said, "I need to borrow a wagon, Pa. For lumber."

"Pray tell what for?" Lachlan said.

"For firewood, Pa. For the Indians."

His father's face grew redder still. "I thought you'd gotten that out of your system, lad. You spent three days on them when you should have been here helping your brothers. Three days for your Christian duty."

"I can't stay here, knowing they need help."

"Well, you're not burning my boards."

Matthias was aghast. "Of course not, Pa. I'll take some of those trees the ice took down. I can hitch up Nell and Bell to the sledge and—"

"Your head's on sideways, Runt," Duncan said. Until he spoke Matthias hadn't realized his three brothers had joined them. "Most of that is green wood and wouldn't burn for love nor money. Or maybe it was your plan to smoke out those Indians. It would take the Nell and Bell the biggest part of a day to drag the sledge there. And then you wouldn't be able to unload the trees. Not without the hoist."

Duncan was right. Something must be wrong with his head to come up with such a stupid plan. He expelled a breath and tried to tamp down his worry.

"You weren't thinking straight, lad," Lachlan said.

"I was thinking those people are cold and sick. They're dying, Pa."

"There's plenty of timber over that way. Why do they need mine?"

"Herman Stodges won't let them cut any. He rides around the camp just hoping to shoot someone."

"Stodges—the stupid fool." Lachlan kicked at a stub of hickory that lay on the ground near his feet. "Then gather up these stubs and take it to the Indians. I suppose I could give you another day."

"I've been thinkin' on that, Pa. But I figure I could fill the wagon to overflowing with stubs, and even so, it wouldn't be enough. The people would burn through them before they could finish cooking one meal. They need good, solid oak to burn."

Lachlan heaved a frustrated breath then folded his arms over his chest and glowered at his youngest son.

"Never mind, Pa. Forget I said it." Matthias rose from the stump to go get back to work.

Lachlan rose, too, and then wrapped his arms around Matthias and squeezed what air he had out of his lungs. "No, son. If it means that much to you…well, I reckon your Christian duty just turned into mine." Releasing him, he took his hat off and scratched his balding head. "Somehow."

Matthias smiled his thanks and worked on getting his breath to come right again. His heart still throbbed, but now it was from relief.

Duncan used a forearm to brush his unruly hair out of his eyes . "What did you have in mind, Pa?"

"Use the eyeballs the good Lord gave you, lad. There's a stack of dry timbers and planks in plain view."

"But, that's Cyrus' lumber, isn't it?" Simon said, looking confused.

"Of course it is. But it's our Christian duty to give Cyrus' lumber to the Injuns."

"How do you figure that, Pa?" Matthias said.

Lachlan smiled slyly. "It will take us a good while to cut enough lumber to replace Cyrus' stack over yonder, now won't it? Why, it might be summer before ole Cyrus gets that fancy new house he's hankerin' for. Just think of the patience the man's going to learn! And we, lads, will be the Almighty's instruments that'll help him learn it."

Angus laughed loudly. "I hope I'm around to see his face when the stingy old coot figures out what's burning to warm your friends, Matthias."

"Come help me hitch up the team, Angus," Duncan said. Then he grinned at Matthias. "While we do, Runt, you might as well go on and grease those pistons."

"Oh, all right," Matthias said.

Simon grabbed his arm and then grinned. "I suppose the mill won't suffer overmuch if I do your chore, Runt. Even though you're so much better at it."

"No, Simon," Lachlan said. "You and Matthias go on and hitch up the second wagon. It'll take both to get all the lumber to the Indians. We'll all go."

"We will?" Matthias said in wonder.

"Son, when we Fraileys do a thing, we do it right. Go on, lads and get started loading the wagons. I'll gather up as many crosscut saws as I can find and come help you."

***

THE PRESENT

"Why did you stop?" Abby said.

"Time for a pit stop," Merrideth said. "Sorry. I should have gone before."

When she got back from the bathroom, Abby and John were slumping in their chairs, hands hanging nearly to the floor, in a fair imitation of corpses.

"Should I start CPR?" Merrideth said.

John straightened in his chair. "No, but remind me why we're torturing ourselves like this."

"Because we want to see what Matthias does next."

"He is pretty wonderful, isn't he?" Abby said. "I've been thinking. Wouldn't it be cool to trace his family back to the first Frailey Christian back in Scotland. To see the prayers of the faithful, the influence that godly parents and grandparents exerted over their children."

"It would, wouldn't it?" John said. "Too bad we won't be able to tell Patty most of the things we've learned about the Fraileys."

"Why not?" Merrideth said. "She already knows about the program, something you didn't bother to mention to me, by the way."

"Oh, yes. Sorry about that," John said. "In the heat of the moment, we felt we had to tell Patty, but I sure don't want her to know that it's working again. Do you?"

"No, I guess not," Merrideth said. "I suppose I'm going to have to get used to keeping secrets from my clients, no matter how cool the information I find for them is."

"But surely we can tell Patty about how kind and wonderful Matthias Frailey was," Abby said.

John put an arm around his wife's shoulder. "You're too tired, honey, or you'd realize that we can't tell Patty anything that we cannot document some other way."

Abby sniffed. "Well, isn't that just horrible?"

"Tell me about it," Merrideth said. "I have to bite my tongue in class so I won't blurt out some interesting bit of history that I know my students would love. It doesn't stop me from learning all I can while I'm time-surfing. Who knows when I might someday uncover substantiation for it?"

"Okay, let's get back to it," John said.

CHAPTER 19

***

DECEMBER 6, 1838

Matthias nudged Champ's sides and his horse obediently broke into a trot the last mile to the camp. When he got there, Running Dog appeared at the side of the trail and waved him on. The camp seemed nearly deserted. The campfires were puny, smoldering things. Presumably the people had gone inside their tents to stay out of the wind.

He left Champ at the livestock corral and walked to White Dove's tent. No one was in sight, except for Awinita who was rocking her baby boy across the way. He was back to crying, his voice hoarse and piteously weak. The pumpkin Matthias left by her tent was gone. Could the child have possibly eaten two whole pumpkins and still be hungry? Awinita looked up and glared at him and then went back to her rocking.

Talisa poked her head out of the tent, but for once, she did not smile at him. She said something in Cherokee over her shoulder and then disappeared back into the tent. A moment later Nancy came out.

"How are you?" Matthias said.

"I am well, thank you."

"I am sorry it took me so long to return."

White Dove's muffled voice came from inside the tent. She was

back to speaking Cherokee. Angry Cherokee, from the sound of it.
"What did she say?"

"She said you are a—well, never mind."

Matthias studied Nancy's face, hoping to discover why White
Dove was angry, but it did not reveal the answer. She wrapped her
arms around herself and shivered. "I do not wish to be impolite,
Matthias Frailey, but I am going back inside now. It is a little
warmer than out here."

"Wait," he said, pointing toward Awinita's tent. "Where's the
pumpkin?"

Before Nancy could tell him, a storm of angry Cherokee words
erupted inside the tent beside him.

"White Dove said why did you pretend to help and then give
the babies rotten pumpkins."

"Rotten? Tell her those were fine pumpkins."

Nancy spoke and White Dove replied. They both sounded
angry.

"She says to tell you that they turned to string, and we had to
throw them all out."

He scratched his head in puzzlement, and then it came to him.
"They froze."

Nancy frowned in confusion. "Well, it is cold, you know."

"Don't you know you can't let pumpkins freeze?" The thought
of all of Alexander Buel's pumpkins going to waste made him want
to hit something. Of course they didn't know that! They wouldn't
have realized. The soldier had said the winters in Georgia never got
below forty degrees. They would never have seen the way freezing
temperatures turned a pumpkin into a watery, stringy mess, not fit
for man nor beast to eat.

"Tell White Dove I said not to worry. My mother sent an even
better gift for the little ones."

When Nancy finished interpreting, White Dove peeked out the
tent flap and said in English, "Sister, tell Matthias Frailey that we
thought he wasn't coming back."

Nancy smiled smugly. "*You* thought he wouldn't come back."

White Dove glowered at her sister.

"All right. Matthias Frailey, White Dove says to tell you—"

"Tell White Dove that I said I would come back, and I did."
She had no need to know that his resolve had ever wavered.

Nancy rolled her eyes. "You tell her. I'm going back inside."

She held the tent flap and at last White Dove came out. "What is this gift you speak of?"

"It will be here as soon as Pa and my brothers…" Matthias began. Then he cocked his head and smiled. "Listen. Can you hear it?"

From beyond the tents came the sound of his mother's spare cow informing the world that it was milking time.

White Dove smiled excitedly. Without thinking he grabbed her hand. "Come and meet Elsie." Then he dropped it in astonishment at his forwardness. Fortunately, she didn't seem offended.

"Your hands smell of cedar," she said.

"I cut some boughs for you from the woods behind our cabin."

She stopped in her tracks and stared at him.

"They're for your priest. For…well, you know."

She continued to study his face.

"Did I do wrong?" Perhaps the priest wouldn't want cedar from a white man for their Cherokee ceremonies.

She took his hand into her own. "You did right, Matthias Frailey. Exactly right."

"Oh, good. And there's another gift, too," he said, hurrying her forward. "But I'm going to need some of the men to help me unload it."

***

THE PRESENT

"Okay, stop," John said, grabbing the mouse. "I mean speed past this part. I'm not going to sit here watching them unload two wagons of firewood."

Merrideth huffed. "Well, maybe I would like to."

"You just want to watch Matthias Frailey flex those big muscles of his," John said.

"I do not." Did she? Yes, she did. But only because she wanted to watch everything he did. And more importantly, she didn't want to miss a single thought or emotion that he experienced. And that was just plain weird.

So she made herself take the mouse and begin fast-forwarding. She set it at a rate that still allowed them to get a sense of what was happening. And what was happening was a lot of grueling work.

Matthias and his father and brothers, along with a dozen Cherokee men, cut the lumber into usable pieces of firewood with crosscut saws. Others carried armload after armload, distributing it to all the campfires.

Merrideth didn't slow down enough to hear what was being said, but their body language spoke volumes. Everyone was all smiles now, even Owl, and Matthias was treated as a hero. Near nightfall the Fraileys left except for Matthias, who seemed set on remaining with the Cherokee. They didn't hear what Lachlan said, but he seemed resigned to his son's decision.

As night fell, the people's campfires lit up the sky over the camp.

"Okay, I'm going virtual again," Merrideth said.

***

DECEMBER 6, 1838

Matthias stared into the mesmerizing flames, tired but well satisfied with the day's work. It was not a huge fire, but seemed like a raging inferno compared to the puny one before. If everyone kept their fires small there would be enough wood to last a good while.

Painted Turtle's family and neighbors sat happily drowsing in the glorious warmth. Even Owl, who was there keeping company with Talisa, wore a contented smile. Awinita's baby slept in her arms, and her little girls leaned on her and each other, their eyes half closed. Elsie's milk, like the firewood, would have to be rationed along the trail. Even if it were summer when forage was plentiful and Elsie was in full udder, one cow could not provide enough milk for every child in the camp. But barring any accidents, she would give them enough for the littlest wayfarers to survive.

Eliza snuggled closer to Matthias and companionably leaned her head on his arm. He felt a strange flutter in his heart.

White Dove smiled at him, and his heart fluttered all over again.

Jacob poked at the fire with a stick. Painted Turtle spoke softly to him. Sighing reluctantly, he dropped it and then sat down beside little Amanda. Matthias covered a smile with his hand. He'd been fond of poking sticks at fires when he was the boy's age.

Painted Turtle stood and spoke briefly. The children got up and stumbled to the tent.

"Time for sleeping," White Dove explained for Matthias.

"And I was just thinking how nice it was not to have to crowd into the tent to stay warm for once," Nancy said, yawning sleepily. She followed her mother and the younger children inside. Then Owl and Talisa walked hand in hand into the darkness so they could say their goodbyes in private. And then it was just White Dove and Matthias. Even the neighbors had gone into their tents, except for an old woman who sat squinting at them from across the campfire.

"Your sister is funny."

"Nancy is the new Cherokee. Mother is tied to the old ways, as is Jacob. Eliza and Amanda are young. I do not know which path they will choose."

"What about you?"

"I am stuck in the middle—neither completely traditional nor completely civilized. I studied at the mission school and learned many new things. Good things. But the old Cherokee ways are strong in me yet. There is much good there, and we must not forget it.

"Of all of our family, Jacob suffers this...this *Removal* the most. Our father taught him to be a hunter. Taught him well. Jacob knows where the wild cats, the bear, and the panthers live in the forest. And how to walk noiselessly, to mimic the sound of a fawn so the doe will come close. His arm is strong on the bow and his aim is true. He could get game for us if the soldiers would let him hunt in these woods around us."

"That little boy who was poking at the fire with a stick?"

White Dove smiled. "Yes, that one. After Father died, Chief Hiawassee took Jacob to begin the training of a warrior. But the soldiers came before he was initiated. And now we go to this place where there are no forests. Who would train him anyway? Chief Hiawassee is too ill. Who will teach him to be a man?"

"What about some of your other men?"

She glanced at him and then went back to staring at the fire. "You wonder about my husband, but you do not ask."

"Yes," he said. "I wonder, but I do not ask."

She started to get up, and so he stood and took her hand to help.

"It is late, and I grow weary of sad talk. I will tell you tomorrow. If you are still here."

"I'll still be here. If the young men will let me sleep in their tent again."

She laughed softly. "Have no fear. You are a hero to them now. You are one *unaka* they'll always welcome." She smiled once more and went into her own tent.

Matthias put more wood on the fire and then went to see if it was true.

***

THE PRESENT

John stopped the action. "I'm going to fast-forward. Watching Matthias sleep would be about as exciting as watching grass grow."

Maybe for you, Merrideth thought. As for her, she couldn't get enough of watching him. "Virtual is better, John."

Abby sighed. "I'd like to remind you guys of time-surfing rule number two. Actually, I don't like reminding you. Why do I always have to be the one anyway?"

"Sounds like someone else is getting cranky, " John said. "But yes, I guess you're right. Even a tent made of Army-issue canvas counts as a bedroom."

"Matthias deserves his privacy, same as everyone else," Abby said. "Even if he's been dead for nearly two centuries."

"Don't say that!" Merrideth said and then felt herself blushing. "It's a horrible thought."

"I know," Abby said sadly.

"I'm sorry. I don't know what's wrong with me—just tired, I guess. Let's get back to it while we still can." Then Merrideth pressed *Fast-Forward*.

***

DECEMBER 7, 1838

Matthias found White Dove sitting near the fire rubbing her back. Her brows were furrowed, but she quickly put on a smile when she saw him. At least he hoped the smile was just for him. Perhaps he flattered himself.

Her hair hung down her back like a length of black silk. She ran her brush through it once and then hurriedly gathered it up and pinned it into her usual bun. Why did all that beauty have to be kept hidden away? It was a terrible custom.

He sighed and sat on his heels near the fire to warm his hands.

She rubbed her back again, then stopped when she saw that he watched her.

"Are you all right?" he said.

"I will be soon. Mother is making me one of her teas. Breakfast won't be for a while. Jacob isn't back from the supply wagon with our rations yet. Nancy is milking the cow."

Eliza and Amanda came scrambling out of the tent like happy puppies. "Come, girls, and I'll brush your hair," White Dove said.

The girls sat down next to their elder sister, and White Dove undid Eliza's braids and began to brush her hair.

You spoke to your sisters in English," Matthias said. "Do they understand it?"

"Quite a lot. We haven't practiced much lately. Until you came."

It was another gift to him, and he felt his heart swell.

Matthias went to Eliza and Amanda and said slowly, "Your hair is very pretty." He turned his eyes to White Dove and added, "It shines in the sunlight like a raven's wing." Just like your sister's, he thought but didn't say.

The little sisters giggled.

"Don't scorn my attempt at a poetic compliment," he said. "It is ever so much nicer than the one my pa would have said."

"What would he say?" White Dove said.

He laughed. "That their hair is blacker than the Earl of Hell's waistcoat."

White Dove's black eyes twinkled and a small smile formed on her lips for a brief moment.

He had hoped for a laugh, but perhaps some of the humor was lost in translation. When she was finished with her little sisters' hair, she shooed them away, and they went running to play with other children nearby.

Painted Turtle came out of the tent carrying a cup and spoon. She smiled distractedly at Matthias and then ladled hot water into the cup from the steaming pot at the campfire. She stirred it and then handed the cup to her daughter.

White Dove sniffed at it suspiciously. Painted Turtle said something to her, and White Dove cautiously took a sip. They exchanged smiles, and Painted Turtle went back into the tent.

"Not as bad as most of her teas."

"What is it?"

"Something for a woman who is with child. It is made from the root of the blue cohosh plant."

"I could get willow bark for you. It grows along Lusk Creek near our cabin. My mother uses it for all our aches and pains."

"It is good that you have willow in this harsh place. Mother is distressed that she has not seen other medicine plants growing here in Illinois. In Georgia, even in the winter there would be roots and bark to gather for her teas."

"It's not always like this. Come spring there will be many plants. Flowers will bloom everywhere. My mother doesn't use them for medicine, but she gathers them and puts them in jars to be pretty."

"Spring time in Georgia is…" She couldn't finish, and he saw that her throat worked as she choked back tears.

When she seemed to have her emotions under control he said, "It must be real nice there."

She wiped at her eyes. "Oh, it is. The young corn and squash turn our fields into green quilts. And when the peach trees bloom…" She stopped again, as if the subject of peaches was just too painful for her to contemplate.

After a moment, she swallowed hard and spoke again. "But before that, there is the festival of the first new moon in March. Our principle chief John Ross sends messengers to all the villages, announcing when it will be. He puts two times seven men in charge of the festival."

"Fourteen."

"I know my numbers, Matthias Frailey. I say two time seven for those are both sacred numbers."

"I do beg your pardon. Please continue."

"It takes much work for them to prepare for the festival. Hunters go out to get the meat for the feast and to prepare the deer skins. Jacob was to go with them next year. On the first night of the festival, women perform the friendship dance. They wear turtle-shell rattles on their ankles and wave cedar boughs as they dance. I was chosen to dance last year. On the second day of the festival we all go down into the river and let it cleanse us of impurities and bad deeds, much like Reverend Butrick's baptism. On the third day we fast. Do you Christians not also do this?"

"Yes, sometimes."

"Then on the fourth day we end our fasting with a huge feast and more dances. The elders tell the children stories of the old times and teach them Cherokee ways. All the old fires in Cherokee homes are put out. That night the priest lights a new sacred fire. Everyone will take coals from it to start their hearth fires again. Then the seven counselors perform the sacred night dance. At the end, the deer skins prepared by the hunters are presented to the festival priests. In the morning, everyone goes back to their villages until our chief calls us together for the next festival."

"How many festivals do you have?"

"There are seven in all. It is time for the winter festival now, but how can our chief call us to it? And where would we dance? Where would the hunters get the deer? And where would we get the sacred herbs for our rituals? If only we had listened to your president instead of our chiefs."

Matthias was shocked. "Andrew Jackson?"

"It is true, although I never thought I would say so. Your Jackson told our chiefs plainly that we must go by May twenty-third or the Georgia soldiers would come to drive us out. Many of our people sold their farms and left. They packed carefully and brought what was necessary for the trip. Already they have been in that Oklahoma country for many moons. Months.

"But Chief Ross said he would go to Washington and tell your President Jackson that we did not wish to leave our homes and our land. He would talk to the men who make your laws. He would tell them that they were breaking their own laws to treat us so. And this, he did. He and many other chiefs went to your capital and talked for many weeks. My husband Jesse Jones—he was chief in our village—he also went with them. Chief Ross sent him back to bring messages to the people from time to time. Always the news was bad. Always the white people still did not listen. But one day Jesse came with good news. The men of your highest laws—I don't know how to say this."

"The Supreme Court."

"Yes, your Supreme Court. They agreed with Chief Ross. They said we did not have to go. And so the people went happily back to growing their crops and feeding their cows and pigs. I went back to reading books and planning the museum. Chief Ross and the others stayed in Washington. But my Jesse came home to me. He said it was no use. No matter what your Supreme Court said, the Georgia soldiers were going to come. Jesse told the people of our village that we must run away and hide in the hills so the soldiers would not find us. Some of the people did, but most of the people stayed in the village because John Ross said they did not have to go."

"Why didn't you hide, then?"

"We did, Matthias Frailey." She rubbed her back and then looked up at him. "But the soldiers found us and herded us to the stockade in Charleston like cattle. We were lucky, I told Jesse, that at least we had time to pack our cart. But the cart was not so lucky after all. Near Chattanooga, a wheel broke, and when Jesse stopped to repair it, the soldiers said to leave it by the road. My husband tried to explain that it held our supplies, things necessary for the trip, but..." She turned away and studied the tea in her cup. "To my mother I say that others found and valued her medicines that we left behind on a Tennessee road. To myself I say that the white soldiers probably stomped them into the ground like trash."

"Perhaps you can find more medicines." His comment did not seem to be of any significance to her. Was he being a naive fool to suggest it? Or was she too crushed by suffering to hope for it?

"We had great need of Mother's things when Fox died. And all the others before him. And we will need them for the ones who will die next on this trail. If we do not perform our sacred rituals, how will our dead find their way to the Great Father?"

She sobbed, and started to turn away, no doubt intending to escape into her tent like she had the night before. But Matthias took her into his arms. Her large belly was awkward between them, but he ignored that. He tried to think of something to say, but couldn't, so he patted her back awkwardly and hoped she would stop crying. It came to him that she had not finished the story. He still did not know what had happened to her husband.

White Dove sniffed. "I am sorry. We are truly grateful for all you have done, Unaka. I will think of you when I am in Oklahoma."

"I want to stay with you." He hadn't known he was going to say it, but the words were true all the same.

She smiled sadly at him. "When we leave, will you follow also to the next camp?"

"I could—"

"And then the next camp? And the next? All the way to Oklahoma?"

He didn't answer, just looked into her black eyes.

"Go home to your family now, Unaka. And tell your mother and father we are most grateful— for the cow and for the firewood."

"I'll bring more tomorrow."

"What about the next Cherokee to come on the ferry to this place? Will you bring firewood to them? And the next? And the next? Until the Cherokee have burned all your father's trees? Go home, Matthias Frailey." She pulled away then lifted the tent flap and went inside.

He stood there staring stupidly at the tent for a moment, and then Painted Turtle came out of the tent looking sadly at him. He wondered how much she had understood of his conversation with White Dove. He tipped his hat and said, "Godspeed," in case she understood that much English. Nancy and the other children were gone, and so he could not bid them farewell.

There didn't seem to be anything else to do but go home.

The wranglers at the corral were back to giving him suspicious looks. He hoped White Dove would explain to everyone about the pumpkins. But at least Champ still liked him, although when they reached the road to Golconda and he had to pick his way around the frozen ruts, he seemed to lose a little of his good spirits.

Or maybe the gelding only sensed his own melancholy. Matthias guided Champ to the road's verge where the going was much easier. Champ was better off, but it did not make the way any easier for Matthias. No matter that he tried to banish White Dove and her family from his tired brain, they kept coming to him. The farther he went, the more unsettled he felt.

He told himself that White Dove was right. She would go on with her people to Oklahoma, and he would go back to his own family. He would pass along her thanks to his parents. And the Frailey family would know they had done their Christian duty to the Cherokee. More than their duty. Of course he would continue to pray for White Dove and her family each day. He would pray that wherever they were, they were warm and that they would make it to Oklahoma safe and sound. And that once they got there, they would adjust to what they found. He would even pray that White Dove would get to eat peaches again someday.

He would wonder about them from time to time, but eventually, his memories of them would fade. Brave Jacob. Funny Nancy. Pretty little Eliza and Amanda. And kind Painted Turtle with her shy smiles. In time, he wouldn't remember the man walking barefoot through the snow, and Awinita's hungry baby, and old people coughing in the night.

Most of all, he would not remember White Dove's flashing black eyes and raven wing hair. And especially he would not remember her courage, strength, and sense of humor while walking through hell.

A sound brought him out of his thoughts, and he immediately realized two things. First, he had reached Alexander Buel's house on the west side of Golconda without even noticing the urine smell. And second, Lieutenant Wheeler and Running Dog were trotting down the road toward him.

The lieutenant hailed him, and Matthias put a smile on his face the best he could.

When they were abreast of each other, the lieutenant tipped his hat and said, "Thanks again for your kind assistance, Mr. Frailey." But the men didn't stop or even slow their pace, and Matthias was left watching their backs as they rode off down the road.

"What's the hurry?" he called after them.

"We're breaking camp," Lieutenant Wheeler called back. "Right after breakfast."

Matthias nudged Champ and hurried to catch up with them. "Why? I thought you said—"

"Running Dog and I have just come from the ferry," Lieutenant Wheeler said. "Berry says the channel is free of ice for the present, and the next contingent is ready to cross. They will be upon us if we do not clear out of camp immediately."

"But you said the creeks are frozen," Matthias pointed out. "What will they do for water?"

"We'll just have to melt the ice. That's all we can do."

"If you can get the firewood to do it."

"I'll get it. Even if I have to shoot someone."

The men continued on, but Matthias reined Champ to a stop in the middle of the road. There was no reason to think the next contingent coming across the Ohio would be in any better condition than the first had been. They would need all the help they could get. But so would White Dove's camp. They would be in chaos trying to pack up and move out before the next group got there. And then they would be back on the trail to Oklahoma once again. Gone forever.

At the thought, a remarkable idea came to him. It was so stunning that it nearly knocked him from Champ's back. He laughed, his breath coming out in little puffs. He wheeled Champ around and nudged his sides. His faithful horse obediently broke into a gallop toward Golconda.

When he reached Cherry Street he found that it wasn't rutted much at all, so he urged Champ again until they were nearly flying. As early as it was, few people were on the street. Mrs. Sweeting was there and scolded him as he raced past. He paid her no mind, only slowing Champ when he came to the church. Good. The horse and buggy tied in front meant Reverend Miller was there, likely working on his sermon for Sunday. He worked at the church, Matthias knew, when he couldn't concentrate at home for the noise of his eight children. Matthias dismounted and tied Champ to the hitching post next to the buggy.

The church door was unlocked, and so he strode in, his boot heels pounding on the wooden floor. "Reverend," he called. "You in here?"

"What on earth?" Reverend Miller came out of the small room in back of the sanctuary, rubbing his spectacles and peering owlishly at him. "Matthias?" He put his spectacles back on and said, "Matthias Frailey, what is going on?"

"I need your help, sir."

"I hear you've been helping the Indians. That is commendable, Matthias, most commendable. Come with me. I have something for the cause."

"Thank you, Reverend Miller. I knew you'd want to help."

Matthias followed him into his office and watched as he knelt and opened a shipping crate behind his desk. When Reverend Miller rose, he held three Bibles and not the food and medicines he had hoped to see.

"Here, Matthias," he said, smiling proudly. "You can take the Word of God to the heathen."

Matthias took the Bibles and said, "Thank you, sir. I'm sure Reverend Butrick will be glad to have them." He tried to look into the crate to see what else it contained, but he couldn't see past Reverend Miller's black frock coat.

"I purchased a crate of Bibles some time back, but I'm embarrassed to say I'd forgotten about them until I heard the Indians had come. Hold out your arms, boy, and I'll load you up."

So there would be no food or medicine, then. Or warm coats or shoes.

"I'm sorry, Reverend, but I don't think I have room in my saddle bags for any more. And anyway… well, right now I have a more pressing need." At the startled look on the preacher's face, he quickly added, "Not that the Cherokee don't need Bibles, yes sir. It's just that…"

"Go on, boy. What do you need?"

"Well, I'd be obliged if you could marry me right quick, Reverend. That is, be ready to marry me if I can talk her into it."

Reverend Miller laughed. "Marry you? Why, you're just a boy."

"I'm no boy. I turned twenty in November."

Miller's eyes widened in surprise as if he'd just noticed that Matthias was a head taller than he was. "I suppose you're not, Matthias. Where's the bride?"

"I'll take you to her." Reverend Miller didn't move, just stood there looking stunned. "Could you hurry to your buggy, please?" In his hurry, Matthias nearly grabbed his coat sleeve before he stopped himself. Then he had a new thought. The buggy would splinter into a million pieces on the rutted road. "No, you'll have to ride your horse."

"Now wait just one minute, Matthias Frailey. If you're set on this, you bring the girl here and get married in church like a proper Christian."

"It's not that I wouldn't like to get married in church, sir. I always thought I would be married right here when the time came, but that's not going to work."

"Why not? Speak plainly, Matthias. You're trying my patience."

"I'm marrying White Dove, and she cannot leave the Indian camp, sir. So we'll have to go to her."

Reverend Miller's face turned purple and his eyes bugged out in a most alarming way. Matthias wondered if he should go get Sam Landis. He knew a little about doctoring.

"Has Satan got you in his grip, boy? You cannot up and marry a heathen girl. And what do you mean, if you can talk her into it? I should think she'd be thanking her heathen gods that a white boy wanted to marry her."

"If I don't marry her, Reverend, they'll make her go on down the trail and she'll likely die. And her baby with her."

"Baby? Why that's even more preposterous."

"It cannot be helped, Reverend."

"Marriage is a sacred institution, Matthias Frailey. Even if I ignored the idea of such an unholy union between the two of you, I'll not be a party to a sham—to a loveless marriage of convenience."

"But I do love her, Reverend. Or I will once we have enough time. And besides, isn't it our Christian duty to save lives?"

Reverend Miller harrumphed and then took off his spectacles and began polishing them again. "I'll think about it."

Trying to keep his disappointment from showing, Matthias said, "I might not be able to be married in my church, but I was sure hoping to have my pastor perform the ceremony."

"I said I'd think about it, Matthias."

There was no sense wasting any more time. Matthias nodded and turned to leave. He paused at the church door and said, "You'll have to come quick, if you're going to do it." Then he opened the door and went out.

***

THE PRESENT

Someone grabbed Merrideth's arm and she cried out.

Abby put a hand to her mouth. "Hush, Merri! It was just John."

"I was just trying to get you to fast-forward," he said.

"Well, you didn't have to assault me," Merrideth said.

"I didn't—whatever, sorry. You seemed really into the past. Too…I don't know what to call the feeling."

"Enthralled?" Abby said. "That's how I think of it."

"That sounds a bit extreme, like we don't have control," Merrideth said.

"Whatever it is," John said. "Let's get back to it. And fast-forward past Matthias' trip back to the camp."

CHAPTER 20

DECEMBER 7, 1838

The camp was as chaotic as Matthias had figured it would be. Everywhere people were gathering their belongings, few that they were. Those blessed with carts and wagons were repacking them. The wranglers were preparing the livestock for travel. Men were taking down the tents and rolling them into neat bundles, which others were stowing on the wagons.

Lieutenant Wheeler sat on his horse shouting in both English and Cherokee to hurry. He hadn't seemed drunk when Matthias passed him on the road, but now he slouched a little in the saddle and his eyes looked decidedly bloodshot. Matthias passed Private McDonal and a soldier he had heard called Smitty. They were assisting an old woman struggling to take down her tent. McDonal shouted impatiently at her to hurry. The bully was probably wishing Lieutenant Wheeler would move on to another part of camp so he could take his whip to her like he had to the blind man at the ferry.

Lieutenant Wheeler's command to hurry applied to Matthias, too. He would have to if he were going to be able marry White Dove in time. When he got to her tent he was surprised to find that no one had started packing yet. Only Eliza and Amanda were there, sitting beside the tent looking frightened at all the noise and confusion going on around them in the camp. They had not had their breakfast yet either. An iron kettle of water steamed at the fire, waiting for Painted Turtle to cook the family's morning mush.

"Where is everyone?" Matthias propped his rifle against the tent and went to squat on his heels in front of the little girls.

Eliza and Amanda smiled and said something in Cherokee. It didn't help, but he returned their smiles and patted their heads.

Then Jacob came, lugging one of the tow sacks the people used to carry their food rations from the supply wagons. The boy's face lit up when he saw him.

Why were they just now getting their food? The boy handed him the tow sack and Matthias saw that there was no salt pork, only cornmeal. He heaved a disgusted sigh. Were the people expected to walk all day without meat?

Matthias smiled at Jacob, even though inside he felt like punching a tree. "We had better hurry and get you all fed."

He started to pour the cornmeal into the kettle of boiling water, but Jacob grabbed his arm, said something fierce in Cherokee, and then handed him a wooden spoon. Yes, he should probably stir it. He seemed to recall that his mother did.

Nancy came into view, carrying a wooden bucket. "You're back. I told her you would be." She set the bucket she carried down by the tent and came over to him. "You have to stir that, you know."

"I did."

"The whole time," Nancy said, smiling with amusement. "Here. Let me." She took the spoon from him and began stirring.

"Where did everyone go?" Matthias said.

"I was over at Awinita's tent giving her some of the milk for her baby. Talisa is off somewhere with Owl. I don't know where Mother and White Dove are."

On the other side of the campfire. Awinita, baby on her hip, scurried about, her whimpering girls hanging onto her skirts. She did not seem to be accomplishing anything useful.

"She's going to need help packing, isn't she?" Matthias said.

"Yes. She always does. The soldiers get quite cross with her."

"What took you so long with the milking?" Matthias said. "Did Elsie give you trouble?"

"No, Elsie is a sweetheart. But it took time to get the milk to those who need it most. Woya and some of the other women came and tried to take the milk. I told them no, but they didn't get my meaning for the longest time."

"The same women who wouldn't help Awinita?"

"The same."

He laughed, imagining twelve-year-old Nancy holding her own against the grown women.

Soft murmuring came from inside the tent and Matthias realized that White Dove and her mother were in there and had been all along.

Nancy looked as surprised as he felt. She handed the wooden spoon back to him and said, "It's ready to eat." Then she lifted the flap and went into the tent. The quiet conversation inside the tent got a little louder.

Matthias stood there staring at the tent until he realized Jacob and the girls were holding their bowls out to him. He spooned some mush into each bowl, and they sat by the fire to eat.

After a while, Nancy came out of the tent looking strange and pale.

He handed her a bowl of mush, and she looked at it as if she didn't know what it was. Then she seemed to gather herself. "Yes, I should eat. You, too, Matthias. It will be a long day."

"I'll eat later." And God willing, it would be at his own home with White Dove at his side. "What troubles you?"

Nancy only glanced at him and then spoke in terse Cherokee to Jacob and the little girls. They gulped the last of their mush and went to put their bowls away.

"White Dove made water in the tent, and mother is giving her more blue cohosh tea." Nancy spoke again in Cherokee. Jacob started to go into the tent, but she blocked his way. She went back in and then came out first with Jacob's and then the little girls' packs. Then she and the boy began gathering up the various personal items around their tent and tucking them into the packs.

Matthias was shocked that White Dove, no matter how pregnant, had relieved herself in the tent instead of the latrine. He was equally shocked that Nancy had revealed her sister's embarrassing mishap to him.

His reaction must have shown. Nancy stopped her preparations and looked up at him. "She didn't...." A smile flickered and was gone. "Her birth waters, Matthias. The baby is coming. Coming soon."

"It is? Now?"

"Now."

Across the way, McDonal and Smitty had come to take down Awinita's tent. The woman began wailing. The soldiers shouted at her, and the children joined in their mother's chorus. Nancy and Jacob continued to pack up the family's belongings.

"I need to talk to White Dove," Matthias said. "This very moment."

"Now is not a good time, Matthias."

Painted Turtle stuck her head out of the tent flap and looked at the commotion over at Awinita's tent. She spoke to Nancy and went back inside.

"What is it?" Matthias said. "Is White Dove all right?"

"I think so," Nancy said. "But Mother says she cannot be moved right now."

Matthias put his mouth close to the tent flap and said softly, "White Dove?"

Painted Turtle popped open the flap, startling him so much that he stumbled back and landed with a thud on his backside. Nancy said something to Painted Turtle, and she retreated back into the tent.

Matthias got off the ground and put his ear to the tent again. He heard what sounded like panting. Then it faded away, and White Dove's voice came softly to him. "What is it, Matthias? I am trying to have a baby, you know."

"I know now is not a good time, with you being busy and all. But you see, the soldiers are coming to take down the tent, and I was wondering—"

"Do...not...let...them—"

"I will not let them. I give you my word." The panting came again, and then a low groan. Matthias pulled his ear away from the tent in alarm.

"Should I put out the fire, Matthias?" Nancy said.

"Wait until we hear from Lieutenant Wheeler. He may want to leave the fires for the new people." He put his ear back to the tent. Painted Turtle was chanting softly.

"White Dove?"

"I have not left the tent, Matthias."

"I was wondering if...well, I was wondering if you would marry me, please." The panting came again. It was louder this time. Did it mean that the baby was almost there? Or that White Dove was disgusted at the thought of marrying him?

The panting died away, and Nancy said, "Ask her again."

Matthias took Nancy's cloaked arm. "I've been meaning to ask you…" He pulled her a little further from the tent. "He *is* dead, isn't he?" he whispered. "She never finished her story, you know."

"Who?"

"Her husband, who else? I mean I assumed so, but—"

Nancy gave him a small worried smile. "Well, I'd hardly tell you to ask White Dove to marry you if Jesse was still alive, now would I?"

Matthias let out a relieved breath and went again to the tent. "White Dove?"

"Go away, Matthias. I have to think about the baby now."

Nancy spoke in Cherokee to her sister, and White Dove responded in kind. Nancy frowned and shook her head.

"What did she say?" Matthias said.

"She said we should go away and stop bothering her. She won't listen to reason. I think it's the tea Mother gave her."

Across the way, McDonal and Smitty had finished folding and tying Awinita's tent. They started purposefully toward White Dove's tent. Matthias positioned himself in front of it.

Private McDonal glared at Matthias. "You again. Are you going with us to Oklahoma?"

"No. I surely am not."

"Well, stand aside so we can get this here tent."

"You go on and get the other tents first."

McDonal drew himself up and took a step forward. "You don't get to tell me what to do, Frailey."

Rolling his eyes, Smitty grabbed his coat sleeve. "Come on, McDonal. It don't make no difference which tent we do first."

McDonal shook his hand off and then poked Nancy in the chest. "Why aren't you packed up and ready to go, little squaw?"

Nancy's eyes lost their lively and intelligent gleam, and her face went blank. Then she lowered her head in a humble way that made Matthias sick to his stomach.

"Keep your hands off her, McDonal," Matthias growled.

"There you go again, telling me what to do."

Smitty shoved his friend away from Nancy. "Come on, McDonal, before you do something stupid."

McDonal wiped at his mouth and glared at Matthias. "We'll be back."

When they were gone, Matthias tilted Nancy's face up so that she would read his eyes. "Do not be afraid. I won't let anything happen."

Nancy smiled. It was a wobbly thing, but a smile nonetheless. "I'm not afraid, Unaka."

"Good." He put his ear back to the tent. It was completely silent. Maybe the baby was already born. But wouldn't it cry or something? "White Dove? Did you have the baby yet?"

He heard a choking sound and his eyes went wide. Then he realized that White Dove was laughing. "What's so funny?"

"You are, Matthias. Babies take a very long time to be born."

"Did you hear what I asked you before?"

"I did, but I thought that I had dreamed it."

"I know that it is a terrible thing to ask you. You grieve still for your husband." The panting came again, so he waited to continue. When it ended, he said, "White Dove? The preacher will be here soon. I hope. And then we can—"

"Matthias, you are being ri…rid…I don't know how to say it."

"Ridiculous?"

"Yes, that word. You are a very nice *unaka* to ask me. But even if I did not still grieve for Jesse, I could not marry you."

"Why not?" Why did *nice* sound so horrible when she said it like that?

"How could I let…my…family…go on…while I…?" Then White Dove lapsed into Cherokee.

"She said something about the white man's luxuries," Nancy said. "I didn't get it all."

White Dove was panting harshly, but Matthias spoke anyway because he found he could not wait another moment to clear up the misunderstanding. "Oh, White Dove, don't worry about that. I will marry all of you, from Painted Turtle down to little Amanda. Then none of you will have to go to Oklahoma."

Nancy nudged him in the ribs with her elbow, and Matthias turned and saw that Private McDonal and Smitty were back. Jacob stood in front of them, trying to prevent them from approaching.

"Sorry, Frailey," Smitty said. "This is the last tent before we move on to the east side of camp."

Matthias saw that it was true. Most all of the tents were down, except some in the distance. The few still standing nearby were being handled by men capable of the task. People were lingering near the fires, waiting to be told when they must resume the journey.

"I'll get this one for you," Matthias said.

McDonal pushed Jacob aside and said, "We're not waiting any longer for this here tent, Frailey."

"Well, you'll have to," Matthias said. "There's a woman inside having a baby."

"She can ride in the wagon," McDonal said and took a step forward.

Matthias shoved him back. "Not yet, she can't."

White Dove cried out in Cherokee.

Nancy grabbed his coat sleeve. "She says not the wagon, Matthias. Galilahi's babe was born dead. Mother thinks it was all the jolting while the babe was being born."

"Then the squaw can born her brat on the ground, for all I care," McDonal said. "We're taking the tent."

Jacob put himself back in front of the soldier, and once again McDonal shoved the boy away. "And *you* brats get started walking."

Matthias lifted his rifle from where it leaned against the tent, and held it in his arms. "You're not getting the tent until I say so, McDonal. Now I suggest *you* start walking."

McDonal, his face murderously red, took another step forward. Matthias leveled his rifle at him. Still he came, so he cocked the gun. The sound stopped McDonal in his tracks.

"You'd shoot me?" he said in amazement.

Matthias wasn't sure what the answer to that question was. Pa had taught him never to aim a gun at something he wasn't prepared to shoot. Could he pull the trigger? He didn't know, so he kept his mouth shut and his rifle trained on the man in front of him.

After a long moment, McDonal said, "Well, we'll just see what Lieutenant Wheeler has to say about that." He stormed off. Smitty followed, shaking his head in disgust. Matthias wasn't sure if it was for him or McDonal.

Painted Turtle came out of the tent and watched them leave. She smiled at Matthias. Then she turned to Nancy and spoke. Nancy interrupted her several times, and their discussion went on for a long while. Then Painted Turtle patted Nancy's cheek and went back into the tent. After a moment, Matthias heard her soft chanting again.

"What was that all about, Nancy?" Matthias leaned the rifle against the tent again, hoping he wouldn't have to point it at the lieutenant.

The girl's eyes were mutinous. "She says that we are to go on with the others where there will be food and warmth for us." She spat the words like bullets. "She says that she will stay with White Dove until the babe is born, and then they will catch up with us. How can she care for White Dove and the babe without a tent and supplies? And they'd never catch up with us anyway."

"That's not going to happen," Matthias said, pacing in front of the tent.

"That's what I said, but she won't listen."

The sound of White Dove's groans came to them. Nancy shepherded the younger children to the far side of the campfire then came back to stand next to Matthias near the tent.

"I've got to have an answer," he said. "Watch for the preacher, would you? I'm going in."

She put a hand on his arm. "I wouldn't do that if I were you. Birthing is a messy and undignified thing. She'd never forgive you if you saw it."

"Then *you* go in there and talk to her. I need to know before they come back."

"Too late."

He turned and saw that Lieutenant Wheeler rode toward them. McDonal and Smitty were half running along behind him, trying to keep up.

Matthias hurried to intercept them before they got any closer to White Dove's tent. If there was going to be a fight he didn't want to disturb her with it.

"You forgot your gun, Frailey," McDonal said. "Now you're not such a big man."

"I left it at the tent so I wouldn't be tempted to shoot you."

Lieutenant Wheeler gave McDonal a disgusted look. "Why are you two soldiers following me like puppies? Get back to work."

"Yes, sir," Smitty said, pulling McDonal with him. McDonal was steaming mad. Matthias figured that if looks could kill, he'd be a goner.

"What's this about a squaw that won't come out of the tent, Mr. Frailey?" Lieutenant Wheeler said.

"It's White Dove, sir. She's about to have her baby in there. Then I'll get the blasted tent to you. I give you my word. Or no, I'll pay for the tent, Lieutenant." Then he remembered that his pockets were empty. "I'll have to go home to get the money, but I'll catch up to you and—"

"Forget the money, Mr. Frailey." The lieutenant burped softly behind his hand. "As you well know, we need every blessed tent that the U.S. government, in its infinite wisdom, saw fit to give us. They're crowded as it is. Besides, it's the woman inside the tent I am more concerned with, because it is my unfortunate obligation— my sworn duty, to be specific—to get every last one of these Indians to the Oklahoma Country."

"She needs more time, Lieutenant."

"That is not possible, I'm afraid, Mr. Frailey. I am commanded not to permit any of the Indians to stay behind when we leave a site. And we are nearly ready to do so."

"But you see, sir, I'm fixin' to marry White Dove. If I can talk her into it. Then she won't have to go, will she?"

Lieutenant Wheeler stared at him. "No," he said slowly as if trying the idea out in his brain. "With the protection of your name, she wouldn't have to go. But marry her, boy? That's mad."

"No, it's this trail, this *Removal*, that is mad, sir. I'd do anything to save them from it."

"You can't save them all, Mr. Frailey."

Matthias looked sadly out over the camp for a long moment. "No, sir," he said, turning back to Lieutenant Wheeler. "But I can save this family."

White Dove cried out, and the lieutenant's expression softened. Then he looked back at Matthias. "All right, boy. There's not much time left, but I'll give you what there is of it. When the last wagon pulls out, that woman will be on it unless—"

"But, Lieutenant—"

"You didn't let me finish, Matthias. As I was saying, *unless* you can talk her into marrying you. Although why she isn't jumping at the chance is a mystery to me."

"Thank you, sir. But I am fully aware of all that I'm asking White Dove to give up in order to marry me."

Not waiting to watch him leave, Matthias hurried back to the tent. "White Dove? Can I come in?"

White Dove gasped. "No!"

Nancy smirked at him. "I told you so."

"How much longer, do you think, White Dove?" Matthias said.

"Mother says another hour…or two…or three. But the pains have slowed, so I will keep my promise."

"To marry me?" he said, surprised.

"I never promised that. But I did promise to tell you about my husband. I will tell you, and then you can go home to your family."

Matthias turned to Nancy and whispered, "What am I going to do? Can you talk sense into her?"

"White Dove?" Nancy said. "There is no time for stories. You must marry Matthias. As soon as the preacher gets here."

White Dove responded in angry Cherokee, interspersed with harsh panting.

"She insists that you should know about her husband." Nancy rose on her tiptoes and whispered in his ear, "I think she must do this before she will allow herself to listen to you speak of marriage."

"Oh." He smiled. Maybe there was hope yet. "Yes, White Dove, I want to hear what happened to Jesse. But Nancy will tell me so you can save your strength for the baby."

Smiling grimly, Nancy pulled him a short distance away from the tent. "When our cart broke down on the road near a place called Chattanooga, White Dove's husband Jesse said to the soldier, 'I can repair this in five minutes.' But the soldier did not want to hear what he said. So Jesse did not listen to him either. He bent to continue working on the wheel, and the soldier hit him in the head with the butt of his rifle. Jesse fell and his blood and brains leaked out onto the road."

Matthias felt like howling. "Which one? McDonal? I will shoot him for sure."

Nancy put a restraining hand on his coat sleeve. "No, not that one. Later, the soldier who killed Jesse was taken away."

"Go on," he said.

"White Dove would not leave Jesse. She would have stayed there and let the soldier kill her, too, but Mother and I pulled her away from there. We told her that she must live so the baby would live. The soldiers dug a hole in the ground and put Jesse in it. But they wouldn't let us gather cedar boughs for his grave, nor allow us to perform our sacred burial rituals. Now…" Her throat worked as she struggled to keep her emotions in check. "Now Jesse may not be able to find his way to the Great Father. It is the thing that most disturbs my sister."

Matthias scanned the camp. There wasn't a single tent left standing but White Dove's. The wagons were rolling into formation. The people were lining up. He should press her again to marry him. Perhaps with her verbal promise alone, Lieutenant Wheeler would let her stay behind. Marrying him could possibly save her life, but how much longer would it take to talk her into it? What if in the end she still did not agree? What if she went on down the trail and lost both her life in this world and her place in the next one because he had taken so much time explaining why she needed him that he ran out of time to explain why she needed the Savior?

He went back and put his face close to the tent. "White Dove? I am very sorry about Jesse. And I am sorry that they wouldn't let you do your rituals for him. Our rituals, yours and mine, they are good things. But the Great Father doesn't need them." She didn't respond, but he sensed her interest. Or maybe he only hoped for it.

"The Great Father you speak of, he knows all things. He knows where you are, White Dove. He knows your suffering on this trail. His son Jesus suffered, too. And it is his suffering that cleanses us of our impurities and bad deeds. Not our baptisms, our fasting, our hymn singing, our churches, our sacred dances. The Great Father wants only for us to believe in his son Jesus. For he is mighty to save. Even if all the rivers of the earth freeze over. Even if all the turtle shell rattles are gone. Even if every last cedar tree and sacred herb are gone. It is his suffering and death that saves us, not all those things."

She began to pant again. While he waited for it to end, he prayed that his words would make sense to her.

"Reverend Butrick speaks of these things," White Dove said. "But your Jesus is a white god, is he not? How can a Cherokee have a white god?"

Matthias' heart beat fast with hope. "Didn't you know, White Dove? Jesus wasn't...isn't... white. He's brown like you. And he's not just my Jesus. He is the way for all to find the Great Father."

"Tell me more about this."

"I will, I promise. But...well, have you thought about it? Marrying me, I mean?"

"I might have. A little."

"Could you try to think about it more? There's not much time left."

She didn't answer.

"My brothers and I built a snug little cabin in the woods. It's nearly finished," Matthias said, picturing it in his mind. "And they'll help me add on so there will be plenty of room for everyone. We'll build a room for Painted Turtle. Jacob can have one side of the loft, and Nancy and the little girls can have the other."

"What about…?" Her panting was louder this time, and the time from the last one seemed shorter. Matthias glanced at Nancy and the other children then whispered through the canvas, "You're wondering about where we will sleep?"

"Yes," White Dove said.

"You'll have a warm bed by the fire, and…I'll sleep with you, if you'll let me."

"What if… I don't… want you to?"

"Then I won't until you do want me to. Only say you'll marry me, White Dove, so I can care for you."

She was silent for a moment. Then she said, "If we don't… remain with the people… Jacob will not…become a warrior."

The panting and chanting reached alarming new levels. Matthias paced until the sound faded. "I can't teach him your ways, White Dove. But I'll teach him everything I can about being a man. My brothers will help, too. I know I'm young, but I'll be a good father to Jacob. The girls, too."

After a moment White Dove gasped, "The girls…won't get to…dance…." She resumed her panting. It sounded harsher to his ears than before.

"The friendship dance? I know, White Dove. I'm sorry about that. But we'll have barn dances. They'll like that. And we'll grow lots of good food—corn, and beans, and squash. The three sisters, like you said. You'll never be hungry ever again. I give you my word. And your milk will flow for your babe, and all the others God will give us. I promise, White Dove."

The panting had ended, but still she did not answer. He could not think of anything more to say. The ties of family and culture were too strong. White Dove would go on down the trail with her people.

He turned away from the tent and saw that White Dove's brother and sisters were waiting expectantly. Funny Nancy, brave

Jacob, sweet little Eliza and Amanda. Would all of them make it to the Oklahoma country? Or would one or more of them fall to disease or mishap along the trail? Would White Dove have enough milk to feed her baby, or would she watch the child sicken and die as the other mothers had?

Nancy looked into his eyes for a moment, and then her face crumpled in dismay when she realized that he had given up on White Dove.

***

THE PRESENT

John reached over and stopped the action. "In a way, I'm relieved," he said. "I was beginning to lose faith in the U.S. Census Bureau."

"Relieved?" Merrideth glared at him. "Matthias' heart is breaking that he couldn't talk White Dove into marrying him!"

"Of course he couldn't," John said. "He has to marry Emmaline."

"Well, it's a horrible ending," Abby said. "What will become of White Dove and her family?"

"It's not a romantic movie, Abby," John said.

Merrideth wiped the tears from her eyes and blew her nose. "He's right, Abby. In real life there are seldom happy endings."

"More than you realize, Merri Christmas," John said.

John smiled, but he looked terrible, Abby, too. The sleepless night and the emotional intensity of what they had just witnessed had taken a toll on them all. No telling what she looked like. Her head ached, and her eyes were so gritty that she could hardly blink.

"Why did you stop, anyway, John?" Abby said, wiping her eyes.

"This is the perfect place, actually. What did you think of what Matthias just told White Dove?"

"You're asking me?" Merrideth said.

"Yes. I'm curious about your reaction."

"He was wonderful. Too bad there aren't more men like him today."

"You don't find him repugnant for foisting his beliefs upon her?"

"Oh, that. You want to talk religion."

"No, I want to talk about Jesus. You do believe in him, don't you, Merri?"

"You know I do, John. Why do I get the feeling I'm on the witness stand?"

"Oh, no, Merri! That's the last thing I intended."

"Good, because I've seen you in the courtroom, Atticus Finch, and I don't think I'd care to have you grill me."

"Just answer this, Merri, was Jesus a liar?"

"Of course not." The thought of it gave Merrideth a jolt.

"Then perhaps he was insane—delusional, maybe—when he claimed to be God."

"No one has ever accused him of that, John, and you know it."

"Maybe not consciously, but they might as well have."

"What's your point? Just spit it out."

"John's point is that you believe in Universalism, kiddo," Abby said.

"Universalism?"

"Let's leave that for the moment, Abby. My point, Merri Christmas, is that if Jesus wasn't a liar or insane, then we have no reason not to believe him when he claimed to be the only way to God. The only way to Heaven."

"He never said that," Merrideth said. Did he? Surely not.

"'I am the way, the truth, and the life. No man cometh to the Father but by me.' It's a rather straightforward statement, don't you think?" John said. "No matter how politically incorrect that might sound."

"The Cherokee culture should have been respected, not obliterated," Merrideth said.

"Of course it should," Abby said. "Don't you think Matthias respected White Dove's culture?"

"But respecting other people's traditions doesn't mean you have to agree with them," John said. "You can't, you know, because Christianity is mutually exclusive. Which is why if what Jesus said is true, and Matthias believed so, then he had a moral obligation to *foist* his religion upon White Dove. From her explanation of the Cherokee belief system, I got that they were not polytheists as I had always assumed. So they believed in one God—the Great Father. But they didn't know about Jesus' redeeming work. And that was good news they desperately needed to hear. Matthias felt that he couldn't let her go down the trail without presenting this truth to her, even if it meant running out of time to marry her."

Merrideth tried to think of a tactful way to get John and Abby off her back. They were her oldest and dearest friends, and she wouldn't offend them for the world, but she was too tired to listen to them talk about religion for one more second. She opened her mouth, hoping nothing insulting would come out.

"Okay, that's all I wanted to say about that," John said, smiling tiredly.

Abby sighed. "I'm happy that White Dove got the chance to hear the Gospel even if she didn't marry Matthias."

"Well," John said. "Now what do we do now? Fast-forward to see who Matthias does marry? This Emmaline person?"

"Yes, Emmaline Jones," Merrideth said. Then the pieces snapped into place. "Oh, you guys! Yes! Emmaline Jones."

"What about her?" John said. "Is your exuberance just a byproduct of sleep deprivation? I'm worried I may start seeing large white rabbits soon."

"Never mind," Merrideth said. "You'll see I'm right."

"About what?" Abby asked plaintively.

"Just humor her, my love," John said, patting his wife's back.

"Ha. Ha. Watch and learn, my friends," Merrideth said and unpaused the scene.

CHAPTER 21

***

DECEMBER 7, 1883

White Dove's soft voice came from inside the tent, and a glimmer of hope rose in Matthias' chest. He turned eagerly back and put his head close to the canvas. "I didn't hear you, White Dove. What did you say?"

"Peaches," she said. "Would we have peaches?"

Matthias laughed with delight. "All the peaches you can eat, and that's a promise."

Nancy slapped him on the back. "Congratulations. I think that's a *yes*. Where's that preacher of yours?"

Matthias sighed. "Apparently mine isn't coming. Can you go find Reverend Butrick?"

Nancy smiled. "Look."

Reverend and Mrs. Butrick's wagon came rumbling up to the tent. They wore similar expressions of surprise and perplexity.

"Why are you not ready to go?" Butrick said.

"Because we were waiting for you, Reverend," Matthias said, grinning happily.

"White Dove and Matthias are getting married," Nancy said.

"That is, if you agree to perform the ceremony," Matthias added.

"Oh, oh," he stuttered. "I'd be honored to." Butrick nearly fell in his haste to get down from the wagon.

Clara Butrick took her husband's hands and safely descended. "Oh, that's wonderful."

"Except that we shall have to leave them all behind," Butrick said. "Have you thought of that, Clara?"

"I realized it at once, dear. We shall sorrow over that later." She dabbed at her eyes and put on a bright smile. "Nancy, is White Dove in the tent getting all gussied up? I mean to say, is she putting on her best dress?"

"No," Nancy said. "She's not wearing much of anything right now."

"Why is White Dove unclothed, pray tell?" Reverend Butrick's expression turned indignant. "Did you get the order of events backward then, Mr. Frailey? Customarily the wedding comes first, then the—"

"I think you are under a misapprehension," Matthias said stiffly. "Nothing untoward has happened, sir, I assure you. White Dove is just concentrating on—"

"Mr. Frailey, I have slandered you, and I do beg your pardon."

"That's all right, Reverend, but if you don't mind, could we get on with the wedding?"

A moment passed. Matthias realized his foot was tapping and made it stop. "We're in a bit of a hurry, Reverend."

"I'm in a hurry myself, Mr. Frailey. Lieutenant Wheeler wants my wagon near the front. We shall commence with the wedding the very moment White Dove comes out."

"I'm sorry, Reverend, but she cannot come out."

"Well, why ever not?"

"I thought you knew. She's...you know." Matthias wrung his hat with his hands.

Mrs. Butrick gasped. "She's having the baby?"

"Right now?" Reverend Butrick said.

"Yes," Matthias said. "But you can still marry us, can't you?"

Reverend Butrick's eyes went round as saucers. "That would be highly irregular, Mr. Frailey. Why, I've never heard tell of such a thing." He turned to Clara. "Have you, dear?"

"No, Daniel, I have not."

Reverend Butrick took a fortifying breath. "But under the circumstances, I don't suppose there's really any reason why I cannot perform the ceremony." He looked at the tent. "If you are sure White Dove's is in there."

"She's in there all right," Nancy said.

"Well, as long as she is willing."

"Yes," White Dove gasped. "I say yes...to Matthias. Now...everyone... please go away."

"I'm sorry, dear White Dove," Reverend Butrick said. "But I have to say at least a few words." Then he spoke in Cherokee, and Painted Turtle answered.

"He asked Mother if she gave her permission," Nancy explained for Matthias.

"Well, did she?"

"Oh. She said she was honored to have this unaka in the family."

"Who will be the witnesses?" Reverend Butrick said.

"I know about unaka weddings." Nancy smiled proudly and then spoke rapidly in Cherokee. At her words, Daniel, Eliza, and Amanda beamed and came and stood by Matthias. "The girls and I will stand witness for White Dove," Nancy said. "Daniel will be your witness, Matthias.

"I wish I had flowers to give White Dove," Matthias said.

"You gave us... something...even better," White Dove said breathlessly.

A moment later, Painted Turtle stuck her head out of the tent, smiled, and handed Nancy two of the cedar boughs Matthias had brought from his home.

Reverend Butrick cleared his throat nervously. "All right, we can begin now."

Nancy tugged on his coat sleeve. "Wait, please." Then she said, "White Dove?"

"Yes...little sister?"

"Don't you think this is a good time to tell Matthias what your English name is?"

"She has an English name?" Matthias said.

"Yes, she chose hers the same time we all did. Even Mother took an English name. But they stopped using them when the soldiers came."

"Emmaline," White Dove said.

Matthias smiled. "It's a right pretty name. But if it's all right with you, I might call you White Dove sometimes."

Nancy smiled mischievously. "Not her Cherokee name

Tsistunagiska?"

"I'll try," Matthias said. "If Emmaline will teach me."

"All right," Reverend Butrick said again. "I could say a lot about the sacredness of marriage between a man and woman, but I'll keep this abbreviated due to the circumstances. I'm sure your own pastor will want to talk to you both, Matthias."

Matthias nodded his head in agreement, although he doubted that would ever care to hear what Reverend Miller had to say on that subject or any other.

Reverend Butrick harrumphed and then intoned, "Then, Matthias Frailey, do you take Emmaline Jones to be your lawful wife to have and to hold from this day forth, in sickness and in health?"

"I do." He'd said it boldly, even though inside he felt like he had when he was five and stood on the bank of the mill pond, trying to get the courage to jump in for the first time. The faces of his family came to him, and he wished desperately that they could be there to see him getting married.

Pulling himself back to the moment, he saw that Reverend Butrick was smiling broadly. "And do you, Emmaline Jones, take Matthias Frailey to be your lawful husband to have and to hold from this day forth, in sickness and in health?"

A gasp came from the tent. And then White Dove— Emmaline—groaned. The question went unanswered. Painted Turtle murmured something, and then the panting and chanting resumed.

Everyone wore concerned expressions, and Matthias felt sure his own face showed the misery he felt. When Emmaline cried out again, he left Reverend Butrick's side and paced back and forth in front of the tent. If only there were some way he could take the pain in her place, at least hold her hand or wipe the sweat from her brow. It was all he could do to restrain himself from rushing into the tent.

Then all fell quiet, as if he were swimming underwater. A part of him knew that the camp was noisy with the people's preparations. And that Nancy and the others talked among themselves in hushed voices. And that his pacing to and fro made a noise. But for him, all was silent as he tuned his ears toward the tent.

Into the silence came the cry of a baby, and with it, finally, the other sounds flooded back to his ears. Everyone spoke at once, laughing for joy over the new arrival. Nancy spoke in Cherokee with her mother through the tent wall.

"It's a boy!" Nancy said.

Matthias hugged the others and grinned like a fool. But his happiness was tinged with sorrow, his thoughts tinged with fancifulness. Were the baby's tears for himself only, to express his outrage at being expelled into the cold world? Or did he cry for the whole Cherokee Nation, for the outrage of their expulsion from their homes?

After a short time, the baby stopped crying, and then Painted Turtle brought him out of the tent and placed him in Matthias' arms. He looked down at the tiny wrinkled face and then at Nancy and the other children who crowded around to see their little nephew.

He knew suddenly that the little cabin in the woods that he had described for White Dove would never do for her. It was too near town, where the Cherokee weren't welcome. Where they had been prodded like cattle down Main Street to the jeers of Herman Stodges and his circle of bigoted friends. No, he would take his family somewhere else, some place where they would never feel shame again. And there he would build a new cabin for them all.

First, though, he would take them home, where Ma would feed them until their cheeks were plump with health, and Pa would put the little girls on his knees and tell them stories. He knew without a shadow of doubt that his whole family would accept them. And Emmaline would see how much love there was among the Fraileys, so that when he left his people behind, as she had left hers, she would understand that he did so out of love for her and not for Christian duty.

"Aren't we forgetting something?" Reverend Butrick said.

"What?" Matthias said.

A soft laugh came from inside the tent. "I do," Emmaline said, and everyone laughed with her.

"Can I come in now?" Matthias said.

"Yes, please, Husband," she said.

**

THE PRESENT

John clicked off virtual mode and turned the sound down.

Merrideth barely restrained herself from grabbing the mouse and taking herself right back to Matthias' time. She struggled to analyze her feelings. On the one hand, she was happy that Matthias had found love, really she was. And happy, too, that White Dove and her family would survive because of his actions. But she also recognized a bit of the green-eyed monster in herself, a definite twinge of jealousy—more than a twinge—that left her feeling ashamed. And even though she sat within mere inches of her best friends, there was a bone-deep loneliness at the knowledge that Matthias wasn't real, not for her. What kind of pathetic woman fell in love with a man made of pixels on a computer screen? A man six years younger than she—that is if he were living in the present—a man that, as Abby had so bluntly reminded her, had been dead for nearly two hundred years.

"That was so sweet I can't stand it," Abby said and then sobbed on John's shoulder. He kissed the top of her head and rubbed her back. But he didn't speak.

Neither did Merrideth. She knew that if she opened her mouth, she would break down and cry. And when she cried, which was seldom, she preferred to do so in private. Among all the emotions her tired brain was trying to process was a painful sense of disappointment that her nation, sweet land of liberty, had perpetrated this crime against humanity.

Other feelings that she hadn't experienced for years reared their ugly little heads again. How could God let such evil happen to the Cherokee? To all the tribes, for they were not the only ones to suffer.

If she expressed that thought aloud, Abby would remind her that "all things work together for good to them that love God." And John would probably go deep, as he was prone to do, and try to engage her in another theological discussion—this time about free will and the sovereignty of God. Ever since the Fall, he would say, the world has been marred by sin, and it is this sin that causes so much suffering and sorrow. She had always struggled to understand how all those conflicting theological ideas could possibly fit together. And at the moment, with her old friend Depression stopping by for a visit, she had no desire to hear him go on about it.

Apparently she was a glutton for punishment, because she couldn't take her eyes away from the scene unfolding silently on the screen. The people were leaving the camp, some on horseback, some in wagons, but most on foot. The men had finally taken the tent down, but Matthias fashioned a cushion for White Dove, and she sat there with her baby on her lap, greeting the people as they passed by. With the sound down, she couldn't hear what was being said, but it was obvious some were angry to learn that White Dove's family would be staying behind with the *unaka*. Others were accepting and happy for the couple. Even Owl smiled and shook Matthias' hand, although Talisa cried and looked shocked that her cousin wouldn't be accompanying her to Oklahoma. Lieutenant Wheeler smiled at Matthias and gave a little salute. But after he passed them his expression turned sad, as did everyone else's.

Finally, Merrideth could take no more. "It's unbearable. I'm turning it off."

She stopped the action and turned to face her friends. Abby had dried her tears, and she and John looked nearly back to their normal cheerful selves. Merrideth wondered what was wrong with her that she could not do the same.

"So when Matthias saw that they wouldn't even let the Wilsons bury their adopted Indian baby in the cemetery, he decided to take them away from Golconda," Abby said.

"No, I think you have the chronology mixed up," John said. "The baby's death wasn't until later after the Cherokee had left the area."

"I just realized that the Susan who sent medicine with Matthias might have been Painted Turtle," Abby said. "*Susan* could have been her English name."

"I bet you're right," John said. "And so they all moved to Eagle Creek, and after however many generations, along came our Patty Ann. Eventually, no one remembered the Cherokee woman in the family tree."

"After the bigotry they experienced in Golconda, I imagine they kept that pretty quiet," Merrideth said. "Many Native Americans did, which is one reason it is so difficult to trace their genealogies." She rose from the kitchen chair, surprised her rear hadn't melded permanently to the seat. "And you don't have to worry about your lie to Nick, John. I am so going to write a book about this."

"Good," he said. "With your first-hand experience, you'll be able to make what happened to the Cherokee real for readers. We need to remember our history, no matter how painful."

Merrideth got a paper towel from the counter and wiped her face. "Yes, we all need to have someone remind us from time to time that it is an evil world we live in. We can go about our normal activities every day thinking life is pretty good, while across the state, or even across town, others are experiencing catastrophic loss. The so-called Indian Removal was nothing less than ethnic cleansing."

Abby left John's embrace and pulled Merrideth into a hug. "Oh, kiddo, you sound so despairing."

Tears welled up in Merrideth's eyes, and she turned away, embarrassed by her loss of control.

Abby continued to hold her. "Yes, there is evil in this world. But we can't forget that there is good here, too. Just think what Matthias Frailey did to help those people."

"You're exhausted, Merri," John said. "Why don't you lie down on the bed until Landis gets here?"

Merrideth sighed. "I forgot to call him. Now he'll really think I'm stringing him along."

"I'll do it," Abby said. "You sleep."

"You're both tired, too."

"Yes, but we got a few winks earlier," Abby said. "Go on. Rest while you can."

"I think I will."

Merrideth took more of the paper towels with her to the bedroom and placed them on the mattress where her head would go, because she couldn't bear to have her face come in contact with whatever crud the last tenant had left behind. Then she lay down and closed her grainy eyes. Her friends' soft voices came from the kitchen. Abby was saying something about the benefits of sleep. John was saying something about Elijah under the broom bush. It piqued Merrideth's curiosity, but not enough to stay awake to decipher what in the world he was talking about.

CHAPTER 22

Merrideth woke to the sound of someone pounding on the apartment door. Then the bedroom door opened and Abby stuck her head in. "Kiddo, Nick's here. It's time to leave."

She wished she had a magic wand that would transform her into a freshly groomed, vibrantly alive human being before she left the bedroom to face Nick Landis. But she was out of magic wands. The thought made her remember how Matthias has wished for a giant to help with the ferry. She was so going to miss him.

Sighing, she opened the door and bravely stepped into the living room.

"Merrideth," Nick said, smiling cheerfully. "I thought your friends had murdered you and disposed of the body."

She smiled weakly. "Do I look that bad?"

"What? Oh, no way," he said anxiously. "You look great."

"Right. I'll be right back."

When she returned from the bathroom, where she had brushed her teeth and washed her face with the Irish Spring deodorant soap John had so helpfully purchased, she saw that Abby and John had returned the apartment to its pristine condition. All their supplies were gone, presumably already packed away.

"Where's my—?"

"Laptop?" John said. "No worries. Safe and sound in the car."

Merrideth felt a twinge of distress. With her laptop gone, she wouldn't be able to say goodbye to Matthias.

"Okay, then, let the tour begin," Nick said, opening the apartment door for them.

Abby and John stepped into the hall. Merrideth's level of distress shot even higher at the thought of leaving the room where she had spent so many hours with Matthias. She told herself to stop being stupid and forced herself to follow them.

When they reached the first floor of the Ferry House, Nick told them what local historians knew about the original building. His description, as far as it went, corresponded with what Merrideth had seen. But it couldn't possibly compare to seeing the inn firsthand. She was sad that Nick never would get to see it or meet his ancestor Sam Landis.

Then Nick led them down to the river bank and showed them where the ferry used to dock. They gazed across the Ohio to the Kentucky shore as Nick explained the system of ropes and pulleys that had helped get the ferry back and forth across the river. He got it mostly right.

Abby got teary-eyed, which of course surprised Nick, who was undoubtedly wondering what it was about the mechanics of the ferry operation that had upset her. Abby's overflow of emotion didn't surprise Merrideth, because she knew her friend was seeing, just as she was, the icy dock and the ragged and hungry people struggling up the embankment.

A concrete wall now protected the river bank from water erosion. On it was the mural Nick had told them about. Although it was artfully done, it was not much like the reality of the 1838 crossing. For one thing, the ferry boat wasn't right. And the scene was too pretty, a sanitized version that didn't nearly capture the Cherokee's suffering and despair. Of course, the depiction in the mural was only meant to be symbolic, and she was glad the city had put it there to remind people of what had happened in Golconda. But when she wrote her book...well, she wouldn't be so polite.

Because of the concrete retaining wall, they couldn't take the same path up the embankment that Matthias, Angus, and the Cherokee had climbed. It took them several twists and turns to reach Main Street. Everything was different, of course, including the facade of the Ferry House. But the modern paved street followed the same course the dirt road had, and that was enough to allow Merrideth to visualize the scene. Some of the people on the boardwalk had mocked and jeered at the people wearily trudging along their street. But Matthias Frailey had stood right where she did now, watching with sorrow in his heart. Then he had figuratively rolled up his sleeves and done what he could to alleviate their suffering. Abby was right. There was good in this world, and she should focus on that, not the evil.

They got in Nick's beat-up Corolla, and he drove them down Main Street for several blocks. Then he pulled over and parked in front of a tan house trimmed in brown. A sign in front said *Alexander Buel House*.

"This is where the Buels handed out pumpkins to the starving Cherokee," Nick said.

Merrideth hid a smile. The Buels' home had, in fact, been a rustic log structure smelling of urine, nothing like the one in front of them. Perhaps later inhabitants had built the present house over it. It happened sometimes. But in any case, the house before them wasn't old enough, and the pumpkins hadn't been given out there anyway. Mr. Buel had delivered them in person to the camp. Merrideth glanced in the back seat and saw that John was about to explode from holding back that bit of information. Merrideth gave him a quelling look and he continued to restrain himself. Abby just smiled.

Nick insisted they take the Buel House tour and that he be their guide. As he had done from the first time they'd met him, he addressed his comments to Merrideth alone, as if John and Abby weren't present. And she continued to treat him courteously, but with nothing that could be construed as a romantic interest on her part. John and Abby, refusing to be invisible, added insightful comments of their own, forcing Nick to divide his attention among the three of them.

The tour might not have turned out as Nick had hoped, but Merrideth found it interesting. Afterward, on the way to his car, she said, "Nick, you should check the precise date this house was built. You could find out at the courthouse, I'm sure."

"I will if you want me to." Nick looked confused but eager. "I'll let you know what I find out."

They drove on down Main Street until it became Route 146.

"We're traveling on what was once James Lusk's road," Nick said. "George Rogers Clark used it in 1778 to reach Kaskaskia, which he captured for the fledgling United States. And then in 1838, the Cherokee traveled it all the way to Green's Ferry on the Mississippi."

While Nick's little car zoomed down the road at a rate of fifty-five miles per hour, Merrideth pictured Matthias, tired and hungry, walking his horse along the same route, heading toward the camp with White Dove atop Champ and her family wearily following behind. A few miles west of town, Nick pulled off onto a small graveled lot and parked near a brown historic marker sign. On it was an insignia that declared the site was part of the historic Trail of Tears. It was appropriate to mark the spot, but still, the logo somehow seemed just a little too cheery to Merrideth, as if it were there to show vacationing families a fun spot to check out.

"This was their first camp in Illinois," Nick said.

The landscape was totally different than what they had seen in 1838, and Merrideth wondered if Nick had it wrong. Fields of corn and beans grew on both sides of the highway. The woodland was almost completely gone. But there were a few trees remaining, and Nick pointed out a trail that led through them. They followed it for close to a mile and came out of the trees into a large bean field. At the far end of it, the hills rose up. And suddenly Merrideth could see that Nick was right after all.

Nick called their attention to the ground where in several spots the ruts made by the wagon wheels could still be seen. "So what do you think? Cool, huh?"

But no one paid much attention to the ruts. They just stood there staring at the place White Dove's tent had been. Once again Abby fought tears and turned to John for comfort.

Nick probably thought she was a nut case. He sent Merrideth a questioning look, but she looked away as if she hadn't noticed. Poor, geeky Nick, all excited to finally take them on the tour, and all they did was stand around looking like someone had died.

"Let's go see the spring, Abby." John started to walk straight to it, but Merrideth grabbed his shirt sleeve and said, "There was one, wasn't there, Nick?"

"There was and is a spring," he said. "But it's grown up in rough scrub. I wouldn't recommend going there in what you're wearing."

"Where did the Cherokee go once they left here?" John said.

"They camped at Allen Springs, now known as Dixon Springs, a mile and a half southeast of the state park. The scouts had to choose places where there was a water source and plain large enough for a thousand or more people. In most there were south-facing hills for protection from the wind, like here," Nick said, gesturing to those before them. "After Allen Springs came Wartrace, Vienna, Mt. Pleasant, Jonesboro, Dutch Creek, and finally Cape Girardeau."

"If I recall my Illinois geography," Merrideth said, "that's not exactly the shortest path from Golconda to Cape Girardeau."

"You're right," Nick said. "They had to find places to ford the creeks where the beds were solid rock."

"So the wagons wouldn't get stuck," John said.

"Exactly."

They stood there, each lost in his or her thoughts. After a few moments, Nick asked if they were ready to go back.

Abby and John said yes, but Merrideth wished she could stay a little longer to permanently impress the site upon her brain. It was where so much suffering had occurred, but also where Matthias and White Dove had fallen in love, said their vows, and begun their life together.

With that thought, came the realization that her own inexplicable and totally inappropriate attraction for Matthias was fading, taking with it her near addiction for his thoughts and feelings. She would have to come to grips with the knowledge that Matthias belonged to White Dove, never to her.

Maybe there was a man for her out there. No one could possibly live up to Matthias, of course. Perfect in the way a fairy tale prince was, he had come swooping in to rescue the damsel in distress with no thought of danger to himself. What did it feel like to be the recipient of such a completely selfless and unconditional love as Mathias had for White Dove?

Merrideth brushed aside her daydream of storybook heroes and concentrated on not twisting her ankle as she followed the others back down the rough path.

When they got back to the Ferry House, the four of them stood on the sidewalk in front and said their goodbyes for the third time. They all shook hands. When Merrideth put her hand into Nick's, she sensed his sadness, but also that he had accepted that there would never be anything more between them than an interest in history.

"Good luck with your book."

"And with *yours*, Merrideth."

"I plan to come back to Golconda. I'll call you as soon as I know when. Maybe we can get together and talk history over a cup of coffee."

"I'd like that."

When they got in the car, John laughed. "What, no kiss for luck?"

Merrideth sniffed. "I don't foresee ever kissing Nick Landis."

"Then why did you tell him you're coming back to Golconda?" John said.

"Because I am. You didn't think I'd quit without rewinding Lachlan back to Scotland, did you?"

"Oh, right."

"But Nick's so sweet, and you have so much in common," Abby said.

"Except the required sparks. It would be like dating my brother."

Abby sighed dramatically. "I guess there's no getting around that."

"No, there isn't," Merrideth said with as much finality as she could put into her voice.

CHAPTER 23

Merrideth woke when John pulled into Patty Anderson's driveway. So much for keeping up her end of the conversation.

She yawned. "How long are we going to stay here? I'd really like to get home. Make that *need* to get home."

"Me, too," John said.

"Just long enough to tell Patty what we found," Abby said.

Patty welcomed them with open arms, iced tea, and homemade cookies. And then she looked at Merrideth expectantly. "Were you able to find anything?"

"After I get a chance to study my notes, I'll send you a genealogical chart with everything on it. But the short story is that we were able to prove that the Lachlan Frailey I found in Golconda *was* Matthias' father. Lachlan and his four sons had a thriving lumber business in Golconda, and when I get more time, I know I can trace your family all the way back to—"

"Merri, for crying out loud," Abby said. "Tell her about Emmaline."

"I was getting there." She smiled at Patty. "Abby's excited because we found a Native American woman in your lineage."

"Really?" Patty squeaked. "How cool is that? I guess it shouldn't be a surprise. This whole area was once the Shawnee's land. Do you suppose I'm related to Tecumseh?"

Abby smiled. "Sorry, you're not."

Patty laughed. "Well, no matter. Even if I were related to the great Shawnee chief, I'm pretty sure my mother-in-law wouldn't think it was cool. Louise is still having a hard time adjusting to the

226

idea of having a hillbilly in the family."

They laughed, and then John said, "Abby means not Shawnee at all, Patty."

"You have Cherokee blood running in your veins," Merrideth said. "Emmaline Jones's Indian name was *Tsistunagiska*, which means White Dove. She came to Golconda in 1838 with her mother, a brother, and three sisters when the Cherokee were forced out of their eastern lands in Georgia and North Carolina."

"The Trail of Tears," Patty said.

"That's right," Merrideth said. "And here's the good part. Matthias Frailey married her so she wouldn't have to go on to Oklahoma."

"Oh, that is so sweet," Patty said. "Why did they end up in Eagle Creek if they had a good lumber business in Golconda?"

Merrideth looked at Abby and John. "Our theory is that White Dove, that is, Emmaline, didn't feel welcome in Golconda."

"They were prejudiced against her, you mean?" Patty said.

"Maybe. Probably," Abby said.

"Matthias wasn't named in his father's will," Merrideth said, changing the subject. "It threw us off at first, but now I have a theory about that. I fell asleep in the car before I could try it out on Abby and John."

"The snoring was atrocious," John said.

"Very funny," Merrideth said. "Anyway, I believe Matthias didn't inherit because his father had already given him money to take his family to a more hospitable location. And he chose Eagle Creek."

"I bet they were happy there," Abby said. "I still remember your beautiful meadow on top of the mountain looking down at the green valleys all around. Standing there must have reminded Emmaline of her Georgia home."

Patty grabbed Abby's arm. "Oh, you guys, I just realized something. I bet that's where they are buried. In that meadow. My grandfather always said there were old graves up there. I never found them. Any markers were long gone by my time."

Abby wiped her eyes with her napkin. "Oh that's a lovely thought. The two of them together overlooking Eagle Creek."

Merrideth could not manage as much enthusiasm, remembering the fact that the Sherman Mining Company had strip-mined it all away. By the look on her face, Patty was probably thinking the same thing. Fortunately, she refrained from saying it aloud. Abby was already in an emotional state as it was.

"I'm really sorry that you all missed the whole Antique Caravan because of me," Patty said.

"Don't worry about it," John said, eyes twinkling. "We saw plenty of antiques in Golconda."

Patty's eyes lit up with a sudden thought. "Speaking of antiques, I want to show you one I acquired. Just this afternoon, in fact. I'll be right back."

When she left the room, Abby whispered, "I do wish we'd had time to get that little antique dresser you wanted for your bathroom, Merri."

"Yes, and I had hoped to pick up that Chicago Tribune for my collection," John said softly.

"You collect newspapers?" Merrideth said.

"He decorates the walls of his man-cave with them," Abby said.

"Sounds lovely," Merrideth said.

"I collect antique science," John explained. "I wanted the article about the solar flare." He sighed. "But I shouldn't complain. After all, I got to see antique science at work first hand. With a little work, I think I could make a steam engine like the Fraileys'. Think of all we could harness it for!"

"The neighbors might complain of the noise, dear," Abby said, patting his arm.

"They'd be glad enough for it the next time we get a solar flare that takes down the whole power grid."

"Wouldn't you be the most popular man in the neighborhood," Merrideth said.

"Here I am." Patty appeared in the doorway carrying a wooden box. It was not large, maybe twelve inches by eight, but John, ever the gentleman, hurried to take it from her.

The box was rustic and handmade of some dark wood, probably walnut. It had a domed lid with a keyhole, giving it the look of a treasure chest. But it was plain and unornamented except for natural worm holes and minor dents, which marred the wood but did nothing to detract from the chest's charm.

John set it on the table. "What is it?"

"A jewelry box, I think," Patty said. "Dad gave it to me today when I stopped by the Garden Place after church—that's the retirement center. Nearly every time I see them, he gives me one of their things, no matter how hard I try to talk him out of it."

"That's sweet, Patty," Abby said.

"It would be, except I think it means he's sensing his end is near."

"Oh, I hope not," Abby said.

"Give them our regards when you see them," John added.

"I will, though I doubt they'll remember you."

"The chest looks old," Merrideth said. "Has it been in your family long?"

"I don't remember ever seeing it when I was a kid growing up on the farm. For all I know Mom and Dad got it at a flea market. I couldn't get anything from either of them about it. At least nothing sensible. The dementia, you know."

Patty lifted the lid. Inside, there were dividers of the same dark walnut that formed little compartments, each of which was lined with faded pink velvet. She removed the compartmented tray, and underneath was another layer of velvet-lined compartments. With the top tray out of the way, Merrideth saw that the sides of the box were lined with faded blue paper.

"What's under that tray?" John said.

"It doesn't come out," Patty said. "I've tried." She tugged on it to no avail. "See?"

"It moved a little just now," Abby said. "Maybe it's just stuck."

John tried, but it didn't come out. "I'd better stop. I don't want to break it."

"Well, anyway," Patty said. "I thought you'd like to see my little antique."

"It's wonderful," Abby said.

Merrideth put her nose nearly inside the box and squinted at the paper lining. What she had assumed was a decorative crosshatch design on it was not that at all. She picked up the box to catch the light better, and found herself holding the second compartmented tray in her hands.

"How did you get that out, Merri?" John said almost indignantly.

Abby grinned. "I guess you and Patty loosened it for her."

Merrideth ignored them and studied the inside of the box. On the lower part of the walls where the second tray had covered it, the paper lining wasn't nearly as faded. The tray must have been stuck for a very long time.

"Patty, do you have a magnifying glass?" Merrideth said.

"I think there's one in Alex's desk. I'll go look."

"Do you suppose the bottom compartment was for secret love letters?" Abby said. "Too bad there aren't any left."

Patty brought the magnifying glass, and Merrideth took it and studied the lining of the box. Then she looked up and smiled at the others. "Maybe there is a love letter. The cross hatched marks are not a design. They're handwriting. It's on one of those letter sheets people used before envelopes became popular. Paper was scarce, I imagine, for whoever built this chest, so they lined it with old letters."

"Waste not, want not," Patty said. "It's something of a family motto."

"It looks like chicken scratches," Abby said.

"That's because it's two letters in one," Merrideth explained. "To save paper, people often replied on the same letter, just turned it forty-five degrees and wrote crossways over the previous message. This person used a different color of ink, probably to make it easier to read."

"So what does it say?" Patty said.

The kitchen phone rang, and Patty rose from her chair. "Excuse me. I've been expecting a call from Alex in Texas."

When she was gone, Merrideth turned back to the letter. After a moment, she looked up at her friends. "You guys won't believe this."

"What?" Abby leaned in closer to look over Merrideth's shoulder. Then she squealed in her ear. "Oh! Oh! John, look."

He studied the letter, and then after a moment shook his head. "You're right, Merri. I don't believe it. Just because her name is in it doesn't mean…It's a coincidence, that's all."

"Did you read the whole thing? Not just one name." Merrideth said. "Four. All of them significant. That's no coincidence. We're looking at correspondence between Matthias and his parents. It's as clear as day."

John snorted his disdain. "I refuse to believe that something like that just happened to survive all these years only to fall into our hands at this particular moment in time."

"After the miracle we experienced this weekend?" Abby said. "Why couldn't it, John?"

"Sorry, I guess I'm a doubting Thomas. Read it out loud,

Merri."

"I think the letter in brown ink is from Mathias' parents. It is in better shape than the other." She read aloud:

"Dear Son,

Your new home sounds like a fine place. You all are so far away, and we miss you something fierce. But we thank God for giving you such a good place to raise your new family. Everyone here is well, so you must not worry about us.
"I can't make the next part out," Merrideth said. "Something, something, something *family way.*

*"In January, God willing, we will have a new little one around the place. Pa sends his love and says to tell you Cyrus is finally getting his new house. Talk around these parts is he's building a mansion, not a house. As for me, I'm quite satisfied in our snug cabin, although it is quiet now that s*omething, something. A whole bunch of somethings.

"Please write again soon, son. The whole family reads every line you write. God bless you.

Your loving mother"

"But it still proves exactly nothing." John said.
"Don't be such a lawyer, John," Merrideth said. "The part about Cyrus' new house cannot be a coincidence."
"Okay, I'll grant you that's an interesting tidbit, but still."
"The other letter is even more conclusive, although less clear," Merrideth said. " A lot of the ink has worn off. It must have been a cheaper brand or something."
Merrideth read:

"Dear Ma and Pa,

We are all healthy and well and something, something, something. The baby arrived something, something problem. We named her Elsie in your honor, Ma. That was Emmaline's idea—"
Abby squeaked at the sound of Emmaline's name. But Merrideth continued reading:
"—although she worries now that you will be offended. Something, something, something—a whole lot of somethings then *firewood.*

"*Nancy is a big help with baby Elsie, and the other children are growing like something, something the woods and fish in Eagle Creek. He says it reminds him of home. I'm hopeful the peach trees in the meadow something, something, something. Emmaline says it is the best gift I could have given her.*

"*Give our love to everyone. God bless and* something, something. And then there's a signature but I can't read it."

"That's four names, John," Abby said. "Cyrus the Golconda storekeeper, Elsie, Nancy, and most importantly Emmaline. Five if you count Eagle Creek. That's too much to be a coincidence. What are the odds that they'd all appear in one interchange of letters?"

"Brett would probably know," Merrideth said."

"Wasn't Elsie White Dove's little sister?" John demanded.

"No," Merrideth said. "Her name was Eliza."

"It doesn't matter," John said. "Either way, this letter isn't from Matthias."

"Why are you being so stubborn, honey?" Abby said. "Can't you see it?"

"He's right, Abby, as much as it pains me to say it." Merrideth set the chest back on the table.

"Why do you say that?"

"Because whoever this Emmaline is, she named the baby after her mother-in-law *Elsie.* Matthias' mother's name was Eileen."

"Oh," Abby said. "Well, isn't that a bummer?"

Patty came back to the dining room, smiling happily. "Alex is going to be home tomorrow night after all."

"Too bad we won't get to meet him, Patty," Abby said.

"Thanks for the cookies," John said. "We had better hit the road."

"But what does the letter in the box say?"

"Not much," Abby said. "But you should read it when you get the chance."

Merrideth promised to be in contact soon. They said their goodbyes, and Patty sent them on their way with profuse thanks and a bag of her homemade cookies for the ride home.

Abby drove this time, and John put the passenger side seat back so he could snooze. Merrideth vowed to stay awake to keep her company. But they were not even out of Marion when she started drifting off.

Images of Matthias, Emmaline, and the Cherokee scrolled by inside her skull like a slideshow. Even the mooing cow Matthias brought made a cameo appearance.

Merrideth sat upright. "Elsie!" she blurted.

The car swerved a little and Abby made a squawking noise. "Merri! You scared me."

John said, "Whaa? Did we wreck?"

"No," Abby said. "Go back to sleep."

Merrideth laughed. "Emmaline's mother-in-law wasn't named Elsie. But her cow was."

John put his seat upright and turned to stare at her. "To honor Eileen. A way of saying thanks for giving her cow to the Cherokee."

"Exactly," Merrideth said.

"All right. I withdraw my objections, Your Honor," John said. "But you realize we can't tell Patty?"

"I know," Merrideth said. "We'd never be able to explain how we knew."

Abby glanced at her in the rearview mirror. "Well, even if we can't tell Patty, I'm so happy for the closure for us. Now we know Matthias and Emmaline were happy together. Isn't God good to let us know that? It's a real gift."

Merrideth thought again of the way Patty's jewelry box tray had effortlessly appeared in her hand when no one else had been able to remove it. Maybe Abby was right about it being a gift. She closed her eyes and settled back into her seat to snooze. In her mind's eye she saw the peach trees Matthias had planted for White Dove blooming in the meadow overlooking Eagle Creek. She smiled.

CHAPTER 24

It was after eight when Merrideth got home, grainy-eyed and craving her bed. But when she stopped off in the kitchen for a glass of water she saw her electric bill, still unopened in its envelope, propped against the vase in the middle of her table. On the back of it, someone had written a poem with a very dull pencil.

There once was a woman with sticky door woes.
They would not open nor would they close
(Without huffing and puffing and stubbing her toes).

Now they go, both to and fro,
With nary a @#$% or even an OH!
All because Brett, that handy-guy,
Loaded his tools and came by.

P.S. I fixed your pantry doors, too.

B.G.

She laughed. She wasn't surprised at the cleverness of his hands, because she'd seen the work he'd done turning Nelda's barn into a workshop, but the poem demonstrated an unexpected cleverness with words.

She checked out all four doors in question and found them in perfect working order, except for the missing knob on the bathroom door. Thankfully, the ones she had bought in Marion matched perfectly.

There wasn't a single wood shaving to indicate the work that Brett had done that day. Furthermore, not a speck of honey-beige foundation remained on her bathroom floor. The room smelled lemony fresh, so he had to have found her cleaning supplies. What all had he seen as he snooped through her apartment looking for them? Why had she not remembered his raging curiosity when she agreed to let him work there while she was gone?

But she had a healthy curiosity, too. She was dying to see *his* apartment. Judging by the condition of his office at McKendree, it was probably a little cluttered. But had he dressed up the plain white walls with art, and if so what kind? Bright, whimsical things like his Aunt Nelda favored? Or as a mathematician and scientist, did he go for geometric modern art? Maybe he was still painting, and she could go over there and offer to help in payment for fixing her doors. Putting aside her fatigue, she hurried through a shower, changed into her oldest jeans and sweatshirt, and drove the three blocks to Brett's condo.

Each time she saw the outside of it, she wondered how he could stand to live there. It was a boxy building made of weird yellow bricks and completely devoid of any architectural details that might have attracted the eye. She parked and went into the entry hall. Faint noises were coming out of the two apartments on the lower floor, but she couldn't tell about those upstairs. The four tenant mailboxes next to the staircase were labeled with apartment numbers only, which probably suited Brett, the numberphile, just fine. However, without a name to go with the number, she had no clue which apartment belonged to him.

She took out her phone and called him. Two seconds after the ring sounded in her ear, it was repeated from behind the door of apartment 1B on her right. Their phones did their dual ring a second time. She put her hand up to knock on his door, but then a bubble of panic rose up in her throat, and she pulled her hand back. What on earth had she been thinking?

Brett would open the door and invite her in. And if she stepped over his threshold, he would see it as an invitation for a relationship with her. He would expect things from her that she had never given any other man. Scary emotional things. Not sex, of course. Not unless they got to the *I do* stage. As if. But still, if she went inside, there was no telling what would happen next. Brett wasn't tame like Nick Landis and certainly not manageable like the men she had dated in the past. And never once with any of *them* had she feared being consumed by passion. What did all that say about her?

On the third ring Brett answered, but by that time, she had already crept back outside, letting the door close silently behind her.

"Hello?"

"Hi, Brett."

The light from apartment 1B escaped past the edges of what looked like a white sheet hanging in the window. So he didn't have his curtains back up yet. If she were the type to spy, she could peek in and see for herself what his apartment looked like. Resisting the temptation, she sat down on the condo's front step. The cold from the concrete immediately began seeping into her bones. The air was cold, too, much colder than the last few nights. The January thaw was over.

"You sound out of breath."

"I'm just excited about having doors that close right. They work great. Thanks. And for the poem, too." Laughing, she pulled the zipper of her coat up a little higher and searched in her pockets for her gloves. "What other hidden talents do you have?"

Fortunately, Brett wasn't the type of man who turned every ill-advised sentence that came out of a person's mouth into a sexual innuendo. After a short pause, he merely said, "That poem ought to prove, if nothing else does, that I'm not related to Nelda."

"Don't say that, Brett. I just know you are."

"It's nice to believe so."

A yearning to show him *Beautiful Houses* nearly swamped her. She could take him back to the 1790s and let him meet James Garretson. Once he saw their similarities, he would never doubt his parentage again. It would be a wonderful gift that only she could give him. But would he—could he—agree not to blab about it? Even if he agreed, could she trust him to keep his word? She had known him less than six months, and for her, that was a mere blip of time to build faith with a person.

If she could time-surf in his brain, maybe she'd find that he was perfectly trustworthy. But what if she were to delve inside his soul and discover that he harbored the same lies and selfish motives that had always ended all her previous relationships? No, it was much better not to know—and to be satisfied with the friendship they had.

She realized he was saying something. "I'm sorry. What did you say?"

"Did you fill up the trailer?"

She couldn't think for a moment what he meant. "Oh, with antiques. We brought the trailer back completely empty. I couldn't find a dresser the right size for my bathroom, and Abby and John struck out, too. We spent all that time looking at the past, and we don't have a single thing to show for it."

"Surely there were other things you wanted."

"Not really."

"What a strange hobby."

"Well, we enjoyed ourselves."

"You and Nick. Wait. Forget I said that, okay? It's none of my business, and—"

"Nick Landis is a local historian that we met at the courthouse. There, I shared a secret. Happy now?"

"Very. If you keep practicing you'll get good at it."

"Abby kept working her match-making wiles on him, too, so you needn't feel like you're special."

"Well, that will keep me humble. Did it work? The match-making?"

"Of course not. Nick is not my type."

"I'd ask you what your type is, but I'm afraid to hear the answer."

"Don't worry. I wouldn't tell you anyway."

He chuckled. "You should come over and see my new walls."

"Are you finished painting, then?"

"All done."

"Sorry. I wanted to get home in time to help you—in payment for my doors."

"Don't be sorry. I didn't fix your doors expecting anything in return, Merri."

It was a selfless attitude, and for a moment she thought again of Matthias Frailey.

"Tomorrow I'm going to rehang all my pictures. I think they'll look good against the new backdrop."

"Do you mean photographs or art?"

"Some of both. My favorite is a photo of Aunt Nelda feeding her chickens and goats. And I have several rural landscapes she painted for me, including an amazing one of her old barn."

"I think I'm starting to picture how your condo looks."

"You wouldn't have to picture it if you came over. I'd let you sit on my couch and help me watch the paint finish drying."

"Sounds entertaining."

"If we lost interest, I could turn on the TV. Maybe make popcorn."

"I doubt we'd need all that, what with your new pillows—in paisley-tie blue—showing off for our amusement."

"Oh, I took them back."

"Why? I was just getting used to them in my mental picture."

"I decided the money would be better spent on shoes. I wanted you to help me pick them out, but when you were delayed getting home, I went ahead and got paisley-tie blue. Since it's your favorite."

"Please tell me you mean athletic shoes."

He laughed. "Yes. Were you picturing Elvis?"

"Maybe."

"And I got three dozen pairs of socks to match."

"Really? That's a lot of blue socks, Professor Garrison."

He belted out a laugh.

"What's so funny?"

"I just realized how that must have sounded to you. The shoes and socks are for my project, not me. I got the idea a few years ago. People tend to help the homeless at Christmas time. But what about after that? So I try to help out with a few things during the winter months. New shoes and socks are always a big hit. Can you believe some of the men are barefoot in this weather?"

Merrideth sniffed and wiped a tear away. "Unto the least of these."

"Exactly. You wouldn't want to help me pass out the goodies tomorrow, would you? We could go after church."

"I'd love to. But I've got to go now, Brett." Before she started crying like a baby in his ear.

"Good night, then, Merri. I'll pick you up tomorrow. Is nine-thirty okay?"

"Perfect."

"Great. And just so you don't think I'm some kind of goody-two shoes, ha, ha, I kept my new paisley-tie blue throw. It's very warm and cozy."

She had been purposely forgetting that. Thinking of it now only made her colder. A shadow moved across the sheet hanging in his window. She pictured him settling back on his couch to watch TV with the blue throw around his shoulders and a bowl of popcorn near to hand.

She shivered in the night. Maybe someday she would have the courage to go into the warmth instead of standing like a fool outside in the cold.

The End

About the Author

Deborah Heal is the author of the *Time and Again* history mystery trilogy and the *Rewinding Time Series: inspirational novels of history, mystery & romance*. Her characters get to visit the past to see the bits that didn't make it into the history books—something Deborah has always dreamed of doing herself.

A former high school English teacher, she firmly believes the maxim "write what you know," which is why all of Deborah's novels are set in her beloved rural southern Illinois. Even so, their historical topics and spiritual themes transcend geographical boundaries.

Although she grew up just down the road from the settings of *Time and Again* and *Unclaimed Legacy*, she was born in Eldorado, Illinois, not far from the Old Slave House featured in her novel *Every Hill and Mountain*. Her novel *Only One Way Home* deals with the Cherokee Trail of Tears, which passed through nearby Golgonda, Illinois. (Unlike the characters in that novel, Deborah's great, great grandmother's Cherokee family remained safely in North Carolina.) Having grown up hearing tales of the Ohio River pirates at Cave in Rock, Deborah wrote about them in *How Sweet the Sound*. And as a fan of Charles Dickens, she told about his visit to southern Illinois in *A Matter of Time*.

Today she lives with her husband Robert in Monroe County, Illinois, not far from where the pioneers of her novel *Once Again* struggled to survive amidst Indian attacks. Deborah is a passionate gardener. She and her husband have three grown children, five grandchildren, and two canine buddies Digger and Scout.

A Note from the Author

Acknowledgments

Thanks, Mom, for lending your help with proofreading at the eleventh hour, but more importantly, for teaching us to be proud of our father's Cherokee heritage. Michelle Babb, your psychological insight into the characters was spot on (should that be hyphenated?, and I couldn't have done "Sticky Door Woes" without you. Thank you, LeAnne Hardy, for taking time out from your own writing to discuss story arc and other important matters.

I am ever appreciative of all the people who tirelessly digitize old history books and other intriguing reference works, making it possible for me to do my research from the comforts of home. It would have been so embarrassing to weep over the plight of the Cherokee in a public library.

The Real People and Events

If by chance you think I exaggerated the suffering of the Cherokee in *Only One Way Home*, you won't think so when you read the first-hand accounts of Rev. Daniel Butrick, Private John Burnett, and others. It's fascinating reading, but be prepared to shed tears of your own. You'll find their accounts and other information about the real people and events of Golconda and the Trail of Tears under the "About my Books" tab on my website.

Let's Keep in Touch

Thanks for supporting independent authors! I'd love to hear what you think of *Only One Way Home*. If you enjoyed it, please write a review for it and post on Amazon and/or Goodreads. I'd really appreciate it if you would "like" and "follow," or otherwise connect with me.

My Website: www.deborahheal.com
Facebook: www.facebook.com/DeborahHeal
Twitter: www.twitter.com/DeborahHeal

But the best way to stay in touch is for you to subscribe to my **V.I.P. Readers List** (on my website). First off, you'll get my free short story "***Charlotte's House***" just for signing up. AND then you'll get more free stories along with insider information about contests, giveaways, and when my books are scheduled to be free or reduced.

How Sweet the Sound

book 3

Note to Self: File under interesting job perks—Trevor Dalton, best dating lead in a while. He's a lot like Brett, only not off limits.

Professor Merrideth Randall has an insatiable curiosity about the past. But unlike other historians, she has the means to satisfy it—an amazing computer program that lets her rewind the lives of people from long ago. So when the topic of Ohio River pirates piques her interest, she packs up her laptop and goes to Cave-in-Rock, Illinois.

There pirates preyed on the thousands of settlers coming down the river on flatboats, heading for new lives on the western frontier. For a time, that stretch of the river was a black hole, where whole families disappeared along with their hopes, dreams, and treasures. And the only way for Merrideth to find out what happened to them is to get inside the head of Samuel Mason, the master mind behind the attacks.

Merrideth's visit to Cave-in-Rock coincides with Hellhound Homecoming, a wild annual gathering of lawless bikers. A confrontation with five of them has her wondering if her curiosity will be the death of her. But God sends a tattooed biker named

Trevor Dalton to her rescue.

Trevor appeals to her in some way that's difficult to explain, even though he's night-and-day different from Brett Garrison, the McKendree College colleague who's still hoping for more than just a friendship with her. Which one should she choose—the man who is safe or the man with a past?

What Readers Are Saying...

"I like the mixture of history, mystery and romance. The author makes you feel like you are there in the book with the characters
This book series is awesome!!! I can't put it down!!" (Nyla M. Rednour)

"This series has quickly become a favorite as it illustrates the timeless theme of sin and forgiveness, while raising the question by many of how God brings healing by faith in Him alone. Readers will definitely relate to Merrideth's struggle with self doubt and worthiness. She is such a realistic character who is searching and growing in her faith."

Check out the History Mystery Trilogy, the prequel to the Rewinding Time Series. Meet Professor Randall as a "bratty 11-year-old" and see the origin of her amazing computer program.

All three novels are available as **Audiobooks**, as well as **Kindle, Nook**, and **paperback.** You can read descriptions of *Time and Again, Unclaimed Legacy,* and *Every Hill and Mountain* on my website. Save money by picking up the Kindle boxed 3-book set on Amazon.

Made in the USA
Lexington, KY
17 September 2016